It was as if that one kiss had turned her life upside down, altering everything she'd thought to be true, everything she'd ever been told about how she should behave and how she should feel.

It was as if she had been stirring from a hazy dream all week and now she was wide-awake. Because no one had ever told her it was possible to feel like that. And now she knew that it was, how could she go back?

"Helena, I'm sorry," Viggo said again, stalking back toward her. "I took things too far. I behaved badly. Forgive me."

She raised her gaze and their eyes clashed. "I don't want you to be sorry, Viggo," she said. "I asked you to do it."

He inclined his head. "Not quite like that," he said wryly.

She smiled, the tension easing a little between them. "No, I don't think it will happen quite like that at the wedding."

They both sobered at the thought.

Because despite that earth-shattering kiss, there was still going to be a wedding. Viggo could hold her, touch her, kiss her and make her feel alive, but tomorrow, she would still have to marry Marianos.

Author Note

Thank you so much for choosing to read *The Viking She Shouldn't Crave*. For this book, I enjoyed going back in time to tenth-century Constantinople, where skilled Viking warriors fought for emperors in return for great riches, and the royal princes picked their wives at bride shows.

My story begins when the bishop's daughter, Helena, is chosen at the prince's bride show. Marianos must marry to sire an heir, and Helena must wed to save her family from financial ruin, but during their first moments alone, the prince's charming facade drops, and Helena's ideas of a romantic union are shattered. She is surprised when his Varangian commander, Viggo, is kind to her, despite his belief that she is marrying the prince for wealth and status. As Viggo helps her win over the prince's affections, she soon discovers it's not the prince's heart but that of his right-hand man she cares about, but any attraction between them is forbidden, and Viggo must resist temptation—he needs the wedding to take place to receive his coin and help his pregnant sister...

I love writing forbidden-romance stories, and I hope you like reading them just as much. Let me know...

Sarah x sarahrodiedits@gmail.com.

THE VIKING SHE SHOULDN'T CRAVE

SARAH RODI

HISTORICAL

Recycling programs
for this product may
not exist in your area

ISBN-13: 978-1-335-83172-9

The Viking She Shouldn't Crave

For questions and comments about the quality of this book, please contact us at CustomerService@Harlequin.com.

Harlequin Enterprises ULC
22 Adelaide St. West, 41st Floor
Toronto, Ontario M5H 4E3, Canada
www.Harlequin.com

HarperCollins Publishers
Macken House, 39/40 Mayor Street Upp
Dublin 1, D01 C9W8, Ireland
www.HarperCollins.com

Printed in U.S.A.

Sarah Rodi has always been a hopeless romantic. She grew up watching old romantic movies recommended by her granddad or devouring love stories from the local library. Sarah lives in the village of Cookham in Berkshire, where she enjoys walking along the River Thames with her husband, her two daughters and their dog. She has been a magazine journalist for over twenty years, but it has been her lifelong dream to write romance for Harlequin. Sarah believes everyone deserves to find their happy-ever-after. You can contact her via @sarahrodiedits or sarahrodiedits@gmail.com. Or visit her website at sarahrodi.com.

Books by Sarah Rodi

Harlequin Historical

"Chosen as the Warrior's Wife"
in *Convenient Vows with a Viking*
The Viking and the Runaway Empress
Her Secret Vows with the Viking
The Viking's Princess Bride
The Warrior's Forbidden Viking Bride

A Season to Wed

The Viscount's Forbidden Flirtation

Rise of the Ivarssons

The Viking's Stolen Princess
Escaping with Her Saxon Enemy

Visit the Author Profile page at Harlequin.com.

For Christina, Lucy, Lotte and Maryam.
I bet few others chat about the things we do!
Thanks for always being there.

Chapter One

Early 10th century
—Constantinople, capital of the Byzantine Empire

'When meeting the Prince, you will use his full title of *Porphyrogennetos*. Upon being introduced, you will curtsy as a sign of respect. And in the presence of the Prince, you will remain at a respectful distance.'

The large, fearsome warrior continued to reel off his list of commands as he paced the gleaming marble floor of the reception hall before Helena and the eleven other women. 'You will speak only when spoken to. Only then will you look him in the eye. And under no circumstances is touching the Prince allowed.'

If Helena had been nervous before, she was terrified now.

She had never come across such a tall, muscular and intimidating man. But then it was only fitting that the Commander of the Prince's elite Varangian Guard emanated such power. He needed to instil fear into his men, and the people, to keep order in Constantinople and across the empire.

'Are these instructions understood?'

The potential brides all nodded in agreement.

'Is the Prince some kind of beast?' the woman beside her whispered. 'If we look at him, do you think we'll turn to stone?'

Helena smiled. 'Even if he is a monster, it would surely be worth it, worth suffering anything, to be Empress of all this,' she jested in return.

The Commander turned and caught Helena's eye. He gave her a long, hard look, his eyes burning like hot coals, making her insides quiver, and she swiftly averted her gaze. Talking of beasts… With a tangle of thick, heavy scars that met in the middle of his right cheek, stern black eyes and dark ink criss-crossing over his bare forearms, the man's brutal exterior both intrigued and unsettled her. She had heard of the Commander's ability on the battlefield—he was a hired mercenary warrior from a faraway place and a soldier of great renown—and she knew only a fool would dare to cross him today.

Helena and the other women were led out on to the terrace in the sultry afternoon heat and she tried to shrug off any concerns. She felt a little shaken by her encounter with the Commander, but she was determined nothing was going to dampen her excitement today. She had spent years of her life in pursuit of this one goal: to win the heart of the Prince.

Stepping out into the sun, glancing up at the majestic Great Palace, the white exterior shimmering like a mirage before her, she wondered if all her dreams—and those of her parents—would finally come true. That she would meet the handsome young Prince, soon to be crowned ruler, and find the husband she so desired. Would he make her his Empress, raise her status and that of her family, and bring her contentment—at last?

Marianos's mother, the Empress Regent, had arranged

today's royal bride show for her son to choose a wife from twelve women in the land, said to be the most beautiful. When Helena had been summoned to participate, her parents had been overjoyed. Yet she had known it wasn't her doing—her family name had secured her place in the line-up. A member of the Prince's clergy, her father was a respected bishop. He had immense influence over his dioceses, even if he was secretly suffering pecuniary difficulties.

But this part, on this bright afternoon—this part was down to her and her alone and she wanted to prove she could do this. That she could enhance her father's position, despite his doubts, and find love at the same time.

Helena soaked up the excitement in the air as her gaze scanned the immense, lively crowd, the magnificent fountains and impressive monuments in the palace square, and she reminded herself to breathe. She had pictured this moment often—she'd look up into Marianos's eyes, enchanted, and he would stare back down into hers and know that she was his destiny. And, as if she'd conjured him up just by thinking of him, finally, he was there—stepping out on to the terrace, flanked by his mother and the Commander, and hope bloomed inside her. The ground shook along with Helena's legs as a thunder of applause erupted from the crowd.

The thousands of people who had turned out to watch the Prince pick his bride probably thought she'd spent just days preparing, bathing in milk and honey so that her olive skin glowed, having her long, dark hair brushed until it shone, barely eating so she would fit into this exquisite green tunic. In truth, for as long as she could remember she had been training for this day. All she had studied for, everything she had accomplished—and suffered—had been in preparation to secure Marianos's hand.

She had grown up learning the Prince's preferences: everything from his favourite colour—the same emerald shade as her tunic—to his choice of foods and beloved pursuits.

It couldn't all have been for nothing.

A slow trickle of perspiration slid down Helena's spine, beneath the delicate silk, as she waited for Marianos's imminent appraisal.

As he strutted closer, she stole a look at him. He had a youthful face, with high cheekbones and a pointy, prominent nose. The rich, luxurious fabrics of his garments and the dazzling jewels decorating them reflected the grandeur of his position—and although at seven and ten he was two winters younger than her, thankfully he was taller. He wore his honey-blond wavy hair long, adorned with a golden crown that glinted in the sun, making him look almost godlike, and his piercing blue eyes arrogantly drifted over the dozen women, perusing them at his leisure.

Here was the man to fulfil her dreams. She imagined herself in love with him already.

She prayed harder that he would choose her.

Marianos began to inspect the other women in turn, stopping to ask each one a question, making them laugh with a witticism. Then he'd turn and whisper something to his mother and the Commander at his side. He was charm personified. The total opposite of his warrior, whose serious face never broke into a smile and whose hand was unmoving from the hilt of his sword, reminding her not to step out of line.

Finally, the Prince came to a halt before Helena.

She could barely breathe. Her fate and her family's—it all depended on this moment. This was her chance to secure the relationship she desired and their standing in Constantinople. To prove her father wrong about her.

'And you are…?'

She looked up into Marianos's ice-blue gaze. '*Porphyrogennetos…*' she bowed, using the title that she knew marked him as the rightful heir '…I am Helena, the only daughter of Michel Arianites.'

And she had always been a disappointment to him. A son had been necessary for succession purposes and she had carried her father's displeasure—his sadness at her being born a girl—all her life. He'd told her she must join the nunnery, but her mother had begged him to allow her to make a good match through marriage instead. While her mother had ambitions for her to ascend the throne, her father had scoffed at the very idea, as if the notion was absurd.

So, a determination had solidified in Helena's stomach. If she was going to marry, she would marry the best. She would marry above her father's station and perhaps be able to pay off his debts. He would be forced to notice her. Accept her. *Love her.* She would no longer be a source of his discontent.

'We respect your father and thank him for his loyalty. Why is it you wish to be Empress, Helena?' Marianos asked. 'Do you seek to rule?'

She swallowed. 'No, I only wish to be your wife.'

Helena had heard Marianos resented the power his mother wielded over him—she did not think he would take kindly to another woman trying to control him. Initially he would want a passive wife who knew her place. But she hoped, if he chose her, that over time she could convince him to learn to trust her, to confide in her—and that they would grow to be a partnership.

'What are your interests?' he asked, as if he had practised a list of questions.

'You.'

Her comment drew stifled gasps from the other contestants and a sharp arch of the brow from Zoe, the Empress Regent. A smirk played around the corner of Marianos's thin lips and, for a moment, the Commander's statuesque pose wavered, his gaze flicking over her.

But Helena wasn't sorry. She knew she needed to stand out. To be remembered.

Marianos clapped his Commander on the shoulder, raising himself up on his toes to do so. 'Did you hear that, Viggo? I am someone else's primary interest. At last, there is someone to rival you,' he laughed.

'Come now, you must have other interests,' his mother said, bringing order back to the situation. 'For the Prince's chosen bride, interests will be vital, so that she can keep busy when he is fulfilling his duties ruling the empire.'

Helena nodded, taking this in. Her heart was in her mouth. Had she been too bold?

'I also love to read, to weave and embroider. I ride and I am not averse to deer stalking—I would love to accompany you on a hunt. I enjoy a feast and dancing, but ultimately,' she said, turning to address the Empress Regent, 'my interest is to make the future Emperor happy.'

Marianos and his mother looked at each other and stepped away, and Helena thought she must have ruined her chances.

She watched as they conversed in hushed tones, picking up the odd word here and there. 'You'd have more control over his dioceses… It would help to counteract any uprisings there… Solidify your power… Very beautiful…'

She tried to refrain from biting her lip. Her eyes were drawn upwards towards the Commander's and she was unnerved to find his dark gaze still focused on her, his eyebrows pulling in, as if she was a problem he was trying to decipher.

All she saw when she looked at him was danger. His longish black hair was pulled back into a band, and he had a thick, neatly trimmed beard which covered the base of some of his scars. She stared back and realised he was a conundrum himself—the right side of his face a labyrinth of deep lines.

Marianos turned towards her again and she snapped her attention away from the other man.

The Prince's fingers gripped the bottom of her veil, before throwing it up, lifting it off her face, taking her by surprise, and she gasped. His piercing gaze stole over her features, his face unreadable.

She held her breath. Would he like what he saw?

Marianos glanced back at his mother and she gave a sharp nod. Then he reached out his hand towards Helena, taking her fingers in his, and the crowd erupted once more.

It seemed he had made his choice.

She was to be his bride and Empress. *Her.* Helena Arianites.

Every woman in the empire dreamed of marrying the Prince. Was he really going to be hers?

She glanced up at the Commander and, though his scowl seemed to have deepened, he inclined his head, acknowledging her as the winner of the bride show, and her heart lifted in triumph.

She would live in the palace. She would be the wife of the most important man in the empire. She would no longer go unnoticed, but instead have everything her heart desired. As would her family.

Marianos drew her forward and raised her hand in his cool, delicate grip, presenting her to his people, and they gave another rousing ovation. It was a moment Helena would remember for the rest of her life. One of pure elation.

She was aware the other women were being ushered off the stage, and she felt a pang of remorse for their disappointment, as that could just as easily have been her. The sea of faces in the crowd blurred before her as happy tears welled in her eyes.

'Thank you,' she said.

She hoped Marianos would look down at her and smile, perhaps lean in and whisper a few reassuring words to put her at ease. But he just stood there, continuing to wave, his jaw set. Was he as overwhelmed as she? Their lives were about to change for ever.

All of a sudden, there was a scramble of action in the crush below. Leaning forward over the balcony, she saw a skirmish. A man drew a knife from the scabbard of one of the guards before throwing it. It happened so quickly, it was all she could do to stand and watch as the blade soared through the air. Her breath hitched as, with sickening realisation, she knew it was coming towards them.

She heard Marianos inhale, a scream lodging somewhere inside her throat, before a shadow fell over them. The Varangian Commander lifted his shield, sheltering them, just in time. The blade pierced the wood with a thump and she froze. Marianos stumbled backwards in shock.

Silence reigned for just a moment, then terrified screams

broke out in the crowd, the mood instantly turning sour as soldiers piled into the square, their weapons at the ready, and people began to shove each other, fighting, or frantically trying to get away. Stunned, Helena witnessed the celebrations descend into chaos.

'Get inside, both of you,' the Commander barked. He unsheathed his sword and leapt down from the terrace into the riotous hordes.

Helena looked on in disbelief.

She saw the Varangian engage the perpetrator. The Commander was a deadly, powerful warrior—and the crowd seemed to hesitate, halting their skirmishes when they saw him. No one wanted to take him on and, with a glimpse of the skills she saw him possess, she could see why.

Marianos began to drag her towards the palace, hurriedly following the Empress Regent, as guards surrounded them. They burst inside the vast but quiet, cool building, leaving the crowds behind, the door slamming shut after them. Marianos released Helena from his grip, casting her off.

'I want that man found and beheaded!' he roared, making her flinch with his sudden outburst. 'As if it wasn't already the worst day of my life. Now someone's trying to kill me?' he bellowed, fury lacing his voice and his actions.

Helena stilled, as Zoe spun round, looking pale. The Empress Regent was no doubt just as upset that someone had attempted to assassinate her precious son and put an end to the joyous afternoon. They all were. 'Viggo will deal with it. You know he will.'

Marianos unfastened his cloak and threw it towards one of his men. 'That rabble should not have been allowed through the gates. I told you! We should never have held this bride show. I hope you're happy now, Mother,' he spat.

The older woman sighed, placing her hands on her hips. 'Yes, Marianos. You have put this off for long enough. It is good it's finally done—that a decision has been made. I am pleased.'

'I'm glad someone is.'

Helena recoiled, taken aback by the marked shift in his tone—and his words. He was like the cuttlefish she'd seen swimming in the local warm waters, which rapidly changed their appearance to evade capture—or trick their prey. Her alarmed gaze flew between the two of them.

She could understand the attack must have unsettled him—it had her, too. Seeing that blade sticking out of the Commander's shield… She shuddered, even now. But the sword could just as easily have hit her, been meant for her.

Her mind scrambled to understand Marianos's dark mood. What had she done to warrant this sudden rebuff?

She looked around, taking in the opulence of the large, foreboding space of the reception hall. The sheer size and beauty of it was meant to impress, but it made her feel small and insignificant—as if she shouldn't be here, witnessing this conversation. The high ceiling was decorated with a stunning mosaic and supported by magnificent white columns, gilded with gold. While her father had considerable influence, her family did not have a vast fortune. She was in awe of it all. And yet Marianos's words threatened to crush her happiness of moments before.

'You will be content, too—once you remember why you are doing this. That it isn't just about you,' Zoe said, coming towards him. 'Marianos, this is about the good of your empire. Your position. Your future. But, most importantly, your succession.' She took a deep breath, as if thinking about her next words carefully. 'I commend you on your decision, you chose wisely,' she said.

Her gaze shifted in Helena's direction, as if she'd just remembered she was still there. Zoe pulled herself upright. 'Now, think no more on what happened. That man's life is over, whereas your reign is about to begin. You have a wedding to plan for. I suggest you take a stroll with your bride and show her to her quarters, where she can freshen up before the feast tonight. After all, we have an engagement to celebrate.'

The formidable woman gave them both one last look before turning on her heel and leaving. And for some reason, Helena wanted to pull her back, to keep her with them. Instead, she and Marianos stood there in heavy silence, watching her go, a frown carved into the Prince's face. A chasm seemed to be opening up between them and Helena felt a prickle of dread chase over her as she waited for him to say something. Anything. When he didn't, she tried to reach him.

'*Porphyrogennetos*,' she said hesitantly, 'is everything all right?'

He whirled round to face her, his eyes chillingly cold, filled with—was that hate? Or repulsion? His hands clenched into fists. 'Does everything seem all right?' he hissed.

She reeled. The change in him was extraordinary; his attractive veneer had cracked. The charm he'd exhibited outside was gone and now ugly words filled its place. She almost expected his crown to topple and begin to slide down his head.

'Let me show you to your rooms and be done with this.'

He crossed the hall, escorted by the guards, and she forced herself to follow. She struggled to keep up with him, out into an open walkway. She tried to concentrate on placing one foot in front of the other, but her legs felt boneless. Every step was an effort. The corridor was long, made up of arches, and filled with sunlight and statues of past Emperors and Empresses who had once walked these halls, reigning here in times gone by. She felt their eyes on her, watching her every move.

Marianos made no attempt to speak with her again and the stifled quiet was deafening, the sound of their footsteps like a drumroll for the dead.

It wasn't meant to be like this. Why was he ruining it?

She had expected he might be superior, maybe even detached, especially as they had never met before—but she had hoped their upbringings would help them overcome any awkwardness. They had a lifetime of experiences to share with each other after all—so much to discover. But this coldness, it whipped her like a blast of icy wind off the Bosphorus.

It reminded her of her father and how he treated her.

Her mind raced, wondering where she had gone wrong and how she could put this right. After many winters of being moulded into the Prince's perfect bride, she felt as if she was failing. But her mother's training hadn't prepared her for this.

Finally, they reached a large wooden door. A guard pushed it open and, stepping inside, she followed Marianos into what was the most luxurious bedchamber she'd ever seen, with a large dressing area and ornate mirrors, and a huge, canopied bed hung with soft, silk curtains that wafted in the breeze. In any other circumstance, she would have been delighted that all this was to be hers.

'It is impressive,' she attempted politely through the thick wall of emotion that had built up in her throat.

'You will be sent for when it is time for the feast,' Marianos said curtly, retreating to the door.

'But, *Porphyrogennetos*,' she said, not wanting him to go, not with this enormous void between them. 'I had thought we could sit and talk for a while—perhaps spend some time getting to know each other?' she asked hopefully.

He sneered. 'I have no interest in that.'

He might as well have struck her.

She shook her head. 'I don't understand. Do you not wish to marry?' Her voice was barely a whisper. She was aware the guards stood behind them—that the men could hear every mortifying word that was being said. But she had to know.

Marianos turned back towards her. 'Did you really think I wanted to go through with that dreadful bride show?' he said, waving his hand in the direction of where they'd come from—the terrace and the palace square. His face bore down on her. 'That I want to wed *you*—a complete stranger?' He gave a bitter laugh. 'No, this is all my mother's doing.'

'But I thought—'

'What?' he spat.

He came closer still, his rage threatening to spill over, and she seemed very much to be the cause of it. 'You are well mannered and educated, yes. Beautiful, there is no doubt. You have interests enough to keep you entertained when I won't have need of you. And I respect your father. I need to bring peace to his dioceses—I need the people there on my side. But really what it comes down to is this—my mother and my advisors say I need a wife of noble birth, a respectable vessel, if you will, to bear my heirs. So that is all. Your only purpose. The single reason you are here.'

Each word was like a shard, wounding her far more than that blade on the balcony could have, for their aim was her heart and her dreams shattered into pieces, like glass falling all around her. Marianos was like one of those beautiful sculptures out in the corridor—from a distance they seemed perfect, but if you looked closely, cracks began to appear beneath the surface.

She brought her hand up to her brow, suddenly feeling ill.

'There you both are!'

Everyone looked up. The Varangian Commander stood in the doorway, watching them. How long had he been there?

His presence seemed to galvanise the Prince, distracting him, taking his thoughts in a different direction. Marianos obviously respected the warrior.

'Viggo! Did you apprehend the man who tried to kill me?' he asked, moving to greet his right-hand man.

'I did.'

'Then you will execute him. Immediately.'

'It is a day of celebration,' the Commander calmly reminded him. 'I'm sure it can wait till after the feast.'

'No!' Marianos bit out. 'I want it done now. I want to know he has ceased breathing before I sit down to dine.' He glanced back at Helena. 'At least that will be something worth celebrating.'

With his final words hanging in the air, he stalked out of the room, his guards following closely behind.

Helena swayed, feeling adrift. He was not the person she'd thought he was. She had spent her entire life fawning over an illusion of a man.

She had longed for an instant connection, but there had been nothing—Marianos hadn't even offered her any words of kindness. He could not have made it clearer—this union had not been his idea. In fact, he was opposed to it and the rejection cut deep.

So, what now?

She closed her eyes and took a deep breath.

She could ask to go home, say that she wanted to devote her life to God instead. No one could argue with that. But she'd have to live out her days in the convent. Trapped. And the very thought made her wither inside. Although perhaps, in some way, she'd still make her father proud.

Or, she could continue along this path. She could still be Empress, even if she couldn't have love.

A small cough drew her attention. '*Kyria*, is everything all right?'

Startled, she looked up to see the Commander was still there. She had been so lost in her thoughts she hadn't realised he had stayed behind. It surprised her even more to see his obsidian eyes were filled with concern.

Tears threatened and she furiously blinked them back, giving him a short nod.

'Helena, isn't it?' he said, stepping into the room, coming towards her.

'Yes.'

'I am Viggo. It seems you've had quite the initiation into

palace life,' he said. 'I can assure you things here aren't always this exciting.'

His gruff voice was softer than it had been while barking out his instructions earlier and it had a gentle lilt of an accent she couldn't place. She tried to give a small smile, but failed.

His brow furrowed. 'The Prince...'

'Is under a lot of pressure,' she finished for him, making her decision. She tilted her chin up, just a little, drawing on the steely determination that had got her through the past winters at home. She could not allow the Commander to see her devastation—she had her pride to think of and he would think her a silly girl. She did not want his pity. She would be horrified if he started making excuses for Marianos on her behalf.

Besides, this had always been about more than just her foolish notions of finding romance, hadn't it? It was about a promise she'd made to herself and her mother. It was about rescuing her father. There were other reasons for this union beyond love and she couldn't give up her family's dreams, even if her own were now tarnished. Not now she'd come so far.

She straightened. She needed to be shrewd. She had to show her loyalty to Marianos, no matter what.

'The Prince has just been through a terrible ordeal,' she asserted, getting her story straight in her head. They had got off to a bad start, that's all.

A look of understanding passed between her and the Commander and he gave a sharp nod.

'I understand. And it would surely be worth it—*worth suffering anything*—to be Empress of all this, isn't that right?'

She heard his knowing, reprimanding tone and her gaze swung up to look at him. She saw judgement darken his eyes and realised he was repeating the words she had said to the other participant earlier today. He *had* heard her.

She lifted her hands to cover her burning cheeks. He must think her awful. That she was just after a title. Riches. But if he only knew the truth—that although she had a duty to fulfil, she truly had hoped for more.

'A word of advice, *Kyria*. There are eyes and ears everywhere in the palace. You'll need to be more careful if you're going to survive here.' He moved to the door, but paused, placing his hand on the frame as he glanced back over his shoulder. 'Congratulations on your engagement, Helena.'

Chapter Two

Pulling Helena's door to behind him, Viggo looked up and down the corridor and, seeing it was empty, he let out a sharp curse.

'Helvete!'

It had been one hell of a day so far and they still had the feast to get through.

He'd been relieved when he'd managed to apprehend the man in the square and put a stop to the fighting, and he'd been able to breathe a little easier when his soldiers had ushered every last spectator out of the gates, sending them home to their families. He'd been eager to catch up to the Prince to secure his safety—but was appalled when he'd approached Helena's chambers and heard Marianos's cold, harsh words.

He didn't know what had got into Marianos lately.

He'd served the Empress Regent and her son for many years, since the day he and his sister had arrived here in Constantinople. He'd proved his worth, working his way up the ranks to where he was now—one of their most trusted advisors and military generals. He commanded a huge army of elite mercenary guards—Norwegian soldiers just like him—and he had won many battles for the crown. In return, Zoe and Marianos had treated him well and rewarded him with coin, knowing they had his unwavering loyalty. But since the Prince's coronation had begun to loom on the horizon and the bride show had been announced, something had been off.

He'd watched the Prince grow from a boy into a young man these past winters. He knew Marianos was spoilt and could sometimes be self-serving, but he wasn't cruel. Especially not to women—beautiful women at that.

'Helvete,' he groaned again, placing his hand on the wall, resting his head against the cool marble.

Truth be told, he hadn't wanted the Prince to choose Helena.

But of course he had! She was by far the most exquisite woman in the bride show. He himself hadn't been able to take his gaze off her since he'd first caught sight of her during the briefing. And when Marianos had lifted her veil, Viggo had felt an alarming punch to his gut.

He'd been drawn to her expressive eyes—green and wide, framed by thick, black lashes that matched her long, dark glossy hair—and when she had looked at him, his heart had come to a standstill, just for a moment. He had never felt such a fierce attraction to anyone—a sudden need to touch her, to see if her bronzed skin was as soft as it looked. He hadn't been able to prevent his eyes from dipping down over her soft, full lips, over the beauty mark on her left cheek, and lower, to the delicate silk that encased the small swells of her breasts, before he'd brought himself up short.

He should not be thinking like this. His head could be severed from his body just for doing so. She was going to be the Emperor's bride. He had no right.

This was unfortunate. More than a little problematic.

Because he took his role seriously. Very seriously. He could not compromise his ability to carry out his duties. He needed to extinguish the flame that had been lit upon meeting her—immediately. To allow any attraction to linger was inappropriate. Dangerous. For when he'd seen Helena be mistreated—within moments of her stepping inside the palace—his outrage had been instant and his loyalty tested. His allegiance had always been to the Prince, but the sight of her forlorn face at Marianos's harsh words, her eyes two huge pools of vulnerability…

No! He would not think of it. He pushed himself off the wall, making a fist with his hand.

It was concerning. He didn't need another distraction. He didn't need another complication in his life. He already had too many responsibilities, too much on his mind. He shouldn't be lingering here.

With that thought, he began to stride down the corridor towards the hall with purpose. They had a feast to prepare for. Everyone would be on edge after the incident today. The situation in the city was fraught and growing worse by the day. The pressure was mounting in the streets. He could feel it, taste it. He would need to double the guards on the gates, making sure the palace was secure. And if things went smoothly, only then would he be home in time to eat supper with his sister.

With every day that passed with Sofie in her condition, he was hating leaving her home alone even more. He was constantly worrying about her.

She was what he lived for. The reason he'd risked the dangerous journey along the Silk Road to Constantinople eleven winters ago. He'd been determined to bring her to this land of riches to give her a better life. And he was still striving for that now, so he ought to focus.

The incessant heat and humidity weren't helping at all. But he hadn't fought so many battles and come so far only to throw it all away on an inconvenient desire now—by losing his head over a woman. Especially not over a woman who had cowered away from him when she'd seen him, most likely repulsed by the web of scars on his face.

He had seen Helena looking at the deep, ugly lines and he didn't like it. He was used to it—people staring—and it rarely bothered him any more, so why did her scrutiny? A woman whose beauty was skin deep. She clearly lacked depth, for he had heard her whispering to one of the other participants about her reasons for wanting to marry the Emperor. It seemed riches and status were the only things of importance to her. And if that was the case, perhaps Marianos's words hadn't impacted her as much as he'd thought. He shouldn't be fooled by her act of disappointment.

Maybe she and the Prince were suited—perhaps this marriage would work. Only, he doubted it. He had seen what such a union could do to people. It had destroyed his parents—*helvete*, his entire family.

Coming to the end of the portico, he glanced out at the dazzling afternoon sun, the brilliant blue waters of the Bosphorus Strait shimmering in the distance, and sighed. He had been here since dawn, and was due a break—and he desperately needed one if he was to be on form tonight. If he left now, he could check on his sister, settle his concerns and be back in time for the feast. He could gather his thoughts and, knowing he'd seen her and put his fears to rest, he wouldn't have to worry about making it back in time for supper with her.

They just had to hold out for a few more days and the Prince would be crowned Emperor. Marianos would be wed. And then Viggo would finally receive his reward—

the silver he had been promised by the Empress Regent to see her son safely to the throne and married. Then, he and Sofie could leave.

The extra coin would give them the means to start afresh elsewhere. He knew it was not what Sofie wanted, not what either of them wanted—to say goodbye to this place they had made their home—but his sister's situation demanded it. He had to use his head and not listen to his heavy heart.

After giving his men their orders, he strode through the busy, baking streets, heading for the city walls and beyond. The celebrations and altercations had quickly died down and with his men patrolling the lanes, a guard on almost every corner, it was good to see there were no signs of any more trouble—for now at least.

As he walked through the door, Sofie's face lit up and she rushed towards him.

'Brother! You're home! Is it all over already? Tell me everything,' she said, gripping his hand. 'It's been the longest day, waiting for news.'

He laughed, pulling her in for a quick embrace. 'I have to get back, I can't stay long. But I had to come—is all well?' he said, taking a step away from her and looking her up and down. 'Any sickness today?'

She shook her head. 'I told you, you're not to fret about me. I am well. Hot,' she said, raising the back of her hand to her brow, 'but well. Now please. Start at the beginning,' she said, patting the chair so he could sit down beside her. She pushed some bread and fruit in front of him while she eagerly waited for him to reveal the details of the day. 'Don't miss anything out. How many women were there?'

'Twelve in total,' he said, taking off his mail coat, relieved to be able to discard the heavy armour for a short while.

'Twelve?' she gasped. 'All beautiful, I expect?'

'Yes,' he said. He tore off a hunk of the loaf and popped it in his mouth.

'And what happened?'

'Marianos spoke to each of them, asked them questions.'

'What did he ask?'

'Just about their interests, their skills,' he said, chewing his food. 'I didn't pay too much attention.'

Not until the Prince had reached Helena anyway.

'And who did he pick?'

'The Bishop Michel Arianites's daughter.'

Sofie's eyes widened. 'Why her?'

Viggo dusted off his hands on his breeches and shrugged, thinking back to the way Marianos had treated Helena in her chambers. If the Prince didn't like her, why had he chosen her? He gathered up his empty bowl.

'Viggo!' Her hand came down on to his arm to stall him from getting up.

'She was the most beautiful, I suppose,' he said, not meeting her gaze.

'But a bishop's daughter. Won't she be…? I mean, isn't she used to a life of study and prayer?'

'I don't know. She seems spirited,' he said.

Sofie pulled back her hand, releasing him, allowing him to take his bowl to the bucket and swill it. He could hardly believe it when Marianos had asked about her interests and Helena had asserted that her sole interest was the Prince—and to make him happy. Viggo had felt a pang of envy tear through his chest. But why should he care?

'I think his mother liked her,' he added. 'Her father is a man of influence. His position could be beneficial for the Prince in the early days of his reign. There is growing discontentment in the city. Many are unhappy by the Empress

Regent's oppressive rule. They harbour resentment. An attack was made on Marianos's life today.'

'What?' she gasped, bringing her hand up to cover her chest. 'Was he hurt?'

'No, I stopped the man.' Just. It had been close. Too close. He kept going over it in his head. How near that blade had come to almost hitting Marianos—or Helena.

'Thank God,' Sofie said, her face pale but relieved. 'Who would do such a thing? *You* weren't injured, were you?'

'No. I wondered what Helena must have thought. It was the first thing to happen after Marianos had made his choice.' The perils of having power… If Helena hadn't realised the dangers that came with Marianos's position before, she might have a better idea now. She should be careful what she wished for.

Sofie nodded thoughtfully. 'Helena. Is that her name?'

'Yes.'

'It's pretty. Does she have dark or fair hair? What did she wear?'

Viggo groaned. 'No more questions now.'

His sister's face fell. 'Please. Just answer these last ones. Then I'll stop. I wish I could have been there and seen it all for myself.'

He came back to sit beside her, guilt tightening his chest. He couldn't bear to see her look so sad. 'I know you miss your position in the palace. And the other *cubicularius*.' He could tell Sofie was craving the conversation and connection of the other women who worked for the Empress Regent. Perhaps he'd kept her hidden away for too long. But what choice did he have? 'I'm sure Zoe misses you waiting on her. But you know I can't let you go back. Not like this. No one can know. It would ruin us.'

'I understand. You have been far too lenient with me already, Brother. I know I only have myself to blame.'

He'd been shocked when his sister had sat him down one evening, not long after he'd returned from a shift, and told him she thought she was with child. Until that night, he hadn't known she'd had any contact with men.

But he didn't think badly of her, only himself. He should have spoken to her about these things, warned her of what men could be like. Instead, he'd spent too much time at the palace. He should have been a better brother—in so many ways.

When he'd questioned Sofie on the father's identity, she had shaken her head, unwilling to tell him, perhaps not wanting to get the man in trouble. She had only told him it was over, that the father of her child was no longer around.

'He told me he loved me,' she had sobbed, as he'd comforted her.

He believed it to be one of the soldiers—and she was probably right not to tell him who, because if he ever found out, he might want to throttle them with his bare hands. Yet he'd kept his anger at her foolishness, and the man for taking advantage of her, inside, promising Sofie they would get through this together. That he would look after her, help her.

But he was still concerned. A woman who had a child out of wedlock was seen as a disgrace. It would be difficult for her to ever get work, or to find a husband. And his reputation would be tarnished alongside hers.

At first, he'd been at a loss as to what to do. Terribly, there was a part of him that had hoped fate would intervene and she might lose the baby. Yet all too soon, she'd begun to feel nauseous and started to show, and he'd known they had no choice—he'd made her leave her position at the palace. He'd bade her stay indoors during the day, only walking out together at night to take in some air.

He knew he was being strict with her, but it was for her own good.

He covered her hand with his on the table. 'Helena has almost ebony hair,' he relented. As dark and shiny as the mane of a sleek black horse. 'Green eyes.' Enchanting emerald eyes. Never before had a woman made such an impact on him. She possessed a voice of soft, dulcet tones that had washed over him like the wind rustling through the leaves of his favourite olive tree. 'And she is graceful. She wore the most elegant silk tunic I've ever seen. It matched the colour of her eyes and was encrusted with tiny beads that glittered in the sunlight.'

His sister sat back, taking it all in, shaking her head in wonder, and he thought he must have satisfied her curiosity enough for now.

'I hope that she will make him happy,' she said.

Could a woman make a man happy? Viggo wondered, as he made his way back to the palace.

The Prince had certainly won a prize in Helena. But because of all that Viggo had seen come to pass between his own parents, he himself had determined not to wed—he'd never wanted a wife of his own. He felt sure it would only lead to the same pain he had experienced growing up. But tonight, he would have to put on a smile and celebrate along with the rest of them, as if this union, as if meeting Helena, was the best thing to have happened to the Prince in a long time.

But not to him… No. Viggo would maintain his distance, keep his focus and make certain everything went smoothly from now on.

Chapter Three

Viggo took in the Prince's unsteady gait and the glassy look in his eyes and knew instantly that he'd had far too much to drink.

He had positioned himself near the top table in the great hall, where he could keep a close eye on Marianos and his bride. With a swell of rousing music, the pair had arrived and all their aristocratic guests had stood to applaud them.

Marianos was holding Helena's fingers in his and a disconcerting resentment smouldered in Viggo's chest. They looked like the perfect couple. Almost. If only Marianos had been able to walk in a straight line.

Viggo clicked his tongue in disgust. After the incident today, Marianos must know they needed tonight to go well—to keep the council on side, given his coronation was imminent. People wouldn't just start to doubt Viggo's capability to keep order and control, but the Prince's, too.

As the hall became alive with conversation again, he shifted his gaze to Helena. He wondered what she was thinking—could she tell the Prince was intoxicated?

She had changed into a different tunic—scarlet and gold in colour—and she had braided her dark hair with gold twine. She smiled as she was introduced to some of the officials, conducting herself well. She looked radiant in the glittering candlelight—and seemed to have recovered from earlier. More so than he, as Viggo couldn't seem to get his breathing in check as she drew nearer.

What was the matter with him? He had met many beautiful women in his time. Taken too many to bed. But no one had ever affected him like this, so instantly, so completely. He was attracted to her, yes, but when he had watched her quietly gather herself in her chamber earlier today and seen the proud jut of her jaw and the determination in her eyes, a curious dart of admiration had also taken him over.

She was strong. A lesser woman might have bolted at Marianos's cold words, although, he reasoned, if she was indeed only here for the title and riches this marriage would bring her, that would be cause enough to stay. She probably would be willing to suffer anything. Besides, it was not as if she could go against the Prince's wishes. No one could. If Marianos said she was to be his bride, Helena had no choice—they would wed.

Marianos flicked his hand for a serving girl to approach him as he took his seat. He raised his goblet to be filled and it was topped up to the brim. But just how much wine had he had already?

Viggo ran a hand over his jaw, feeling unsettled—his apprehension stirred by dark memories from his childhood. Now he avoided alehouses and people who drank too much at all costs. They were the worst. He was still disturbed by the sound of tankards clashing, or the smell of ale on someone's breath, making his stomach turn, and raised voices and heated arguments alerted him to imminent danger.

His father had always been too inebriated to look after his family properly. It was why his mother had eventually left them. And it was the reason Viggo had been forced to grow up quicker than most. He'd had to take care of his sister and be on guard, in control, for as long as he could remember. He'd had to protect Sofie from the brute's flying fists each night when he returned from the tavern. He'd always taken the brunt of the man's anger, so Sofie didn't have to. Perhaps he owed those spats to his skill on the battlefield now—he knew how to defend himself and how to attack when it was necessary. He knew how to take a life…

A ceremonial affair, the rest of the royal party took their seats according to rank, as a decadent display of food was laid out before them on the golden plates, and he gave a thought for those people out in the city who were going hungry tonight. It was the reason the perpetrator gave for his attack today—that his wife and children were starving. That he'd wanted to make the Prince—and his mother—pay. Viggo wondered what would happen to the man's poor family now.

He leaned in discreetly to whisper in Marianos's ear. 'Are you feeling yourself, Marianos?'

'Yes. Come, join us, Viggo,' the Prince said, his manner garrulous, almost excitable.

'No, *Porphyrogennetos*. I am on duty.'

'I insist,' Marianos said, slamming his hand down on the table. 'Pull up a seat. It is my engagement feast, after all.'

Viggo glanced across at Zoe and she gave a quick nod for him to oblige. She was a formidable woman. She ruled the empire—and her son—with an iron fist, so he was surprised she conceded to Marianos's demand now. Perhaps she couldn't face another scene tonight either.

Viggo looked towards the guards on the door and all around. He took in the familiar faces of the nobles, all of whom he knew by name—all of whom he had won over through his success in battles, lining their pockets with gold. Everything seemed to be in order, so he would humour the Prince for just a moment.

'Sit,' Marianos said again, before guzzling more wine.

Viggo reluctantly lowered himself into the seat opposite Helena and he was immediately poured a drink, which he knew he wouldn't touch. He never did. He had to stay alert. And when a bowl of food was placed before him—venison and vegetables—he couldn't bring himself to eat it. He would not allow himself to be distracted.

'So tell us, is it done?' Marianos asked, leaning forward conspiratorially. 'Did you end the man, Viggo?'

'My noble son! This conversation is best saved for another time,' Zoe said, placing her hand on her son's arm. 'People are eating.'

'This conversation pleases me, Mother, therefore I shall pursue it.'

Viggo felt the entire table of officials turn to stare at him, awaiting his response. He was aware of Helena's spoon hovering by her mouth.

'My men carried out your commands as directed, *Porphyrogennetos*,' he said.

'Excellent.' Marianos clapped. 'Make sure his head is displayed for all to see. Let that be a warning to others. You say you like hunting, Helena?'

'Yes, *Porphyrogennetos*,' she said hesitantly.

'Well, that man in the square today was like the deer that roam our royal forests. If not controlled, they can overgraze. Thus, it's best we cull them to control their numbers. Enjoy your venison,' he sneered. 'Let us have some music to celebrate, yes? Musicians. Play something lively.'

Helena lowered her uneaten spoonful of food.

Zoe engaged her son in hushed conversation and Viggo hoped she was telling him to go a little easier on the wine. He was not impressed. He wasn't sure the Prince was ready to take on the crown just yet—he was still young. He would certainly need the help of his trusted advisors. He longed for him to rule wisely—he had hoped to help him, but he wouldn't be able to now he and Sofie were leaving. He prayed Marianos would take a less brutal stance than his mother and show his subjects kindness.

'I wanted to thank you, Commander. For saving our lives today.'

Viggo looked up, surprised to see Helena was speaking to him, her voice smooth, like golden honey, trickling over him, quickening his pulse.

'It is my duty to protect the Prince—and now you, *Kyria*.'

'I hope no one…else…got hurt?'

'Everyone is well.'

He turned to his left, hoping to speak to the man at his side in an attempt to avoid Helena—for the sake of his own erratic heart—but the official was already deep in conversation with another.

'Why did he do it—the man in the square?' she said, lowering her voice, drawing back his attention. 'Did he give a reason, before…?'

He sighed, knowing he had no choice but to answer her, and inclined his head. 'Taxes have been raised. There is much tension in the city—people are dissatisfied. There have been many riots of late,' he said in a hushed tone that matched her own. 'But you do not need to worry. You are safe here in the palace.'

Her beautiful brow crumpled. 'I had no idea. Why have taxes been raised?'

She had a lot to learn about how Zoe and Marianos governed the empire, he realised. Not that it would concern her—he felt sure she would be kept far away from the politics of it all. Coming from a wealthy family, she perhaps wouldn't have seen how the poor were going hungry—though, did they not appear at her father's church door each day, seeking help? After all, it was his dioceses that were the largest and affected the worst. Which was why the Prince needed to keep control there.

Viggo cleared his throat. 'To pay for the coronation—and the wedding, I believe.'

Helena's eyes widened. 'I see.' She put down her spoon completely.

Viggo walked the streets daily. He made it his duty to know the people personally and take an interest in the mood of the lower classes, and he felt he had gained their respect over the winters that had passed. Due to the broiling heat of late, disease and poor sanitation were rife. He and his men had been doing all they could to help.

After all, he had been just like them once, when he'd first arrived here. He could relate to their suffering—he knew better than most what it was like to live on the streets and he would never forget what those desperate hunger pangs were like. He'd once had to fish, hunt and forage for the little food they'd had and he'd often gone hungry so Sofie could eat instead.

He had spoken to Zoe about the situation in some of the poorer neighbourhoods in the city and she had promised to hand out leftover food—which she had done, yet days later had raised taxes. He was still simmering about it. It was the only time they had exchanged angry words. The only time he'd thought about walking away. But he needed the coin. He had to think about Sofie. He had to sit this out. Just a few more days.

The clinking of a goblet drew back Viggo's attention to the hall and he was disturbed at how the world had fallen away when he'd been speaking to Helena; he'd been wholly captivated. He was even more perturbed when the music stopped playing and Marianos rose to his feet, as if to make a speech. This was not good.

'*Kyries kai Kyrioi*, I'd like to make a toast to my mother—and my bride.'

Viggo sent Zoe a look, but as all the guests began to pound their fists on the table in support of their Prince saying a few words, there was not much they could do.

'I want to thank my mother for putting on today's show and thus finding me my beautiful bride.' Marianos's face was flushed and he was having difficulty articulating his words. 'I mean, heaven forbid, Helena and I would not have met otherwise,' he slurred. 'But to my mother, my happiness is everything.'

Marianos's voice was laced with scorn and derision, and Viggo winced. He looked around at the councillors. They were all smiling. Perhaps the Prince's wry tone wasn't so obvious to those who didn't know him as well, but he could hear the seething resentment beneath the pointed statements. Marianos was furious with his mother, but why? He must know that as his coronation was looming the council felt it was vital to establish a clear line of succession. It meant stability—a legacy that would extend beyond Marianos's reign.

And yet he could understand the hesitation. It was why

Viggo was glad he hadn't been born into royalty. He certainly wouldn't want to be forced into marriage.

'And to my bride, Helena,' Marianos continued, turning to look at her. 'Pure, perfect. Isn't she a vision? Any man's dream.'

The guests all clapped for Helena and Viggo stole a glance at her. She was all the things Marianos described, yet she had gone very pale.

'Do you know what she said today? She said her sole purpose is to make me happy.' His words drew a cheer from the guests. 'Well, aren't I the lucky one?' He raised his tankard up in the air and the wine sloshed over the sides. 'To my mother and my bride.'

'To the Basilissa Zoe and Kyria Helena,' the people in the room said, clambering out of their chairs to raise their own cups.

Marianos took a step back and stumbled, and Viggo launched himself round the table. He could not let him fall.

Helena leapt up and instinctively reached out her arms, catching the Prince as he lost his footing, and she struggled to hold him up. His weight threatened to overwhelm her, but Viggo's movements were swift and he was at her side in an instant. She immediately felt the effects of his help as he lifted the Prince, supporting him under his shoulder, his solid arm coming across her own. The contact sent a strange shiver of awareness through her body and she retrieved her arm, pulling sharply away.

His reprimanding eyes bore down into hers. 'Sit back down, Helena. I've got him.'

The Prince rested his head on Viggo's shoulder and closed his eyes. 'I'd like to go to bed now, Viggo,' he muttered.

'*Kyries kai Kyrioi*, I think my future husband has enjoyed celebrating our engagement a little too much,' Helena said, thankfully drawing a laugh from the guests. 'If you'll excuse us, the Prince needs his rest. It has been the longest, but most wonderful day. We'd both like to thank you for celebrating with us.'

'Please, continue to enjoy the feast,' Viggo said in his deep, authoritative voice and the impact of his calm leadership on the room was reassuring. The officials began to retake their seats, unperturbed.

Viggo quickly escorted Marianos out of the hall and Helena followed closely behind. But as soon as the door shut behind them, Viggo turned on her.

'Go back! You do not need to be here, *Kyria*. I can deal with this.' He shifted the sleeping Prince in his arms, getting a better hold of him.

'And how would that look, if I abandoned my future husband in such a state?'

'Proper!' A muscle worked in his jaw. 'You are not married yet and your presence is required by Zoe and the council.'

She floundered. 'Truth be told, I am glad to be out of there,' she said, wringing her trembling hands. 'I promise, if you just give me a moment, I will return shortly.'

His eyes narrowed on her. 'Are you well, *Kyria*?'

'Yes. I just need some air. It is loud, cloying in there. Everyone was staring.' She had been under scrutiny all day and she felt bone-achingly tired herself.

'Wasn't that your goal? I thought you wanted the admiration that this role will bring you,' he bit out, the judgemental tone returning.

She stepped away, stung. She supposed she had thought

she'd welcome it, the attention, after years spent locked away, kept out of sight, but instead she felt on edge, not knowing what the Prince would do next.

She turned to go.

'Just for a moment, then.' Viggo relented and she rallied. 'The royal chambers are this way.' He gestured with his head and effortlessly hoisted Marianos up once more. He began to walk, taking long, powerful strides down the corridor.

'It was good of you to step in,' Helena said.

'My primary duty is to ensure his safety,' Viggo replied.

When Marianos had announced he was going to make a toast, she'd looked up at the Prince, hopeful that he'd had time to calm down after the assassination attempt today and that he would finally acknowledge his happiness about their engagement. That he would atone for his earlier behaviour and treatment of her. But when she heard the mockery behind his supposed kind words, her hopes had been dashed once more.

She'd clenched her hands under the table, hurt. Angry, too. She didn't deserve this. After all, he was the one who had summoned her here and chosen her to be his bride.

Excruciatingly aware they were being watched by every important man and woman in Constantinople—including her own mother and father—she'd felt her skin heat, her heart begin to pound, unable to trust what he was going to say.

Her mother had been jubilant when she had met with her this afternoon. And her father, shocked to silence, as if he couldn't quite believe his daughter was going to be Empress. That he would have to bend the knee to her—the daughter who had always been a burden to him, whom he'd made to feel unlovable.

While she couldn't deny it had given her a thrill—a deep sense of satisfaction that she had proved her father wrong—there was a niggling doubt in the back of her mind, saying at what cost? Taunting her that perhaps she was the fool, for the consequences that might be associated with her achieving this goal could be great.

But at that moment, nothing could have made her reveal the sham of the engagement to her parents. Even if she was deceiving her family and lying to herself, she had to maintain the façade—her pride demanded it.

This union was still her chance of escape. For so long, she had felt confined to her father's home, kept under his strict, oppressive rule. She could finally be free. She could participate at court, enjoy performances, view art and walk through gardens. She could help her family while making something of her life—even be remembered for something when she was gone. Anything would be better than spending her days stifled in the convent.

And she hadn't given up hope of trying to win the Prince round. Perhaps she could force her dreams into reality, somehow. She just needed to be patient. After all, if she was expected to have his children, there would need to be some element of care and compassion, wouldn't there, for a child to be born?

Her mother had told her marriage wouldn't be easy, but she'd thought her mother had just been unlucky being matched to her father and that things would be different for her. But if she had to work harder to make this a success, then so be it—that was what she would do.

When she'd met Marianos in the corridor to go into the feast together, she'd done so with renewed hope, walking nervously towards him, optimistic that she might find him in a better mood. She'd felt the gazes of the statues of past Emperors and Empresses upon her, as if they were sizing her up, wondering whether she was up to the task ahead of her.

All day, she'd tried to make excuses for his behaviour, putting it down to awkwardness, distress at the assassination attempt. But when she'd approached him, her heart had sunk, for he hadn't been able to look her in the eye. He'd reluctantly taken her hand, and he had made her feel just as her father always had—invisible and unworthy.

Then he'd stood to speak and she was so afraid of what he would say in front of the room full of strangers. She didn't want his cruel treatment of her to undermine her position before she had even secured her footing here—she just had to hope the guests didn't understand the true meaning behind his words. She herself had found them hard to comprehend—after all, he'd been slurring. Swaying. In the end, she felt perhaps he'd only humiliated himself.

Viggo carried Marianos along the quiet corridors and, finally, kicked open a large wooden door. The chamber was not too dissimilar to her own and she watched from the doorway as the Commander carefully laid the Prince down on the silk and removed his shoes. It was an act of care, not duty, she thought—and the relationship between the two men intrigued her. Viggo blew out the candles on the table and then retreated from the room.

He pulled the door to and met her gaze.

'You have had a moment, now we should return you to the table. Next time, you should stay where you are. It is not your responsibility to tend to the Prince in this state.'

'Next time? Does this happen often, then?'

Viggo frowned. 'Actually, no. He does not usually drink like this.' He inclined his head. 'And while I still assert you should have remained in the hall, I admit you handled the situation well.'

'As did you. You seem to have strong peacekeeping skills—as well as being lethal with a sword.'

He grimaced. 'I grew up having to calm tempers brought on by too much ale. I have seen first-hand how it can destroy lives. Yet I'm certain this was just a one-off for the Prince—a case of too much indulgence.'

Was he was trying to reassure her?

'Let's go. You need to eat something before they take your bowl away.'

Had he noticed she was yet to touch her food? She hadn't been able to stomach it—she had been reeling from the fact the man who had thrown that blade today had been put to death. Just like that—with a snap of Marianos's bony fingers. And it had suddenly dawned on her just how precarious her position was here. How swift the Prince's cruel commands could be carried out. If she displeased him, what would Marianos do to her?

They began to walk slowly back through the quiet corridors.

'I am glad I have had the chance to speak to you alone. I wanted to explain myself, for my careless words earlier on today.' She swung her arms nervously by her sides. 'I want you to know, despite what you heard me say—in jest—I had aspirations of love, not riches or power.'

'That's convenient to say.'

She stopped walking and turned to face him, looking him in the eyes. 'It is the truth.'

'I've seen how wealth and power corrupt. I strive to protect the Prince from such people.'

'And you think I'm one of them?' she gasped.

He shrugged. 'The description fits.'

She felt winded. 'That's not me!'

He looked up and down the corridor, then his gaze came back to rest on her face. He crossed his arms over his chest. 'Why are you telling me this? Why are you trying to prove your innocence to me?'

She wasn't sure—she just felt as if she needed his approval. Perhaps it was because she knew he was important to the Prince and Zoe. Because she could see he held such power here. Or because, despite his judgement, he had been the only person to show her any kindness when he'd lingered behind in her chamber earlier today. She couldn't explain it, she just knew she wanted him to like her.

'Because I do not want us to get off to a bad start, too.' She paused. 'Where are you from?'

He frowned at her change in direction. 'Norway.'

'What brought you here?'

'Family. To give them a better life,' he said. 'I was determined to rise above my circumstances, to make a name for myself.'

'Then perhaps our reasons for being here are not so different. But that does not mean my hopes for a love match weren't genuine, that they didn't make the daunting prospect of marriage much less scary for me. Or that I am not devastated that my ideas of a romantic union have been shattered within hours of my engagement. I honestly hoped Marianos had picked me because he thought he could care for me.'

Viggo stared down at her. She was so aware of his proximity, his chest almost brushing against her. He was so close, she could smell his spicy, lemony scent and she was disturbed by the strange flicker of interest he ignited when he looked at her. She found his face oddly fascinating. She wanted to ask how he got the deep, peculiar scars to his right cheek.

He inclined his head. 'If you were having second thoughts, there are ways…reasons you could give…' he said, his voice a warm whisper. 'I've seen what bad marriages can do…' A muscle flickered in his jaw. 'I'm just saying, you don't have to go through with this.'

She tipped her chin up. 'Actually, I do. This isn't just about me.' She shook her head. 'Although I cannot believe they are taxing people to pay for a wedding the Prince doesn't even seem to want…'

Viggo sighed and released his arms. 'I'm sure that he does really, Helena.'

'Do you intend to tell Marianos what you overheard me saying today?'

He raked his hand through his hair. 'I don't think that will be necessary.'

Relief flooded her. That was something, at least. 'Thank you.'

'Come on, let's get you back,' he said.

They walked the rest of the way in silence. When Viggo pushed open the door and escorted her through the hall, the rush of heat and noise hit her, as the nobles all stood again, watching her as she made her way back to the head table.

Viggo held out her chair for her and she sank into it. His hands braced on the arms and she had the curious notion that he lingered, just for a moment, before his hands skittered across her shoulders as he moved away. She gave an involuntary shiver.

'Please, continue,' he said to the room.

She was aware he didn't join them in taking their seats,

but instead took up his former position a few feet away, standing sentinel over the hall. Watching, on guard.

She picked up her spoon. Her stomach was growling. She forced herself to gather up a little of her cold food. He was right, she needed to keep up her strength.

Zoe leaned in to whisper in her ear, so only she could hear. 'This is your fault, Helena.'

The spoon didn't reach her mouth. She swung to meet the Empress Regent's eyes.

'The Prince would not need to ply himself with wine if he were content. A satisfied man would be happy in the presence of his bride,' the woman said.

'But we've only just met,' she gasped. 'I've only just arrived here.'

'And if you wish to stay, if you truly wish to become Empress, you will fix this.'

Panic thrummed in Helena's chest, Zoe's words ringing in her ears like her father's church bells, pealing out in alarm.

'You have five days…five days before the coronation and your wedding to win him round. If not, well…you are not irreplaceable. Your head could be the next to end up in a basket just like that commoner today.'

Chapter Four

Helena felt her hair being swept out of the way, the cool metal of the axe against the back of her neck, panic squeezing the air from her lungs. She lifted her hands to her throat, gasping for air, before sitting bolt upright in bed, her eyes wide, her body drenched in sweat.

It had been two days since the bride show and her dreams were getting darker each night. She had to do something about her predicament and fast.

For the past two mornings she'd been bathed, groomed and dressed up in beautiful tunics, her hair styled to perfection. She had been expected to carry out menial tasks and any preparations for the wedding—she was brought flowers to choose between, food to sample. She'd only seen Marianos briefly for various rituals, but he had barely made any effort to speak to her—in fact, despite her efforts, she had felt as if he'd gone out of his way to avoid her.

She was at a loss as to what to do, feeling desperate as Zoe's words rang in her ears. She watched people go about their day with purpose, while she tried to find mundane things to do to keep busy.

She dined alone in her room in the mornings, ate alone in a small hall at night. She walked alone—apart from her bodyguard. It felt as if she'd swapped one cage for another.

She used to be a prisoner in her father's home, now she felt like a prisoner in someone else's. And how was she meant to fix the situation, as Zoe had demanded, if she wasn't even allowed to get near the Prince?

Well, she'd had enough of the confinement of her four walls. She had to take action. She couldn't waste another day. Frustrated, she threw off her silk sheets and tugged on her clothes—she was not in the mood to be fussed over this morning. She was perfectly capable of dressing herself. Then she pulled open the door to her room.

The guard stood to attention. '*Kyria mou*, the Prince has requested you stay in your quarters today,' the young man said.

'I will be taking a stroll around the palace gardens this morning,' she said, ignoring him. 'You can stay here or accompany me—either way, I'm going.'

She would not be detained. Not again. She was starting to think even life in the convent was better than this, as at least there she had the company of the other nuns.

She walked along the portico, the guard on her heels trying to keep up with her, pleading with her to turn back, but she kept going. The palace occupied an enviable position over the city and her gaze automatically sought out the spires of the cathedral, the impenetrable Theodosian walls and the grand arena. She ought to feel lucky to be here, she thought, as she followed the length of the pristine walkway, finding it offered discoveries of frescoes, statues or pretty plants around every corner. The vast tiered gardens were the jewel in the crown's estate, with incredible views far and wide. She hadn't had the chance to explore them properly and this would give her the space to think, to come up with a plan as to what she was going to do.

The scents of the fig and olive trees, the sight of the beautiful roses and irises lifted her spirits and she found a secluded corner to sit in for a while, watching the scores of ships cross the Bosphorus, though a commotion at the far end of the garden soon caught her eye, disturbing her peace. She saw a contingent of Varangian soldiers running towards the gates, their armour clattering, boots crunching over the ground.

'What's going on?' she asked, looking up at her guard.

'I don't know, but we really ought to go back inside,' the young man said, shifting uncomfortably. 'The Prince said…'

She turned back to the sound of footsteps running and instead began to follow the noise, her interest piqued. What were the Commander's men doing?

'*Kyria* Helena—' the guard said, exasperated.

She rounded the corner of the topiary hedges and came to a halt as her gaze travelled across the helmet-covered heads of a company of men, to the imposing man stood in front of them. The Commander was barking out instructions and her breath hitched.

Viggo's uniform was always immaculate—his gleaming chainmail covering his chest, his burgundy cloak tossed over his shoulders. She studied the dragon emblem on his armour that was meant to strike fear into their opponents. Everyone took notice of him, everyone followed his orders. And it looked as if they were readying for battle.

She had only caught glimpses of him these past few days, directing his men in the hall, talking with the Empress Regent or officials at the end of a corridor. He was always on the move, taking action. If he saw her, he would acknowledge her with that slight incline of his dark head, but he had made no effort to approach her again.

She couldn't help but stop and stare now. What was going on?

As he was talking, his blistering black gaze found hers and she swallowed. He never missed anything, she realised.

When he'd finished delivering his instructions, the gates opened and the men began to file out, but he stalked over to her.

'What are you doing here, Helena? This is no place for a woman. Get back inside.'

'What's happening?' she asked.

'The people are rioting again. There are fires in the city.'

Her heart lurched and she sent him a look of concern, but she was grateful he hadn't withheld the information from her.

'My men will soon get it under control.' He sent the guard who had been chaperoning her a stern look. 'Theodor, escort Helena back to her chambers immediately.'

Casting a furtive glance over his shoulder, she saw people had thronged the streets, men, women and children heading towards the palace. It looked as if they were about to meet Viggo's men head on, to make a stand.

'You won't hurt them, will you?' she gasped.

'That's not my intention. We're just trying to diffuse the situation, for their own safety.'

'I haven't seen the Empress Regent or the Prince today,' she said, hoping he would offer her a little more insight, before the guard could whisk her away. 'Do they know about this?'

He nodded. 'They are aware of the disturbance and remain indoors, safe. You must now do the same.'

A thought struck her. Viggo knew the Prince better than anyone. His whereabouts. His moods. He was closer to him than most. Viggo had been the only one to properly acknowledge her, to show her a sliver of kindness here. Perhaps, and she knew the chances were slim, but maybe he would help her.

But was his character to be as admired as much as his reputation as a fierce warrior? Could she trust him?

He served the Prince loyally. In return, Marianos listened to his counsel—she had seen the camaraderie between them and the deep affection. But might that work in her favour? She could certainly do with an ally right now. Might Viggo be persuaded to speak to the Prince on her behalf?

The thought grew in her mind as the guard ushered her back to her room. But how would she find a moment to speak to Viggo alone? The Commander was always occupied—in demand. Surely he wouldn't want to be bothered by her? And as he'd told her days before, the palace had eyes and ears.

By the time her evening meal was served, she had convinced herself Viggo was the answer to her problems. That he would be able to facilitate a line of communication between her and the Prince. She just needed to find the right moment to speak to him, somewhere they couldn't be seen or heard.

'Any news on the rioting today?' she asked Theodor, who stood behind her as she ate.

He stepped forward. 'The men have not long returned. I believe the Commander has brought the situation under control. The rioters have dispersed. Viggo is debriefing the Empress Regent and Prince now, before he leaves.'

'Leaves?'

'His shift is almost over.'

'Do you and the other guards not live here?' she asked.

'No, but close by, in our own residences.'

'Who guards the palace at night?'

'A mixture of the Varangian Commander and General Markou's men—he is head of the Byzantine forces. There is a fresh contingent of guards for the dark hours.'

'I see.' She pondered this as she pushed her food around her plate. 'When I'm done, I'd like to go to the palace church to pray, if that would be all right?'

'Certainly. I'd be happy to accompany you.'

Stepping inside the modest chapel, Helena cast a thought for her father—she thought he would have loved to look round the church, to study the magnificent icons and mosaics on display. He would have liked to have conducted a service here.

'You can wait here,' she told Theodor at the door, as she ducked inside. 'I'd like some privacy to pray. I won't be long.'

She felt guilty lying to him—he was young, far too young to be a soldier, risking his life for the crown. He seemed like a gentle man. But she had no choice. She had to try to find the Commander and speak to him tonight. This couldn't wait a moment longer.

Once inside the building, she slipped out the back, to the area where she had seen the soldiers gathered earlier today. And just as Theodor had told her, some of the guards whose shift was over for the day were gathering up their belongings, readying to leave.

One in particular stole her attention.

The Commander was praising the men for their achievements today, telling some of them to patch up their wounds as soon as they got home.

Hanging back in the shadows, Helena was glad she had worn her thick woollen cloak that hid her tunic—but would it be enough to disguise her? Out of the corner of her eye, she saw a uniform on a hook and sent up a prayer of thanks. She snatched up the helmet and burgundy cloak. It would help her to blend in as one of the men.

Her heart was in her mouth. She would surely be punished for her disobedience if the Empress Regent or Marianos were to hear she had left her room after dark, let alone the palace. She dare not think of the consequences if she were caught. But right now, she was desperate. She could see Viggo was about to leave and she had just three days remaining. Three days to win over the Prince. She had to speak with the Commander, urgently.

As the group stepped out of the gates, fear rippled through her—and an exhilarating sense of independence. She'd never done anything like this before. Never been out alone at night—or even in the day. She crept through the dark streets of the city, lingering a short distance behind the men, but close enough so as not to lose them. Her instincts had sharpened and she was studying her surroundings, taking everything in. The soldiers broke off from the group, one by one, as they approached their homes. But it was the man at the front she kept her eye on, her thoughts racing, her heart pounding.

Viggo spoke to various guards on street corners, asking about any disturbance, but all was quiet as they strolled past dwellings, families gathered together inside. The happy scenes made her heart clench for a future she had longed for.

She stole a look at the palace behind her—its domes and towers dominating the skyline. Once, she had looked at it in awe, desperate to step inside the high walls. Now, it seemed an oppressive place. A building that held her prisoner. Another place where she went unnoticed and ignored. That couldn't be her life. If she were to have any chance of making a good marriage, she had to fix this, as the Empress Regent had said. And hopefully Viggo could help her.

The only way she could see of reaching the Prince was to go through the Commander. This idea of hers had to work. She dared not think what would happen if he said no. But it was quite possible—no man had heard her out before.

As the group whittled down to just a few men, she fell right back, following Viggo at more of a distance. For a moment, she thought she'd lost him, but when she rounded a corner into a prestigious street, she saw him turn up a path and enter an attractive residence. It wasn't huge—just two storeys high—but the views it must offer from the back rooms, over the Bosphorus, would be one of the best in the city. It was mere steps to the shore.

Was this where he lived?

She stood and watched the property for a while, trying to pluck up the courage for what was to come, uncertainty making her shiver. The street was quiet, but she had to make sure no one had seen or followed her. She didn't want to get the Commander—or herself—into trouble. When she was sure there was no one about, she tentatively followed in Viggo's footsteps, up the path. She removed the helmet and burgundy cloak, took a deep breath and knocked on the door.

Her stomach was in knots. She didn't know what Viggo would say when he saw her, standing on his doorstep. No doubt about it, he'd be shocked—furious. She just hoped he wouldn't slam the door in her face.

The door opened a little and she was startled when a woman peered round the frame.

'Yes?'

It took her aback for a moment. She hadn't been expecting anyone but Viggo to answer. Was this his *dominia*—his housekeeper?

She could only see her face, but the woman was pretty—very pretty. Was he married?

Helena's ribs seemed to squeeze tight in shock. A strange frustration flared that she hadn't known this. She had sneaked out, come all this way—but she didn't know anything about the man. What a fool she was! She hadn't thought this through at all.

She took a step back.

'Can I help you?' the woman asked.

A burning sensation seared Helena's stomach. She shouldn't have come.

'Sofie! I told you not to open the door!' came a familiar voice from inside. 'Who is it?'

And then the girl disappeared from sight and Viggo was there, opening the door wider, filling the doorframe—his chest bare. She stopped breathing and his brow shot up when he saw her. Frozen with surprise, he stared at her and she at him.

'Helena? What—?'

'I'm sorry to intrude,' she said quickly. She felt her cheeks burn. She had never seen a man in a state of undress before. Or a man with ink on his magnificent, formidable body.

He stepped towards her and looked up and down the street. Then he saw she was holding a Varangian cloak and his scowl deepened.

'What are you doing here? And out alone at night—so far from the palace?' he said, disturbed, his voice verging on anger.

'I walked. I followed you. I had to speak to you.' She rushed to explain and it came out in a flurry.

He stared down at her. 'Did anyone see you?'

'No.'

'Are you certain?'

'Yes.' She wrung her hands. 'I didn't know what else to do. Please. I need your help.'

Giving the street once last look, he cursed and gripped her arm, the shock of his firm touch making her gasp. He pulled her inside and closed the door behind her.

He released her and, as Helena's eyes adjusted to the candlelight, she took in the building's interior, trying to look everywhere but at him and his broad bare chest, his scars and incredible ink on display. In fact, it looked as if his scars had been used as the basis of the inked design, the shape of the dragon following their lines.

The reception was comfortable, with seating. There was a large table and kitchen area, with private rooms off it, and beautiful handmade mosaics decorated the walls. It felt warm, homely.

Catching sight of a bowl and bloodied rags on the table, she couldn't help it—her gaze flew back to his body and she saw his arm was bleeding.

'Are you hurt?' she gasped, pulling down the hood of

her cloak, her concern making her forget her awkwardness for a moment.

'It's just a scratch.'

He grabbed his tunic from the back of a chair and tugged it on, covering up his chest and his injury—but it was too late. She'd already seen his wound and the vast expanse of his golden skin. She couldn't erase it from her mind.

'From the rioting today?' She forced out the words.

'Yes,' he said, pulling down the material over his taut stomach, but the ties at his neck were still loose, his tunic hanging open, his sleeves rolled up.

'Is this where you live?' she asked.

'Yes.' He frowned.

He looked different like this, at home, in his own surroundings. Even more dangerous somehow.

'Start talking, Helena.'

But she was acutely aware of the woman stood behind him, staring at her. She could hardly ignore her, yet Viggo had not volunteered to introduce them.

Helena was trying not to stare back at her. She was extremely pretty, yet young. Surely too young for Viggo? And she had unruly hair, dishevelled clothing—unlike his usual immaculate appearance. It was as if the woman didn't care what she looked like, or hadn't been expecting a visitor. Flour dusted her cheeks, as if she'd been baking. She was not the type of woman Helena would put him with at all. Didn't he deserve someone more…?

She halted her thoughts. She wasn't sure why she was thinking unkind things about her. But as she stared some more, one thing was strikingly obvious—the woman had a swollen stomach. She was with child.

Helena inclined her head to acknowledge her and Viggo

followed the direction of her gaze. He swung round, saw the woman standing there and swore again. 'Sofie! I told you to stay out the back.'

'Sorry. But you said the name Helena and I… I couldn't help myself. I so desperately wanted to meet you,' she said, rushing forward, taking Helena's hands in her own. 'The woman who is going to marry the Emperor. *Kalispera.*'

'Kalispera,' Helena replied. And then she turned to Viggo. 'Is this…are you married?' she asked. She felt the heat climb in her cheeks again that she had been so blunt. She tried to think back to what he had said the other day. *I've seen what bad marriages can do.* Was he unhappily married?

'Good God, no. This is my sister, Sofie,' he said.

She released a breath, unsure why she was relieved. 'It's nice to meet you,' Helena said, smiling now, her eyes drifting down over the woman's body again. 'You're with child.'

It came out as a statement, rather than a question, and Helena instantly wished it back, realising she'd been too bold, especially when Sofie looked anxiously at her brother.

Viggo frowned. 'Look, Helena,' he said, hastily stepping towards her. 'You should not be here. If anyone were to see you…'

'You won't tell anyone, will you?' She released Sofie's fingers and moved towards Viggo, her eyes pleading with him.

He ran his hand over the back of his neck. 'No. I don't think that would do either of us any good, do you?'

She swallowed. 'Thank you. For your discretion.'

Viggo glanced over his shoulder to talk to his sister again. 'Sofie, would you mind giving us a moment alone?'

The woman nodded. 'I'll just be in here,' she said, shuffling into one of the back rooms. 'I'm glad I got to meet you, Helena,' she said, before disappearing and closing the door.

Helena looked up at Viggo and could tell he was trying to rein in his anger. His ebony eyes were flaming. Now they were alone, she couldn't get the image of his inked bare chest and the large muscles in his arms out of her mind. What were all those marks—the ink and the scars—all over his body?

'Do you want to explain to me what you're doing here, in my house? Why you followed me? You being here could get us both killed! And for heaven's sake, why are you walking the streets at night when there's rioting going on?'

'Theodor said you'd got the situation under control. That the rioters had been dispersed.'

'For now.' He stepped towards her. 'What's this about, Helena?'

She bit her lip. 'I really am sorry. If there was another way…'

'Could you not have spoken to me at the palace?'

'I tried. You're always…unavailable. Constantly surrounded by soldiers or the Prince. And I'm barely allowed out of my room,' she said. 'I'm going out of my mind with boredom, by the way,' she threw at him, as if he were to blame.

His lips twisted. 'You have a wedding to prepare for,' he said. 'There must be a lot you could be doing.'

'It is all prepared! Almost everything is organised—Zoe has done it all—apart from her actually trying on my wedding tunic. Besides, what I want to say, or ask you, I didn't want anyone to overhear.'

He loomed closer still. 'What is it?' he said. 'Now that you've come all this way, you may as well spit it out.'

'I wanted to talk to you about the Prince,' she said, wringing her hands. 'You've seen what it's like. He has chosen to distance himself from me and there's just days to go until the wedding.' She paced away, towards a large ornate mirror. She was distracted by her reflection. Her cheeks were pink, her eyes bright and her hair had come loose from her braids after wearing that helmet, tendrils framing her face. 'Zoe has told me I need to rectify the situation, yet Marianos won't let me near him to see or speak to him.'

'I'm sure he will come round,' he said. But then he frowned. 'Unless… Are you saying you want to break off the engagement?'

She whirled round, leaving her reflection behind, crossing the distance between them. 'No. This union is vital.' To her and her family. Her pride. 'Even though I know this marriage will not be what I had envisioned—that Marianos is indifferent to me—I will not give up on it, or him.'

His jaw clenched. 'Then what are you doing here?' he said, his voice turning glacial.

'You fight for him—risk your life for him. You must think he's worth it.'

'I do,' he said, his voice clipped. 'Over the past few winters, I have tried to guide him. I believe, I hope, that he will become a leader to be proud of. The ruler we all need him to be.'

She nodded. 'I want to help,' she said. 'Only, to do so, I need you to help me first.'

His brows rose. 'Help you? How?'

She stepped towards him. 'I am at a loss as to what to

do—how I can get close to him. Marianos looks up to you; he respects you. I was hoping you could speak to him, navigate my connection with him. Help me understand his needs?'

'His needs?' Viggo's obsidian eyes widened—he looked incredulous.

'Please,' she said. She reached out and touched his arm, shocking the both of them.

He stared down at her fingers curved over his inked forearm and she instantly snatched her hand back—the heat of his skin strangely burning hers.

'I wouldn't have come here if I hadn't been desperate. But if I can't win the Prince round, if this marriage doesn't go ahead…' She wrung her hands once more. 'I will be ruined.' Her family, too. She looked up at him. 'Zoe has made it clear how unstable my situation is.'

His scowl darkened. 'What did she say?'

She gave a little shake of her head.

'Helena,' he said, stepping towards her. 'Did she threaten you?'

'I need to know I can trust you,' she said.

'Isn't it a little late for that?'

A pained expression flittered across her face and he relented. 'You have my word. Whatever you tell me stays within these walls.'

She swallowed and nodded. 'She said that if I don't win Marianos's affections, if the wedding doesn't go ahead, then she will see to it that I end up the same way as that man in the square.'

Viggo cursed.

Helena's touch—it had surprised him. To feel so awakened by the contact, and in the same moment hear that her life had been threatened, it troubled him. Deeply.

This, on top of the fact he was reeling from Helena even being here at all. In his home. He shook his head.

Seeing her at his door had caught him off guard. She was putting them all in danger. But when she'd uttered the words, 'I followed you. I had to speak to you', his heart had clenched between his ribs.

Then, to make matters worse, she'd seen his sister—and her swollen stomach. It had shaken his usual composed demeanour. What had Sofie been thinking? He'd gone to great pains to keep her hidden for the past months. She knew better than to put herself at risk of being seen. Yet he'd turned to see her standing in the kitchen, staring at Helena, as if she was transfixed, unable to help herself.

Now Helena was the only other person who knew his sister was having a child. *Helvete!* It complicated things, massively.

And as if that wasn't enough, she wanted him to assist her in winning the Prince's affections. His frustration had flared. It was too much. Especially when there was a part of him that had hoped she'd come here to ask for his help to get her out of her engagement.

But, no, of course not—why would she? She had the chance to be Empress. He knew better than to believe her story that she wanted to marry for love and could guess at her real motivations for the marriage—the allure of power and wealth beyond her dreams.

How foolish of him to think she'd had a change of heart.

He was suddenly excruciatingly aware of how small it was in here—not the type of dwelling she was used to stepping inside at all. He rubbed the back of his neck, feeling uncomfortable in his own home. Old feelings of worthlessness that stemmed from his childhood threatened to surface. That he wasn't enough. That he didn't have anything to offer anyone. He caught sight of a pile of clothes thrown over a bench and he moved to tidy them. Next, he cleared the bowl of dirty water his sister had been cleaning his wound with off the table.

'Do you want to sit?' he asked.

'No, I'm all right. Thank you.' Helena held her arms stiffly around her body and he thought she must be nervous—after all, she had taken a big chance coming here. He didn't know whether to be flattered or furious.

'Do you mind if I do?' He pulled out a chair and slumped into it. He needed to focus.

Helena was right, he did know Marianos better than most. He had served him for years and had learned much about him—cared for him. Yet he had a sudden desire to vent the Prince's unworthiness to her, even though he knew he wouldn't.

Besides, even if he didn't like the idea of Helena and Marianos together, he needed them to marry so he could claim his reward—and so Zoe wouldn't follow through with her appalling threat.

He was sickened she'd said such a thing. He knew the woman was ruthless, but still, it made his stomach churn.

Helena pulled out a chair after all and sat down opposite him. She clasped her hands together and leaned in across the table, and he got a waft of her sweet, floral scent. 'So will you help me, Viggo?'

He swallowed. He really didn't want to say yes. She was asking for his help to bring them together, when what he really wanted to do was to keep them apart. But what choice did he have?

It was unfathomable to him that she needed his help to begin with. He couldn't understand why Marianos had chosen her, then inexplicably rejected her.

'So you're really determined to go ahead with this?' Despite the way she had been treated by Marianos and Zoe so far. It made him angry on her behalf.

What if he didn't succeed? Would Zoe really carry out her threat?

'I know it won't be easy. But if I need to get the Emperor on side to keep my head…' she said, her lips curling upwards.

He sent her a stern look. 'Don't make jests like that, Helena.'

He thought that would be the worst order he could ever receive from Zoe. It would be one he would refuse. He closed his eyes briefly. 'I will do what I can to help.'

'Really?' she said, her face instantly brightening, the taut lines on her face softening. 'Thank you, Viggo.'

'But I do have some conditions.'

It was Helena's turn to sit back. 'All right. What are they?'

'One. You will not say anything of you coming here or anything you have seen tonight.'

She shook her head, as if not fully comprehending.

'About my sister.'

Realisation dawned in her eyes.

'She worked at the palace as one of the Empress Regent's *cubicularius*. Because of her condition, now she cannot. We have said she is sick—we would rather no one knew about her being with child. If you were to reveal what you have seen here tonight, it would bring shame on me and my position if those in the palace were to find out. My reputation would be ruined. My relationship with the Prince would be tested.' Sofie's secret could not get out before he received the coin he was owed. 'Can I trust you not to say anything?'

Her forehead creased. 'Where is the father?'

'Never mind about that.'

'Sofie is not married?' she gasped.

He saw her eyes widen in shock and he reached across the table, placing his hand over hers. 'Look, Helena—'

He could understand it. He had reacted just the same when he had found out. He had been so afraid that Sofie's honour—and his—would be sullied. That they would both be ostracised by society, as they had been in Norway because of his father. *Because of Viggo's own actions.* Well, never again. He would not subject them to that. He was determined that by the time the baby came, they would be long gone. They would start again somewhere no one knew them, where no one would judge them.

So, he needed to be sure Helena would keep quiet.

'I understand. I won't say anything,' Helena agreed and he released her hand. Though he could still feel the softness of her skin, the heat from their touch.

'Thank you.'

'And the second condition?' she said. He was aware of her moving her hands into her lap, out of his reach, her voice sounding a little shaky.

He raised a single dark brow. 'I told you to stay in your room today. You ignored me. From now on, you will do as I say. No arguments. And right now, we need to get you back to the palace, before someone realises you're missing. There will be no more running around at night, do you hear me? I can't protect you, help you, if I don't know your whereabouts. Do we have an agreement?'

She nodded and smiled tentatively, and he tried to ignore his chest squeezing, his responsive flickering pulse.

'We do.'

Chapter Five

Helena sat in the cosy kitchen as she waited for Viggo to change. She could hear him bickering with his sister through the door, Sofie insisting on bandaging up his wound before he left.

'He really doesn't need to walk me back,' Helena said, as Sofie appeared from out of the back room with the bowl of water and bloodied rags.

'Of course he does. You're to be Empress. You can't be roaming the streets on your own at night.' She put the bowl down and washed her hands. 'Besides, my brother wouldn't have it any other way. That's what he does—he takes care of people.' She shrugged, coming over to the table and pouring Helena some water.

'Let me do that,' Helena said, standing to take the jug out of her hand.

Sofie relinquished the vessel and Helena filled two cups.

'It's out of habit, you know. He grew up doing it. He was left in charge of raising me, when he was just a boy himself. He thinks I don't remember that he would make do with less food, less everything, so I wouldn't go without. But I've never forgotten it. He never went off exploring, playing with his friends, instead staying home so he could look after me.'

'Where were your parents?'

'Our mother left us when we were little. Our father withdrew from life—always trying to solve his problems in the bottom of a barrel of ale,' she said. 'Viggo really is the best brother. He protected me from a lot of things. He took me away from there and brought me here when I was five, to give me a better life.'

So in a way, they'd had similar upbringings—they had both been unwanted by their families. It explained Viggo's comments about ale the other evening. And now she knew, beneath that brooding, fierce warrior exterior, there was a softer, compassionate side to him that was trying to protect his sister and keep her secret.

The same part of him that had agreed to help her.

Helena felt better about her situation already, knowing she had the Commander on her side. That she wasn't alone in this. She guessed that's how Sofie must have felt growing up.

'What's the age gap between you?'

'I am ten and six. He's ten years my elder. We struggled for a while when we got here—but Viggo made friends quickly in the city. They helped him to raise me while he did various things to earn coin. And he trained hard, finally getting into the Varangian Guard.'

Helena took all this in. It must have been incredibly hard for Viggo.

'I never had any siblings. I should have liked one, I think.' Helena smiled sadly. 'I wonder whether you will have a boy or a girl?' she asked, nodding to Sofie's stomach.

'I would like a boy…' she said, resting her hand on her bump.

'But she won't mind, as long as it's healthy. That's the

most important thing,' Viggo said, emerging from one of the rooms off the kitchen, back in his uniform.

Helena straightened.

Viggo caught his sister's waist lightly with his hand and gave her a kiss on the cheek.

He was still the same, intimidating man she had met in the gilded reception room the day of the bride show, but while she felt she could breathe a little easier now he was in full regalia, his burnished inked skin hidden from view, the more she knew about him, the more her heart seemed to race when he was near. It was peculiar—she found herself envying the camaraderie between him and his sister.

'Ready to go?' he asked, looking over at her.

'Yes,' Helena said, rising to her feet. 'I'm sorry you're having to do this.'

He turned to his sister. 'Lock the door behind us,' he said.

Sofie rolled her eyes. 'Don't worry about me.'

Viggo passed Helena her cloak and she took it from him, their fingers brushing. She pulled it on, then he handed her the Varangian cloak to put over the top.

'Where did you get this?' he asked.

'I saw it hanging up. When no one claimed it, I decided to borrow it.'

He loomed over her and placed the helmet on her head. 'You'd better wear this, too,' he said. 'We don't want anyone recognising you.'

'I don't know how you see anything in this,' she said, wrinkling her nose under the brass plate, wobbling her head from side to side.

His lips quirked and his hands came up to tighten the buckle on the leather chinstrap. 'This helps to hold it in place.'

She stopped breathing as his large fingers brushed against her throat, gently working against her jaw, causing her skin to heat. Why did that always happen? Each time he touched her, her heart skittered. His dark eyes stared down into hers with quiet intensity and she wondered if he could tell her breathing had stalled.

Finally, he was done and moved away to open the door. He glanced up and down the street, and she was glad of the blast of cool night air against her burning skin.

'Right, let's go,' he said.

They began to walk at a pace down the quiet lane. It was late. The only sounds were their two sets of footsteps and the waves from the Bosphorus crashing on to the shore behind them. When a lone gull let out a screeching call, she jumped. She kept looking around, especially behind them. But she hoped most people were tucked up in their beds, asleep by now.

Viggo was probably cursing her that he wasn't doing the same, especially as he was risking his position—and his life. It was honourable of him to do this. She hoped he knew she appreciated it.

The further away from his home they got, the more aware of him she became—that it was dark, they were alone and he hadn't spoken. His spicy scent drowned out the fresh, salty air and his arm kept brushing against hers.

'What happened today, with the rioters?' she said, trying to fill the silence.

'Keep your voice down,' he bit out. 'If people were to see us, hear us…' He shook his head and she shuddered. They walked on, but after a while, he relented. 'Sometimes the people just want to be heard, to express their dissent,' he whispered. 'If only Zoe, or Marianos, would listen. I have no choice but to bring my men out into the streets to keep control. When the people see the soldiers march out of the gates, they often lose their nerve. Most of them, anyway. But I don't believe everything needs to be settled with the sword. In instances like these, violence doesn't usually help.'

She thought back to the gash to his muscular arm, images of his broad chest filling her mind again. She wished they wouldn't. 'You were injured.'

'Happens all the time.' He shrugged.

Was that how he got all his scars—even the ones on his face? She turned to look at them again in the soft glow of the moonlight. The lines seemed to spread out from a central mass, almost resembling the shape of a star, like the ones in the sky above.

He stopped walking and turned to look at her, catching her staring.

'I've seen you looking at my scars. Do they bother you, Helena?'

'No!' she croaked, shaking her head, embarrassed.

He nodded and carried on walking.

'Are they all battle wounds?'

'You could say that.'

As they rounded the corner, they saw two men patrolling the street. He reared back, gripping her arm and pulling her down so they were crouching low, behind a bush. It sent a ripple of apprehension through her—or was that due to the fact their bodies were close, his pressing against hers?

'Who are they?'

'They're General Markou's men. We'll have to go another way. We can't risk having to explain this to anyone.'

'What, you and me taking a midnight stroll?'

He stared at her. 'You think this is funny?' he asked.

She bit her lip. No, no, she didn't. If her mother could see her now, she'd have a fit. If Zoe were to discover her… She shook her head, grateful it was still attached to her body. She licked her lips, wrapping her arms around her waist.

His eyes dipped to her mouth, before he nodded to a spot over her shoulder.

'There's a passage, just over there. We'll go the back way. Stay behind me. Keep within the shadows.'

She didn't like the look of the walkway he was suggesting they take. 'Shouldn't we wait for the men to leave and go down the main street? Isn't it quicker?'

'You agreed to do as I say, remember? No arguments. We're doing this my way.' She felt the whisper of his warm breath across her face. And when he took her arm in his large hand, tugging her with him in that firm but gentle and extremely disconcerting way, there was nothing she could do but obey.

It was pitch black in the passage, dank and narrow. They had to feel their way along the walls. She didn't know this route. 'Is it safe?' she whispered.

'Safer than walking alone out here in the first place,' he ground out. 'Yes, it's safe. You're with me.'

'I'm not familiar with this neighbourhood.'

'No,' he snapped. 'You wouldn't be.'

She was aware of his steady breathing, the warmth emanating from his body moving just ahead of her. Her movements were jerky and she kept bumping into his broad, solid back.

'Sorry, I can't see anything,' she whispered, cursing her clumsiness.

She was glad when they reached the end of the alley and stepped out into a moonlit courtyard, until the metallic smell of blood hit her. At first she wondered if Viggo's wound was bleeding again, until her eyes adjusted to the pale light and she saw bodies lying in the street, with people sitting around them, weeping.

The hairs on the back of her neck stood on end and she felt Viggo tense. He instinctively reached for the hilt of his sword.

'Wait here. Stay hidden,' he said.

She didn't want him to leave. She reached out to grab hold of him, to make him stay, but he was already gone. All she could do was watch, helpless, as he walked across the street, picking his way between the wounded, while she took in the destroyed buildings all around. What had happened here?

She was struck by the squalor and poverty of the neighbourhood, compared to the magnificent palaces and residences of the upper classes. She had never even dreamed there were places this bad. That people lived like this. And in that instant, she knew she was spoilt. She had nothing to complain about. Her life in the convent hadn't been so bad. At least she'd had a warm bed to sleep in, food to eat and a roof over her head. Now, marrying a man who was indifferent to her—whose mother was ruthless—was nothing compared to what these people had to deal with.

Was this why they had been rioting?

A thought hit her—had Viggo's men done this? Was this how he'd stopped them? He'd promised he wouldn't hurt them and yet the evidence was clear…

Some adults were holding children, or weeping over bodies. Others were tending to their wounds, or trying to patch up the broken walls of their residences.

He should be ashamed.

She watched as Viggo approached an old man, who held his head in his hands, and she could not do as she was told.

She couldn't just hide here, in the shadows. She needed to know what had happened; she wanted to hear what was said. Had she picked the wrong ally?

These people needed help—could she assist them? Unable to breathe in her helmet, she released the strap and tore it off. Drawing in a sharp breath, she tiptoed across the courtyard, passing one lifeless body, then another—some women, others children. Bile rose in her throat. She had never seen a dead body before.

She saw Viggo crouch down. 'What happened here?' he asked.

The man looked up into the Commander's eyes. 'Viggo!' he said. 'You are too late, my friend. They showed no mercy. They were just boys,' he said, gesturing to the bodies that lay on the ground in front of him. 'Hungry boys,' the man cried, huge sobs racking his body. 'They didn't mean any harm.'

Viggo placed a hand on his shoulder. 'I am sorry for your loss, Niketas,' he said.

Did Viggo know these people? How?

'Here,' Helena said, passing the man a blanket she had found discarded on the ground.

Viggo was up on his feet like a shot. 'I told you to stay back,' he barked.

'And I want to help. Did your men do this?' she threw at him.

'No!'

His eyes blazed down at her. But before he could chastise her further, more people came out of the shadows, from all directions, holding makeshift weapons. Men, women and children began to surround them. They had dirty, hunger-panged faces and anger in their eyes.

Suddenly, she was afraid. Did these people mean to harm them?

Viggo held out his arm to push her behind him. 'Get back,' he said.

One man approached Viggo and went to hit him with his wooden baton, but Viggo stepped out of the way and the man fell. Another approached, taking Viggo on, but he stopped the blow, twisting the man's arm, wrestling him to the ground.

'My men and I are not responsible for this,' Viggo roared.

A third tried to tackle him, but Viggo was too fast. He was careful not to hurt them, yet he managed to put each one down. They were no match for him.

The man who had been sitting, inconsolable, tried to stand and Viggo put an arm under his shoulder to help him up.

'Hear him out,' the man said. 'It was not the Varangians. They are not to blame for this. Viggo is on our side. This was General Markou's doing. His men did this.'

Helena stepped back. So Viggo wasn't at fault?

The crowd began to quieten.

'These were not our orders. Neither the Prince—nor I—commanded this,' Viggo said. 'We did not intend for anyone to get hurt today. We just wanted to control the crowd. Regain order.'

'What about the Prince's mother?' another one asked.

'She takes, takes, takes from us,' a woman cried.

'I do not know. But I promise, I will look into this—what happened here. You have my word,' Viggo said. And that calm he exuded—that she had seen him instil in the officials at the feast the other night—had the same effect here. She felt terrible for condemning him so quickly. 'At first light, I will send my men to help you with your wounds and your homes.'

He was a good man, she realised. She wouldn't judge so quickly again.

'What about the dead?' someone called.

'We will bury the bodies. You will have your chance to say your goodbyes.'

The man Viggo had called Niketas gripped his arms and embraced him before stumbling away and Helena realised the gravitas of the situation. These people were weak with hunger. Zoe—and Marianos—had raised their taxes yet they couldn't even afford to feed themselves or their families. Some had no homes. It was despicable.

She suddenly felt contrite—that she had moaned about her situation to Viggo. What did she possibly have to moan about? Apart from the fact she was meant to be marrying the man who was responsible for this suffering. What must the Commander think of her?

She raised her hand to her throat, where a huge lump grew. She felt the royal jewels around her throat, strangling her. She needed to do something. She needed to make amends for Marianos's brutal rule. She gently tugged at the silver and it came away. She stared at it in her hand, wanting it gone. She walked over to the woman holding her children and placed the trinket in her gaunt hand, closing her fingers around it. 'To help you rebuild what you lost,' she said.

And then she did the same with the jewels in her earlobes and the rings from her fingers—she tore them from her body, before handing them out. Excited whispers rumbled around the crowd. These decorations meant nothing to her, yet she knew they were worth a lot to these people.

They could change their lives. She would tell Zoe she'd lost them, she didn't care what the woman would say.

'Εὐχαριστῶ.' Thank you, people exclaimed. *'Εὐλόγησον.'* Bless you.

She couldn't stop. She carried on around the courtyard, handing out her tablion, made of precious metal, and her bracelet, encrusted with jewels, until Viggo caught her by the arm.

'Enough now,' he said gently. 'There'll be nothing left of you and I'd like to get you home in one piece, if that's all right with you?' His tone was disapproving, although his eyes glittered down on her in admiration.

She felt a tug on her tunic and looked down to see a little girl staring up at her.

'You're her, aren't you? You're the Princess Helena?' she asked, wide-eyed.

More mutterings erupted around the onlookers as the people began to comprehend who she was.

Viggo gripped her arm harder, in warning—it was like a burning band of steel, but she cast him off.

She got down to the girl's level and looked into her eyes.

'I am she,' she whispered.

'Have you come to help us?' the girl asked.

'I will do my best.' She removed her diadem, adorned with pearls, and placed the headband on top of the girl's gentle blonde curls. 'For you,' she said.

The girl gasped, feeling the smooth little beads with her tiny, grubby fingers.

'We must leave now,' Viggo gritted out, hauling her up.

She could see she was attracting attention, causing a stir—the exact opposite of what he'd wanted. But she hadn't been able to just stand by and do nothing.

With a final promise to send his men, Viggo tugged her with him down another dusty street, launching her forward at such a pace it was clear he wanted to get her away from there. She could feel the tension rippling off him.

'Do we have to walk so fast?' she asked him, her legs aching.

When he didn't answer, she tried to pull her arm out of his hand to force him into slowing his pace, but he just held her harder.

'Will you please slow down?'

He stopped and turned on her, grasping her shoulders, his face livid. He gave her a little shake. 'Slow down? Have you gone mad?' he barked. 'Do you have no regard for your safety at all? You're supposed to be asleep in the palace. Safe inside those walls. I told you to stay back. To keep hidden. And yet you defy my rules every chance you get. Do you want Marianos to know you were out here this late at night, mixing with commoners?'

She blanched. 'No, of course not!'

'It looked that way to me. Speaking to the people, showing your face, handing out your trinkets.'

'I wanted to help.'

'It won't *help* anyone if they execute you for it!'

She reared back.

Is that what he was worried about—why he was so incensed? Was he concerned about her safety?

'I'm sorry,' she said and he released her.

He drew a hand over his face and took a breath. 'He wouldn't like it. *I* didn't like it. It's dangerous. You could have got hurt.'

'I'm sorry,' she said again. 'You're right. It was foolish of me. But it isn't fair that those people are suffering because of my wedding. That they're going hungry. That those children were killed because of it…'

Her voice cracked and tears filled her eyes. She frantically tried to blink them away. When one escaped, she drew her hand furiously across her face. She didn't want him to see her cry. She couldn't believe she was letting her emotions get the better of her. But until this week, she'd had no idea of the suffering that was going on and she was angry about it.

Viggo brought his hands back up to her shoulders, but this time his touch was gentler, his thumbs stroking over the material of her cloak instead.

'You're not responsible for that. Those people aren't suffering because of you, Helena. But because of Zoe's cruel rule and Marianos's General.' A muscle flickered in his cheek. 'My men would not have treated them so.'

'Why did he do that?'

'I don't know—we rarely agree on how to resolve things—but I intend to find out.'

She sniffed.

'What you did back there, it was good of you,' he added, a crease appearing in his brow, as if she had surprised him, as if he was still trying to understand her.

'I had no idea this kind of thing was going on,' she whispered. 'Maybe, if I do become Empress, I could make a difference somehow. I don't know how…perhaps I could start with donating some of my royal wardrobe. I have no need of it all…'

Viggo inclined his head. 'You'd do that?' he asked. 'You'll have nothing left.' He smiled and her stomach whooshed in response. It changed his entire face from brooding, dangerous warrior into… He was no beast. He was strikingly attractive.

'We can arrange for the guards to distribute them. It's a good idea, Helena. Not just a pretty face, are you?' he teased, ducking down a little to look into her eyes.

He thought her pretty?

'I'm sorry I raised my voice. Forgive me?'

She nodded, confounded that this great warrior was apologising to her on a dark, moonlit street. It had been the most surreal night of her life and her feelings were all over the place.

He looked down the street. 'We're almost there. Do you think we can get you back without any more incidents?'

After they turned the next corner, the Great Palace loomed into view and, as they approached the guards' entrance, she was relieved to see all was still. But would they be able to get through the gates, no questions asked?

'I've been gone a while. I left your guardsman outside the chapel. I asked him to wait while I prayed. Do you think he might have raised the alarm when he realised I wasn't inside?'

Viggo shook his head. 'I don't hear any signs of the men being sent out to look for you. If I were Theodor, I wouldn't want to be responsible for having lost you. He's young, keen. Fear might have kept him silent. With any luck, he might still be there, hoping you'll return.'

'How are we going to get past the guards?' she asked, looking up at the men manning the gates, hearing a tremor in her voice, her movements stiff.

But Viggo had already placed her helmet back on her head and was ushering her through. He acknowledged the men and they waved him in, trusting him. Yet she was glad his hand never once wavered from her elbow.

Chapter Six

'Let us look at your strengths,' Viggo said, stalking round the large wooden table as Helena broke her fast. 'Why do we think Marianos chose you at the bride show?'

'I don't know.' Helena shrugged, popping an olive into her mouth, drawing his eyes to the parting of her beautiful plump lips. His stomach constricted.

He was regretting not getting any rest last night—it was affecting his ability to focus.

'Well, first and foremost, your beauty.'

She blushed furiously.

After seeing Helena back to the palace, he'd been exhausted when he had finally made it home again, yet sleep had eluded him, his mind racing with everything that had happened. Thoughts of what General Markou's men had done taunted him, his rage simmering. The man's heavy-handed approach, while perhaps stopping the people from rebelling in the short term, would only stir up more anger. People had lost their lives—loved ones.

He couldn't get the image out of his mind of Helena tugging off that helmet, stepping out into the square, showing her face for all to see and putting herself at risk. His heart had been in his mouth. When those men had approached and begun to attack him, he knew they were hurting, wanting to lash out, but in that instant, he'd thought only of Helena and his need to protect her.

He'd sent his men back out there first thing. And he had asked to speak with Zoe and Marianos this morning about Markou's actions. But he was struggling to concentrate. Helena was distracting him. When Theodor had told him she was breaking her fast alone, he hadn't been able to resist putting his head round the door to the dining chamber. Her face had lit up when she'd seen him, making his chest tighten as she'd welcomed him inside.

'Your looks must have attracted Marianos in the first place, so we have that in our favour. We just need to remind him why he chose you. You'll get the chance later today as he has agreed to make your first public appearance together—at the Hippodrome.'

She gasped and clapped her hands together, suddenly excited. 'Thank you, Viggo.'

Progress had been made in the space of the morning. The chariot races were the Prince's favourite entertainment. He should be in good spirits. It might just help to bring Marianos and Helena together—only Viggo wasn't sure how he felt about that. He was uneasy about them going ahead with such a big event in light of the tensions in the city. But he also didn't like the thought of watching on while Helena conversed with Marianos, trying to get closer to the Prince and win over the man's affections, despite the fact Viggo had promised to help her.

His mind kept returning to how he'd foolishly insisted they take that passageway last night and he'd had to suffer her body bumping against his in the dark, her small, perfect breasts crushing against his back while her soft floral scent had exasperated his senses. He had almost growled out loud in frustration.

'I'll wear something he'll like—and it'll be a chance to use my womanly wiles, or whatever my mother calls it,' Helena said, waving her hand in the air.

He raised an eyebrow.

'You know what I mean,' she said, suddenly flustered, as if she couldn't believe she'd said that out loud. 'Mother says all men like to feel noticed. That I should compliment him on his looks, often, and always laugh at his jests.'

Viggo's heart clenched. 'Is that so?'

'I don't know if it's actually true or not,' she said, bumbling now.

He couldn't help but smile. She was so sweet..

Since they'd come to this agreement, she seemed to have relaxed a little around him, dropping her guard slightly, and he was glad. She suited her surroundings, the walls and furniture adorned with silk, just like her slender figure.

'What else has your mother taught you?' he said, crossing his arms over his chest and leaning back against the table.

'She is a woman of unbridled ambition. While every girl is raised with the expectation that they will marry to enhance their parents' position, of course my mother set her sights on the Prince,' she said, rolling her eyes. 'So my training began at a young age. Whatever new interest she heard Marianos had taken up, I was forced to like. My tastes had to change in accordance with his whims.'

Viggo frowned. 'That's a bit extreme, isn't it?'

'I don't know. It worked, didn't it? Well,' she said, her brow furrowing. 'To an extent.'

He ran a hand round the back of his neck. 'So all those things you said at the bride show, were they true? Do you like to read and sew and dance and hunt?'

'How do you remember all that?' she asked, surprised.

And then she shrugged. 'Yes, that was all true.' But then she wavered, as if she couldn't tell a lie. 'Perhaps not the deer stalking so much. I can't bear to see animals get hurt, and I was never allowed to step too far from the convent.'

'Is that why I've never seen you at court?' Viggo asked.

'Yes.'

He shifted his position, crossing and uncrossing his legs, feeling ill at ease at what she was telling him. It sounded as if she'd been kept captive all her life and raised purely for the pleasure of one man. It made him feel queasy. What about her? Had her needs not mattered to her parents?

'So this union—is it what you want, or what your mother wants?'

She bit her lip. 'It is vital to me and my family.'

'Why?'

She put down her spoon. 'All my life I've been insignificant…'

That was not what he was expecting her to say.

He shook his head as if to instantly refute her claims, but she held up her hands and continued. 'I know what you're going to say, but it's true. The day I was born, I have been told my mother couldn't stop crying, because my father so desperately wanted me to be a boy. I have always been a major disappointment to him. He didn't want me. He wanted a son. He has made that clear my whole life.'

Viggo frowned. 'He mistreated you?' Perhaps they weren't so dissimilar.

'He just never cared for me.' She shrugged sadly. 'He never gave me the time of day. He didn't think I was worth bothering with. A boy would have brought status and continued the family line, but my father and mother must have fallen out of love, for they never had another child.'

His heart went out to her. His mother and father had never cared for him either. How could they have and done what they did? He'd often wondered why his parents had ever had children in the first place.

'Then we have that in common. I was never my father's priority.' He wondered why he'd revealed that. He didn't usually tell anyone about himself, or talk about his upbringing. He scowled. 'Anyway, you were saying…?'

'My father wanted me to go into the convent, but my mother…she was determined to push me in this direction. And she brought him round to her idea, telling him the sooner I had children, the sooner his precious legacy would be preserved.'

'So you're doing this for them?'

'Not just that.' She bit her lip. 'I told you before, I truly was hoping for a love match,' she said, her cheeks heating once more. She stared down at the wooden table, rubbing her thumb across the grain, as if it was the most interesting thing to focus on. 'I love the fables,' she admitted, shrugging one slender shoulder. 'I had hopes to meet the handsome Prince and become a princess. Doesn't every girl?' She tried to smile, but it didn't reach her eyes. 'I guess it was naive of me.'

'Not naive,' he said, crossing his arms over his chest. 'But I think that love you speak of is rare. Perhaps reserved only for stories of make-believe. And to find that with a man you met on a palace balcony for a moment in front of thousands of people…?'

She gave a sharp nod. 'So, you're not married?' she asked, looking up at him.

'No. I will never marry. I refuse to make the same mistakes my parents did.' He grimaced and wondered if she could hear the burning resentment beneath his words. 'They were always fighting. Never had time for us. When people hurt you, or you see over and again how they hurt each other, I think it puts you off ever wanting to take that path yourself.'

You close your heart off to protect yourself.

It's why he avoided relationships. He refused to let anyone in. He wouldn't be hurt again. It was why if he wanted a woman, he bedded one he didn't care for, who wasn't likely to return any affection for him. It kept things simple. For so long he had striven for independence—now he had it, he would never return to relying on anyone again.

'How is it that your parents could marry?' he asked. 'I thought bishops had to be celibate.'

'Celibate?' That little crease appeared between her brows again, as if she didn't know what the word meant. Dear God. Was she really that innocent? She really had lived a sheltered life—and had a lot to learn. He would dearly love to be the one to teach her. Unfortunately, that job would fall to Marianos. He dug his fingers into his arms and frowned at the direction of his thoughts.

'I thought bishops had to be married to the church, not a woman,' he said.

'They were married prior to his ordination.'

'I see.'

'I've had a lot of time to think these past few days. The thought of spending my life in the convent—I'd suffocate there,' she said, shaking her head. 'I can't go back.'

Just how bad had her childhood been? At least he had been able to make the decision to leave his home. He had fought his way out and got away. He'd been determined to live a better life. Helena hadn't had that chance—until now. Was this her fighting for her freedom? Did she see marrying Marianos as her way out?

'I thought back to what the Prince told me the other day. That it is my duty to provide him with a child. My father always said the same—that if I wasn't going to go into the convent, I could at least provide him with a grandson. Perhaps that is my purpose in life.'

Viggo went to shake his head, then he looked down at Helena's plate and saw she hadn't eaten some of her fruit.

'Don't you like that?' he said.

'I've never tried it,' she said. 'I'm not allowed.'

'Not allowed to eat pomegranate?'

She shook her head. 'The Prince doesn't like it.'

He looked at her, incredulous. He came off the table towards her. 'Are you trying to tell me you know all his likes and dislikes—and only eat the same things he does?'

'Yes, my mother made sure I kept only to his preferences.'

That was too much. It sounded as if her mother had prioritised Marianos's wishes over Helena's—and for how long?

'How did she know such things?' Did the woman have a spy within the palace walls?

'Court gossip and gatherings where the Prince's character and habits were often discussed,' Helena said. 'Personal connections in the palace. And she has very keen observation skills.'

'You know that's not normal, don't you?'

'What?'

'To live vicariously through someone else. You must have your own experiences. You know that, yes?'

Did she not want that—to live a little—before she married? He had wanted that for his sister. He felt angry that a man had taken that chance away from her—she was still so young, yet she was now going to be a parent herself.

Helena nodded, but he wasn't unconvinced.

He turned and placed his hands on the table in front of her and leaned in. 'Helena, I think your mother is wrong.' Her eyes shot to his. 'Have you ever thought you might be more interesting to Marianos if you liked the opposite of what he does? That it might give you things to talk about—a difference of opinion—rather than always agreeing with him?'

She stared up at him. 'I never thought about it like that,' she said.

He came off the table and stood up. 'So, what do you like that he doesn't?'

'I don't know.'

He clicked his tongue. 'Well, we need to find out. Start thinking about it, today. I'll need to know everything about you if I'm to help you succeed with this.'

'Everything?' she asked, her eyes wide.

'Everything…' he winked '…but later. I'm meeting with Zoe now.' And he wasn't looking forward to it. He really hoped they hadn't given Markou those orders to hurt those civilians yesterday. He hoped they hadn't known about it and would be as appalled as he was. 'I'll try to find you in my break.'

He swiped an apple out of her fruit basket and grinned, heading for the door.

'Will you tell them you were there—last night?' she asked and he halted his exit.

'Not if I can help it.'

'I was thinking about it… If they won't lower the taxes, I want to try to redistribute the wealth that has been taken. Somehow. Try to get food and clothing to those in need. I meant what I said last night about handing out my royal wardrobe.'

Viggo inclined his head. 'That's good of you.'

He was starting to believe she hadn't meant what she'd said to the other contestant the day of the bride show. That she had only been jesting and she didn't care for riches. He had been astounded when she'd started giving away her precious trinkets last night. He couldn't help but admire her strength—and her kindness.

Could it be that she had been telling the truth…that she really had wanted to marry the Prince for love?

He wasn't sure how he felt about that—which was the lesser of two evils. He wanted to hold on to his assumptions about her, but she was smashing them down with every word she spoke.

Love.

He'd seen love give way to turmoil in his parents' marriage, so he didn't trust it as a basis for a union. He wanted to warn Helena against it, but he wouldn't. Whatever her motives, he too had his reasons for needing this wedding to take place. Even if he didn't like it.

'Doing such a good deed could win you favour—with his subjects and potentially the Prince himself. If you can show him that you can help him gain their support…'

Helena had won over the people so easily, so completely last night. But then, he could see why. After all, wasn't she doing the same with him? They had all be in awe of her, wanting to see her, speak to her, get close to her. But he couldn't believe how reckless she'd been. What was it with his sister, and now Helena, not being able to do as they were told? They might not have any care for their safety, but he did.

He didn't want to see Helena hurt. He'd rather Marianos's feelings warmed to her, that she married the man—

no matter how galling the thought of it was—as anything was preferable to Zoe carrying out her appalling threat. Helena didn't deserve to be treated that way. She was a good person, he realised.

He really didn't want to like her, but it was impossible not to. And he wondered again why Marianos wasn't smitten with her already, why he was even having to step in and persuade the Prince to spend time with her, and help Helena win him over. The man was a fool!

'I've earned Marianos's trust with my unswerving loyalty. If you can show him you can be just as loyal, through such gestures, he will soon see your value,' he said, taking a bite of the apple.

'I can see you've been doing a lot of thinking,' Helena said.

'What can I say? I'm not just a pretty face, either.'

She smiled. 'Thank you, Viggo.'

'One more thing before I go…' He walked back over to her and came down on his haunches by the side of her chair.

'You'll be late,' she said.

He took her spoon from her fingers and he scooped up a dollop of the pomegranate seeds. He held the spoon up to her swollen lips. 'Try it.'

She shook her head, her lips pressed tightly shut.

'Helena. You need to understand yourself before you think of anyone else's wants or needs.'

She relented, rolling her eyes. She opened her lips and his stomach tightened. He put the spoon inside her mouth. He liked that she trusted him enough to let him.

He removed the spoon and she closed her lips, slowly crunching the seeds. And he could imagine the tart but sweet juice exploding on her tongue.

'Well?' he asked, studying her closely, watching her face for her reactions.

'Nice,' she laughed when she finished it. 'Refreshing.'

He grinned. 'See?'

'I'll be walking in the gardens at the sixth hour,' she said.

'I'll find you.'

Hearing the sound of Viggo's deep voice calling her name, Helena's stomach flipped, and she turned and saw him walking towards her in the palace gardens. She smiled, pleased to see him, and the closer he got, the harder her heart began to clamour. It was because they were a team—conspirators, in on a secret together, she thought.

But as he drew nearer, she saw he wore a deep scowl and there was visible tension in his corded neck. Something was wrong.

Had something happened with Zoe and Marianos?

Or was he still reeling from everything that had happened last night, the way she was? She was still struggling to comprehend what she had witnessed in that neighbourhood, wondering what she could do about it. It had been playing on her mind all morning.

When they'd arrived back at the palace, she had almost wilted in relief when she'd seen Theodor, still waiting for her by the chapel door. She was so grateful he hadn't sounded the alarm, she could have thrown her arms around him in thanks, but she hadn't, for then she would have had to do the same to the Commander for getting her back safely and the thought of doing that unsettled her. Every time they touched something happened to her body—it was as if it came alive, her blood on fire, and it was disturbing.

'Is everything all right?' she asked him when he reached her.

'Things have been better.'

'What happened?'

He shook his head. 'It's unimportant,' he said, pressing his lips into a tight grimace.

Which meant he didn't want to tell her. She looked away, trying not to feel disappointed that he didn't want to share it.

'How was your morning?' he asked.

'Fruitful.' The heat was stifling so she had sought the shade of the palace. She had requested her ladies-in-waiting start to go through her wardrobe with her to see what could be given away. But in truth, the morning had dragged as she'd counted down the moments until she and Viggo had agreed to meet.

He glanced around, cautious of what people would think if they saw them together, even though they were just talking. 'So, did you complete the task I set you? Have you decided which is your favourite flower in the gardens?' he asked, getting straight down to the matter at hand. Her preferences.

'Roses,' she said, decisive.

'Nice try. They're the Prince's favourite. Pick another.'

'I don't know,' she said, looking all around. 'There's too many to choose from. These are bold, I like them. Yes, maybe these?' she said, moving over towards some vibrant blooms on spiky stems.

'They're hyacinths, known for their sweet scent. Good choice. I know it's a tiny thing, but it's important you know your own mind, Helena. I think it will be beneficial to you here.'

She had been thinking about what he'd said this morning, about how it would be more interesting to Marianos if she had her own thoughts. She had never considered it like that, but she could see how Viggo might be right. After all, she was interested to hear Viggo's opinions, drawn in by every detail he told her about himself. If he just agreed with everything she said, she could imagine it would be rather tiresome. There would be nothing to discover.

'What's your favourite flower?' she asked.

'I don't have one, but I do have a favourite tree.'

She looked up at him in surprise. 'Which one is it?'

He glanced around again—he always acted with extreme caution. She knew why. There was a lot at stake. 'Let's walk there. I'll show you. It's more secluded—away from prying eyes.'

Although people married for strategic reasons all the time, Viggo had seemed annoyed on her behalf that her mother had raised her to be Marianos's bride. Helena had spent her life complying with her parents' demands to finally gain their approval—and, ultimately, their love. She'd never heard anyone say her mother was wrong before, but now that Viggo had said it, she could see his point—her mother had taken it to the extreme and Helena felt a flare of anger about her lost childhood. Her wasted youth—all those days spent in pursuit of appealing to a man's needs, rather than playing or reading or riding, focusing on her own interests and pleasures. She wasn't sure her mother had ever stopped to consider her feelings and what she wanted. Now, she wasn't even sure she knew what she wanted herself. She felt so confused.

She had thought being picked to be Marianos's wife was her dream, but was it? Or was it just her mother's ambition? She couldn't be sure. It had been her goal for so long, but away from her mother's constant observation, and after meeting the Prince himself—and Viggo—everything felt skewed.

Confined within the monastery, she had been kept apart from the city and what was really going on, and from having new experiences and adventures. Would she have that here—freedom, without restrictions—within these even taller walls? Would she ever see more than the inside of this palace? Would she really be able to make her own choices, as Viggo was suggesting?

She wasn't sure. These past few days had opened her eyes to so much. There was a whole world out there she hadn't known existed and hadn't begun to explore or understand. People she'd never met. Places she'd never seen. Pomegranates she'd never tried!

They walked across the gardens and she tried to shade her eyes from the burning sun at its highest in the sky. She felt her skin prickle—the silk of her tunic was clinging to her in the heat and she wondered how Viggo could bear to wear his armour in these sweltering conditions. They took a quiet path, out of sight of the palace. Although she knew it was forbidden for them to be alone together, and therefore dangerous, it felt good to be free of the guardsmen's watchful gazes for once.

'It's this one,' Viggo said finally, as they approached a tall specimen, bringing her out of her reverie.

'It's an olive tree!' she said, coming to a stop before it. A very large olive tree. It wasn't the prettiest of trees—it had a gnarled and twisted trunk, but lots of branches and silvery-green leaves offering welcome shade.

'You know it?'

'My father uses the oil to anoint the sick.'

He nodded.

'Why this one?' she said, moving beneath the canopy, seeking shelter from the intense sun, her skin feeling damp, her breathing restless.

'It's my favourite spot in the palace. No one comes here,' he said, as if to reassure her they wouldn't be seen. Perhaps she should have felt wary, but she didn't—in fact, a shiver of nervous excitement ran through her that she was here alone with him, going against the rules.

'Foolishly, I feel attached to it. It had weak roots and fell during the quaking of the earth we experienced a few years back, but we replanted it, tended to it, and after giving it a lot of love, it developed new shoots.' He shrugged. 'I like that despite the harsh conditions it has suffered, it has endured and gone on to thrive.' He paused and inclined his head in that way she'd come to know and like. 'Maybe people can do the same.'

She smiled. She had just been thinking that the tree was a reflection of himself. She thought about what he'd said about not being his father's priority growing up and what his sister had revealed about their upbringing, and she wanted to ask him about it. She willed him to tell her more, longing to learn more about him.

She sat down, wiping her brow with the back of her hand. It was too hot to walk any further. 'What was the journey like, from Norway to Constantinople? You must have seen a great many things.'

He ran his hand around the back of his neck—she noticed he always did that, when he was deliberating whether to speak of something or not. She was pleased when he finally kneeled down to sit beside her. 'We left the vast fjords of Norway in a boat of thirty. I was quite a strong boy and they needed an extra pair of arms to row, but my sister—even though she was little, they just saw her as extra weight. I had to beg them to let her on. We sailed the Baltic, encountering many different settlements, then the rivers Dnieper and Volga, making it up past the rapids and the many tribes there. It was daunting. I felt responsible for Sofie's safety. The journey was long and hard, but I was set on my destination. By the time we reached the Black Sea, I finally allowed myself to believe we might make it. And when we arrived, I was in awe of this place,' he said, picking up a wilted leaf and crunching it between his fingers, before letting it drop to the ground. 'I thought it held all the answers. Everything we'd need.'

'And did it?'

'It was the right decision to come.'

'Why did you leave in the first place?' she asked, running her hand through the cool, shaded blades of grass, wondering if he would reveal anything of his family to her, what his sister had mentioned.

He shifted his position. 'If you loathe your life, you have to change it—don't you? No one else is going to do it for you. Things were bad at home. One day, I decided enough was enough. We left shortly after that.'

'You said your parents had an unhappy marriage? That you weren't your father's priority growing up?'

He leaned back on his elbows, stretching out his long legs, and she was acutely aware of his proximity. His large, solid body was just a breath away, his spicy scent enveloping her. 'No, ale was.'

'I noticed you did not touch your wine the other evening at the feast.'

'I was on duty,' he said. 'But even if I wasn't, I would have abstained. I'm not one for raucous feasts. I don't drink. I've only ever seen it bring out the worst in people. Seen them lose control.'

'Is that why you're in a position where you seek to control everyone now?' she said, offering him a wry smile, and he looked at her in surprise.

'Is that how you see me?'

She shrugged, smiling, bravely lying back, too, gazing up at the sun dappling through the leaves above. But she stole another look at him. Now she knew him, just a little, the web of scars on his face were no longer alarming. They no longer frightened her, just intrigued her—she desperately wanted to know the story behind them. She was greedy for more information about him.

'Why come here, of all places?' she said.

'It was known for being the land of riches. Somewhere someone like me could make a name for themself.'

'That's important to you?'

He turned to look at her. 'Everybody wants to be somebody, don't they?' And then his brow furrowed. There it was again. That look. Something was definitely troubling him. 'Isn't that why you're here? Why you're marrying the Prince—to make something of your life?' Yes, perhaps she did want to be someone, but she also had other less selfish reasons for being here and going through with this union. 'Otherwise, you would find a match elsewhere.'

'Unfortunately, that's not possible,' she blurted out. 'My father has no coin for a dowry…'

He reared, shifting up a little on his elbows. 'What?'

She felt her cheeks heat that she'd revealed her father's secret. These things weren't discussed in public. Yet she'd said it now. She couldn't take it back. And she felt she could trust Viggo. That he wouldn't repeat it. Especially as she knew secrets of his own.

He sat up fully. 'How can that be? Your father is a wealthy man.'

She shook her head. 'You'd think so.' She lowered her voice. 'Although he has influence, he has accumulated much debt. From what I can understand, there has been a misappropriation of funds. And now he's on the verge of ruin—at risk of losing everything.'

Viggo ran his hand over his jaw. 'I had no idea. The Prince does not know this.'

'I know and, if he were to find out, it would make me less of a prize to Marianos. The dowry is meant to prove I come from a respectable, noble family—that I am a worthy match.'

She sat up to join him. 'So I need to keep it secret. We all keep secrets for our families, to protect them, it seems. And this marriage…it could change my father's situation. Yes, he will get into more debt paying the dowry, but the hope is I would be able to pay back what he owes discreetly once I am Empress and secure my family's future. It will save them from ruin. Perhaps…' She ran her fingers over the grass again. 'Perhaps then my father will finally notice me…'

Viggo leaned back. 'So you are doing this for him? It doesn't sound as though he deserves it.' She looked up at his furious words. 'That dowry should belong to you, providing you with independence in the marriage, Helena.'

'I know. But you won't say anything, will you?' she rushed to say. 'If word got out, it would risk the reputation of the church. There would be uproar in the Bishop's dioceses…'

'It would destroy your reputation,' Viggo finished for her.

'Yes.'

'Helvete!' he cursed. He seemed appalled, his anger seeming to boil up beneath the surface. Surely he wouldn't be that cross on her behalf—was something else troubling him?

She couldn't bear it any longer. She had revealed her concerns to him. She needed to know what was bothering him in return.

'How did your talk with Zoe and Marianos go? What did they say about General Markou? Did something happen?'

His scowl deepened, darkening his face.

'I know you don't want to share it, but don't you think I have a right to know?' she said sharply. And then she reached out to touch him lightly on the arm. 'Viggo, tell me.'

He stared at her fingers, then up into her eyes. A muscle flickered in his jaw. 'I told them. About the death toll in the city last night. How it wasn't my men. How General Markou had gone against orders.'

'And?'

'They didn't care.'

'What?' she gasped.

He shook his head. 'I expected it from Zoe. But Marianos—he is not himself at the moment. He's full of anger. I don't know where it's come from, whether it's his age, or the changes that are about to take place. Anyway, he refused to listen to me. He said General Markou was handling the situation how he wanted. I had a few choice words to say,' he said. 'He didn't like it.'

'What happened?'

'He said he was going to switch some of my duties with General Markou.'

'What?' She knew instantly that this would have upset him more than he was letting on. That it would have wounded his pride. Everyone knew Viggo was Marianos's best warrior. He didn't deserve this disappointment.

Viggo was right, Marianos's actions were disconcerting. 'Which duties?'

He curled his body upwards, moving away from her, getting to his feet. She wondered if he wasn't going to answer her, then he looked down, meeting her gaze.

'He said he wanted me to watch over his bride, his happiness, instead of him for the next few days and that it would be insubordinate of me to go against his orders.'

She raised her brows and scrambled to her feet to join him. 'His *happiness*?' They both knew Marianos didn't mean that.

'I have been his private bodyguard for three winters. I was in his guard for another five before that. And the previous three years I spent in training with various mercenary groups. I don't know why he would make this change now, just a few days before the wedding.' He shook his head. 'The intention is clearly to sideline me, though I do not know why.'

She shook her head, troubled. 'I'm so sorry, Viggo,' she said.

'There are worse duties, I suppose,' he said, attempting to offer her a wry smile. 'But while I am more than happy to watch over you, Helena, I can't help but feel something is going on that I don't know about. Something I can't quite put my finger on—that I know I'm not going to approve of.

It's like waiting for that ominous dark cloud in the distance over there to approach and burst its seams.'

'I understand,' she said. 'Although I'm glad I'm deemed so important I now have a commander as my private bodyguard,' she said, gently bumping his arm with hers.

They looked at each other and the air seemed to crackle between then. Her breath was suspended.

'Speaking of which—we should get on with what we came here for—lesson number two,' he said.

Only number two? It felt as if he'd taught her so much already. About herself. About everything.

'Your mother has obviously taught you how to carry yourself with grace and poise, but confidence and command—that's what I teach my men. If you can carry yourself with authority, like they do, and speak with assurance, like you did at the feast the other night, you'll make Marianos stand up and take notice of you. You don't want to show him any signs of weakness. You don't want to be someone he can overlook.'

'But aren't I meant to be modest and reserved in public—seen but not heard?'

'Supposedly. But if I had to take a wife, I'd want her to know her own mind, to be compelling, captivating—someone I was proud to have on my arm. Someone I felt confident introducing to people, knowing she was capable of enthralling a room, building alliances and asserting influence.'

She nodded, giving full consideration to his suggestions.

'To this point, we need to utilise your family. You need to remind Marianos how your father can help him gain support in his dioceses. How *you* can help him win favour with the people. I saw you do that just last night.' He inclined his head. 'I know you can do this, Helena.'

'I hope you're right.'

'The things your mother said, about using your womanly wiles, is true to a point. Touching your face, or your hair, will draw his attention to those parts of you.'

'I want to draw attention to my hair?'

He inclined his head. 'Yes. Most definitely. And a light touch to his arm every so often can create a connection—and leave a lasting impression.'

She leaned into him and placed a hand on his forearm, causing a sudden jolt—a tingle through her body. 'How do you know all this?'

He stared down at her fingers on his skin before looking back up into her eyes. 'I've been around a lot longer than you.'

Then she smiled.

'You were practising.' He inclined his head. 'Very good.'

It took effort to move her hand away.

'Ask him thoughtful questions and when he replies, be attentive. It shows a man you're interested. It will build his trust.'

She thought she had done this with Viggo—but then, it was easy to ask him questions, as she was genuinely interested.

'And remember, the Prince gets a lot of compliments about his looks. His servants are always praising him. You don't want to just blurt out the first thing that comes into your head. Think about it, find something else to comment on—his intelligence, or a quality like his humour—it might come across as more sincere. After all, we're all more than our looks, aren't we?'

She nodded.

'Try it on me,' he said.

'Now?' she said, panic thrumming through her.

'Yes.'

'All right,' she said, twisting her hands.

'Stop fidgeting.'

She swallowed.

'Are you finding it hard to say something kind about me?' he asked, his lips curling upwards.

'No. I just…want to say the right thing,' she said, stumbling over her words.

'Well, you won't want to keep Marianos waiting on these compliments, Helena.'

'All right, all right…' She took a deep breath and looked up into his eyes. She shook her head a little. 'Viggo…you…' She gave a little cough.

He raised his brows.

'When I first I met you, I thought you were fierce, even frightening. Everything a warrior ought to be.'

'Helena—'

'Wait—' She raised her hand. 'I'm getting to it. But I have come to see you are more than a sword to defend me or a shield to protect me,' she said. 'Your presence makes… everything feel all right. Your eyes, your heart have a gentleness to them that offer an unspoken promise that I'm not alone.'

His brow furrowed as he stared down at her.

She stepped back, concerned she'd been so outspoken. 'Was that all right?'

He cleared his throat. 'I think you're a natural, Helena.'

He looked all around, that hand running back around his neck, then up at the sky. 'We'd better get you back, before we're found alone out here,' he said, moving away from her. 'I don't think my new role as your bodyguard is due to commence until this afternoon, so we've probably been long enough. And you'd better get yourself dressed and ready for the Hippodrome. I'm going to go and do a quick scout of the arena—check it's secure before the crowds arrive. After last night, I don't know what the mood of the people will be like today. Sometimes, the crowds can get rowdy, the event disorderly. Just…stay close, so I can ensure your safety, all right?'

She nodded. She liked that he seemed to genuinely care about her. They heard a rumble of approaching thunder as they began to make a move. The weather seemed to be reflecting her emotions. 'I'm nervous. And a little excited,' she said. 'It's my first public event. I've heard it's quite a spectacle. I want the people to like me. I hope Marianos doesn't shun me in front of everyone.'

'There will be plenty of opportunity to engage him in conversation between races. Make sure you cheer for the same chariot as Marianos—remember, you will be supporting the blues, the commoners will cheer for the greens—it will be something you and the Prince can bond over.'

She bit her lip, and they carried on walking in silence. But before they rounded the corner that led back to the palace, he turned round to face her, halting her in her path. 'Despite all I've said, just be yourself.' He reached out and cupped her chin in his hand. 'How could anyone not like you, Helena?'

Chapter Seven

'You need to present yourselves as a united front,' Zoe said, as Helena and Marianos were ushered down the private walkway that connected the Great Palace to the imperial box at the Hippodrome. It allowed the royal family to enter the arena safely, avoiding the hundred-thousand spectators who were also piling through the gates. Viggo and General Markou followed just paces behind, keeping guard.

'Smile. Wave. Look like you're in love,' Zoe said.

Viggo's nostrils flared. Walking behind Helena, he allowed his gaze to travel down her body. She looked more stunning than ever, dressed in a gold tunic with emerald beading that he knew matched her glittering eyes. Her thick, dark hair was swept off her beautiful face, pinned up in an intricate style.

When she smiled at Marianos, Viggo felt his stomach harden, his muscles bunch. Seeing them together for the first time in days was affecting him more than it should and he gripped the hilt of his sword harder, taking out his frustration on the metal, his knuckles turning white.

He knew he'd told her there would be chance for her to talk to the Prince, that they could bond over the races, but he suddenly wished his words back. He didn't want her to converse with Marianos at all, he wanted to pull her back, keep her to himself—because surely the moment she spoke to Marianos, the moment she smiled, or laughed, the Prince would be taken by her. He couldn't understand how anyone could not be.

He tried to shake away his thoughts. He had to remind himself he should be pleased if that happened. That's what he and Helena both wanted, wasn't it? She needed the wedding to go ahead to secure her position here, for herself and her family, and he needed the union to take place so he could receive his reward. He had to think of his sister and her unborn child.

Still, he didn't have to like it.

While he knew she had only been practising, the compliment she had given him earlier, out by the olive tree, had left him momentarily speechless, because it had felt real. Genuine. And it had touched him more than he cared to admit that anyone should say he made them feel safe.

A sudden flare of anger at the unfairness of the situation lit inside him, especially after being overlooked for General Markou today. He couldn't understand how that had happened and he couldn't let it lie. It felt like a personal rejection and one that tapped into his deep-seated fears from his past, reminding him of how his parents had both disregarded and abandoned him, and he'd begun to doubt his abilities or worth. He was offended, but determined to discover the true cause of why Marianos had pushed him aside. Like always, he would question everything, trust no one.

He and General Markou had often been at odds as to how to handle things in the city. The General always wanted to use much harsher tactics. In this instance, it would just make things worse.

Marianos had made Viggo's role even harder with this

new command, because even though the Prince might not want him around, he would still need to watch over him to make sure he was safe. Out of duty. Out of care. And to receive his coin. It wouldn't be so easy to protect him if he wasn't allowed as close to him. And now he had another task—he had Helena to guard over. Watching both of them wouldn't be easy. But then, hadn't he been doing that all week anyway? Helena had consumed his thoughts since she'd arrived here—her whereabouts, her safety.

He surveyed the Kathisma one more time before he allowed Marianos and his entourage inside. The royal box offered the best view of the arena and Helena was delighted, clapping her hands together. It was indeed a spectacle. The excitement in the arena was palpable, the noise of thousands of people talking deafening and Helena's eagerness for the races to start must have been infectious, for Marianos seemed to emerge from his dark mood of late—just enough to exchange a few words with her and his mother. Perhaps an event like this was what was needed to bring everyone together.

Viggo took a breath.

Finally, the races began and, watching them from his position against the back wall, Viggo suddenly saw the results of all those years of training Helena's mother had given her and perhaps his own instruction, too. She hadn't needed it—she was perfect as she was. Yet now he was thinking they'd taught her a little too well.

While everyone was focused on the riders, the chariots racing around the track at dangerous speeds, as if they were battling to the death, Helena cheered them on, matching Marianos's enthusiasm. When the Prince launched himself out of his seat, she did, too, and Viggo couldn't tear his gaze away from her fingers—every so often, they would lightly graze Marianos's arm—and he felt the urge to put himself between them and break them apart. Did the Prince's body react instinctively to her searing touch, as his did?

What was wrong with him? She was only doing what she had been told to do. What he had told her to do! He wasn't being rational. He should be assessing the danger in the arena, the mood of the crowd—but instead he was consumed with the concerning nearness of their bodies, aware of Helena's every move.

He didn't think they suited each other at all. In fact, they just seemed wrong together. Marianos was far too blond, too slight, too young. Surely Helena needed someone stronger, someone older, someone more mature, to open her eyes to the world?

Someone like him? a little voice asked.

That was absurd!

Did he really think he would be more suitable? Or that she would even choose someone like him, someone with deep ugly scars, over the handsome Prince? How could he compete with someone she'd been readied to marry since she was young? Someone she had been tricked into thinking she knew everything about and loved?

He felt uncomfortable at his own line of thought.

Since when did he want to compete with the Prince? How could anyone? Marianos was God's sovereign ruler. He was perfect. He could offer Helena everything Viggo could not. She wanted an emperor, not a scarred warrior.

A killer.

Of course she wouldn't want him. No one ever had.

Yet she'd said he made her feel safe. He thought it was the nicest thing anyone had ever said to him.

But if she ever learned of the terrible things he'd done, she would turn and run. She would be right to. So it would be best if she never found out.

He shook his head. Why was he even thinking like this? He had never wanted a woman at his side. He did not want to take a wife. And Helena was never going to find out about his past. He had to face facts—this wedding was going to happen whether he wanted it to or not. He was powerless to stop it, so he had better start getting used to the idea.

When the blue team won the first race and everyone got out of their seats, going wild, part of him hoped Helena's dancing eyes would glance his way, that their gazes would meet and she would offer him a smile, letting him know she was aware he was still there. But she did not and he felt foolishly disappointed. Instead, she engaged in conversation with the noble men and women Zoe and Marianos introduced her to, asking them questions, drawing their interest. She was good at this—better than she thought she was.

The threatening clouds were growing ever closer and Viggo saw lightning strike in the distance. A storm was brewing, just like inside him. He hoped the event would be over by the time the thunder reached them. He willed the finale to take place, for he wasn't sure how much more of seeing Helena and Marianos together he could take.

When the races started up again, the atmosphere in the stadium was charged. The commoners were rooting for the green charioteers to triumph. It would be a sign that the lower classes could prosper.

He watched as the blue chariot took a tight turn, almost colliding into the other.

'The riders have no fear!' he heard Helena gasp through her fingers.

And just as he thought they were out of difficulty, the chariots collided again, causing a spectacular crash. Wood splintered everywhere, the riders falling beneath the wheels, and the crowd were on their feet, both aghast and in awe.

He watched as Helena sagged. 'The poor horses,' she said, turning her head away, unable to watch. Finally, she sent a fleeting glance his way.

Marianos was oblivious. He was jeering, enjoying the sport of it.

Viggo clenched his fist. He wanted to come off the wall, to go to her, to ask her if she was all right. He wanted to distract her from the blood and gore on display, but he knew that he could not. It wasn't his place.

He glanced out into the stadium. The spectators were becoming more agitated, some pushing others, accusing them of foul play—that the one team had deliberately crashed into the other. The collision had triggered uproar in the crowd. His men would need to keep control. But it was ludicrous—here he was, standing guard over an entire city of people and all he could focus on was one. He couldn't keep his feelings in check.

'You seem distracted, Commander.'

He turned to look at Markou beside him. He'd almost managed to block the man out.

'No. Just taking it all in,' he said. He hoped he hadn't given himself away.

'If Helena was my new consignment, I'd be taking it all in, too.' Markou let out a low whistle between his teeth.

Viggo clenched his fists, trying not to rise to the bait; he knew the man was goading him.

Just a few more days and this would all be over. That's what he needed to focus on. He would be leaving. He wouldn't be forced to facilitate or watch this romance play out between Marianos and Helena any more—and he would no longer have to worry about the Prince, or endure the insufferable man beside him. So he could ignore Markou's comments, they were irrelevant.

'I thought when Marianos asked me to be his right-hand man today, I'd won the prize. He was finally casting you aside and recognising me for my worth. I'd finally done it, I'd overtaken you. The indomitable Viggo.'

Viggo cracked his neck from side to side.

'But looking at her now, I'm not so sure I got the real prize. Perhaps I'll ask to switch, then I can be the one to keep an eye on her and guard her door tonight,' he sneered. 'Maybe I can convince her to let me inside...'

All of Viggo's protective instincts were triggered, and he turned and shoved the brute into the wall, but at the same time, the violence escalated in the crowd and everything began to take a turn for the worse. He gripped the man's mail coat, pulling him towards him. The man was burly, but Viggo was taller, stronger. 'You'd better get your men in here, fast, and help me get control of the situation, or you'll be out of that new role of yours before it's even begun.'

He released him and signalled for his troops to file into the arena and Markou's men followed behind. But as if God was punishing the city—and its rulers—for their behaviour, the ground started to rumble with a deafening roar. The violent shaking made it hard to stand up and objects began to tumble all over the place, chalices of wine smashing to the floor. Outside, the spectators stopped fighting and began running for their lives, screaming, trying to grab hold of something for support or scrambling down on to the tracks of the arena itself.

Helena looked up at him, in wide-eyed panic, seeking him out amid the chaos, and Viggo knew instantly what he had to do. All thoughts of a reward and rivalry now gone, the only thing that was important was getting her, and everyone else, to safety. He yelled at Markou to help Marianos. The General had flattened himself against the wall, terribly pale, clearly afraid, and Viggo had to shout twice to get him to move. Finally, together, they bundled the Prince, Zoe and Helena out of the royal box.

They raced down the private walkway, as he yelled at anyone they passed to get down on their hands and knees, to move to the centre of the arena, away from falling debris, or to take cover somewhere safe.

The ground continued to roll beneath them and Helena tripped and fell. Viggo stopped to help her up, taking her hand in his. He pulled her up just as the wall of the walkway began to crumble, tumbling in front of them, separating them from the others, and yelled at Markou to keep going.

'But the Prince. Shouldn't you go?' Helena gasped.

'You're my priority now,' he bit out. He had to get her to safety.

He glanced all around, looking for a place he and Helena could take shelter, to wait this out until the intense shaking stopped. With dread hammering in his heart, he pulled Helena into a nearby field. Tugging her down, so they were sat facing one another, he tucked her body into his, hip to hip, bent knee to knee, and he wrapped his arm around her shoulders, protecting her.

'Just hold on. It'll be over in a moment,' he said, and she did as she was told, clinging on to his arms, burying her head in his chest.

Helena had never experienced such a bad quake. She hadn't thought this was how she might die. Only, being wrapped up in Viggo's arms, she wasn't sure if she was frightened because of what was happening, or because of the feelings rushing though her as his body pressed firmly against hers. She liked the feel of his arms curved around her shoulders, his large hand holding her tight.

She had never been this close to a man before, so close her face was pressed up against the skin at the base of his throat, so close that she could breathe in the peppery scent of him. She was fascinated by his chest rising and falling beneath her cheek, the rapid beat of his heart.

When the ground had started to tremble, her first thought had been of him and she'd turned to find him, their eyes colliding. She was so glad he was here, that he had stayed behind with her, and the words he had spoken kept reverberating around her head.

You're my priority now.

To be the sole focus of this man's attention… It made her feel safe and terrified all at once.

The rumbling and shuddering went on and on and she gripped his arms tighter, seeking his strength, until finally, the juddering ebbed.

She couldn't move. Her body was trembling, the noise still roaring in her ears.

'Are you all right?' Viggo asked, his hands stroking her back.

He gently raised his head away from hers.

She nodded and lifted her gaze to look at him. It was a moment of great relief.

'You're safe now, Helena. It's over.'

He raised his hands to smooth over the tendrils of her hair that had come loose.

He had saved her. She was so glad he was here.

But they could still hear the sound of structures creaking in the distance, a loud clattering as objects fell and broke, things crashing all around the arena. People were screaming, weeping.

He ran his hands over her arms. 'Are you sure you're not hurt?'

'I'm fine,' she whispered. Although she felt unsteady, disorientated.

She thought about her mother and father—were they safe? And Marianos and Zoe—had they made it back to the palace unharmed?

'We have to go and help,' she said.

He nodded. 'I will. After I've got you back to the palace.'

'No,' she said, pulling away from him, but he didn't release her from his hold. 'I'm coming with you.'

'Helena. It's too dangerous.'

'You'll be there. You said I need to have my own thoughts, make my own decisions. This is one of them.' Only when she pushed him away and stood, her leg spasmed in pain and she winced.

'You are hurt!' he roared.

'I'm not. Not really. It's just from where I fell,' she said.

'Let me see.'

She reared back. 'No!'

He drew a hand over his face. 'This is not the time to argue with me, Helena. If you're hurt, I need to see it.'

She bit her lip.

'For God's sake, woman. Show me.'

She glanced around, checking no one could see them, then sighed. She gingerly rolled her tunic up her leg, exposing her skin. She had never been so brazen before.

Viggo reached out to take the back of her knee in his hand and she gasped, all pain gone. Instead, she just felt heat. She looked furtively around them again. If anyone were to see, their actions might arouse suspicion.

'Your knee is bleeding. You must have fallen on it pretty hard.' He frowned. 'Let's get you back. I'll arrange for a healer to clean it and patch it up.'

'No,' she reasserted, dropping the material, covering herself up, forcing him to let go of her leg. 'I told you. I'm not going back. The people out there need our help. Someone needs to take care of them.'

He rose to his feet, looming over her. 'And who is going to take care of you?'

She tipped her chin up at him, stubborn, ready to fight him, but as his words filtered over her, she instantly thought of his sister—and how she had spoken of her brother always looking after her. She inhaled sharply, suddenly worried about Sofie and the baby. 'Will your sister be all right?' she asked.

He frowned. 'I hope so,' he said. 'Usually the tremors aren't so bad on the outskirts of the city.' But she could tell he was worried.

'Do you want to go to her?' she asked.

'I will send someone to check on her,' he said. He took her hand in his, just for a moment, giving it a squeeze. 'Right now, I'm needed here.'

The scene in the arena took her breath away. The landscape had transformed in mere moments. Large sections of the Hippodrome had been reduced to piles of rubble and dust. They had lost the heat of the sun and the storm had reached them, the rain now lashing down on the desolate place—but at least it was helping to put out some of the fires that had ripped through the buildings.

There was debris everywhere and hordes of people were hobbling about, distraught, bleeding, in shock, panicking as they looked for loved ones or seeking help for their wounds. At least the disaster had put an end to the fighting and men, women and children were rallying round, helping one another.

Helena and Viggo got to work, checking people for injuries, assisting those who were trapped and tracking down children for worried parents. It was a mammoth task. Viggo's and Markou's men worked together, clearing the bodies, trying to move some of the rubble and making temporary canopies to keep people dry who couldn't yet return home.

They'd sent word for the palace kitchens to make cauldrons of pottage to be brought out and little campfires were burning all around. In a way, it was a heartwarming sight. That even at the darkest times, people could come together.

By nightfall, Helena's feet were aching and she was exhausted, her skin soaked through to the bone. Her teeth were chattering. Looking down at her tunic, which was covered in mud—she was a far cry from the woman who had stepped out into the royal box earlier today, hoping to make a good impression.

She had met with so many people and heard their stories, shared in their conversations, and she had tried to offer them hope or console them in their devastation. She prayed she had helped to make a small difference.

Some had spoken to her, not realising who she was, and it was good they felt they could speak freely. Others who recognised her seemed shocked that she should be here, showing solidarity and that she cared. Many came up to thank her, to embrace her. Each time they did, Viggo was right there by her side, on guard. She knew he wouldn't let anything bad happen to her.

She kept thinking back to his comment earlier today, when he had told her the people and Marianos would like her. His flattering remark had boosted her, the approval in his eyes giving her confidence. She couldn't have made it through today without him.

She glanced around, looking for him now, and her heart surged when she saw him wrapping a blanket round two children. He glanced up and they shared a look, and she smiled. He made his way over to her and she felt an even stronger connection to him than before—that their bond had been fortified by their shared ordeal.

'There's not much more we can do for tonight. The arena is secure and the people are safe. It's time to get you back now,' he said.

He said it as a suggestion, but his tone told her she was not to fight him on it.

'I know,' she relented.

Was it absurd that part of her wanted to stay out here, with the people, with him, rather than return to the gilded cage of her palace chamber? She wouldn't dare voice it. The whole arena of people would no doubt think she had lost her mind.

'Look at you, you're shivering,' Viggo said. He glanced

around, before giving her arms a quick rub. She wondered when he had determined it was all right for him to touch her and when she had decided she didn't mind.

Entering the palace, they were escorted straight to the hall. It was empty, save for Zoe, the Prince, Markou and a few of the council members. And for the first time, Helena felt as if she was received with relief, not irritation.

'Where have you been?' Zoe said, approaching them. 'We have been concerned.' Even the Empress Regent didn't look herself, the shock of the day's events perhaps knocking her a little.

'It was carnage out there,' Viggo said, while Helena surveyed the hall. Fortunately, it was still standing. There didn't look to be too much damage and she was pleased. It would have been heartbreaking to see such a magnificent place and all of its history destroyed.

Marianos acknowledged her from where he stood across the room, but he made no move in her direction to ask if she was unharmed.

She'd been pleasantly surprised the Prince had spoken to her during the races, yet, if she was honest, she hadn't been able to muster up the same enthusiasm she had felt that first day, when she had stepped into the palace ahead of the bride show. She had seen a side to him she didn't like and it had tarnished her feelings towards him.

Instead, she had been aware of Viggo standing guard behind her throughout the entire event, as if his eyes had been burning into the back of her head. Had he been watching her, or had she imagined it? Had anyone noticed that she had sought him out, the moment things had turned sour in the arena?

She liked him, she realised. Too much. Suddenly, she was afraid. Afraid her feelings were written all over her face. If her growing affection for him was even so much as suspected, it could have terrible consequences. Serious ramifications for both their reputations, their families—even their lives.

Her parents would never understand or forgive her for it and she instantly felt guilty—for her feelings were a betrayal of the life her mother and father had chosen for her.

If she tried to walk away from this royal union, the backlash from the people of the city—the very people she had just helped—would be great. They would call her a traitor. And as for Marianos and Zoe—she had seen first-hand how ruthless they could be. She and Viggo would be punished—tortured then killed.

So what was she thinking? Marrying Marianos was her chance to make her family proud. She could offer the people hope. Was she really going to put that in jeopardy—for what? A man who had told her numerous times he wasn't interested in marriage.

She renewed her efforts to feign indifference. She needed to pretend she didn't care for him—that their connection was purely formal.

'I'm glad you made it back to the palace all right,' Viggo was saying to Zoe. 'Was anyone hurt? Was there much damage?'

She saw he and Markou exchange a glance and the Byzantine Commander nodded his head in appreciation. That was something. She had seen the brute cower as the first tremors had taken over, frozen in fear.

She listened as Viggo filled in the council on the state of

the Hippodrome, the mood of the people and what would still need to be done when the sun came up on the morrow.

'I would like to ask permission to send some of the men home, so they can check on their families,' he said. 'They're all worried.'

'You should do the same, Viggo,' Marianos said, approaching them at last, and Helena wondered if the events of today had finally had some effect on the Prince. He seemed quieter—more pensive than usual.

Viggo nodded. 'I will. And I think Helena will need some hot food and a warm bath.'

'You should have brought her straight back here,' Zoe chastised him.

'He tried, but it was not the Commander's decision. I insisted on helping the people,' Helena said, interjecting, not wanting him to take the blame for her stubbornness. Not wanting them to see that there was anything between them. Because there wasn't. There couldn't be. She had to fight these growing feelings and push him away, starting right now.

'Help?' Zoe said. 'If you want to help, you do so from inside the palace, not out there, on the ground. You are going to be Empress after all. We in the palace keep our distance from the commoners. You have a lot to learn.'

'That's true. I do.' Helena tipped her chin up. 'But I think the only way we can truly help is from being out there, getting to know them—listening to the people and their needs.'

Everyone turned to look at her, surprised by her words.

'Their needs?' Zoe laughed.

'Yes. The people are starving and there's no food to eat. Many have just been wounded or lost their loved ones. The situation is fraught. We need to help them, any way we can.

They are the backbone of this city and their support secures the stability of Marianos's reign. It is imperative we show them we care. We must pull together and unite.'

It was the first time she'd ever stood up to the Empress Regent. She didn't know what had come over her, only seeing how the people were suffering, she knew she didn't much value this woman's opinion if Zoe was to blame for it. Viggo hadn't just made her start to question her own decisions, but others', too. She had to stand up for what she believed in.

'Helena is right,' Marianos said, coming closer.

Now it was Helena's turn to be surprised. He was standing up for her? Listening to her? This was progress indeed. It was everything she'd been hoping for. Everything she and her mother, and she and Viggo, had been working towards.

Zoe's eyes narrowed on her. 'Well, if you've caught your death in time for the wedding, don't blame me. I hope it was worth it,' she said.

'Will the wedding still go ahead as planned? In light of all this?' Helena gasped. There was a part of her that had hoped the day's events meant she'd get a reprieve, that the ceremony would be delayed, if only for a short while. But she had to stop thinking like that. The sooner the wedding took place, the sooner she would make her family's dreams come true. When she was married, it would help her to stop thinking about the Commander.

'It is more important now than ever that the coronation and wedding go ahead. Like you say, we need to bring the people together. This will give them something to celebrate. Nothing changes,' Zoe said.

Helena could at least take solace in knowing she was doing this for the people.

'Viggo, you must go now and check on your sister. I insist,' Marianos said. 'Please escort Helena to her chambers on your way out.'

Helena was stunned. It almost sounded as if the Prince cared.

They took their leave and Viggo ushered her along the portico, back towards her room, and although her legs were weary, her mind was whirring. She felt torn—torn between these new, frightening feelings she was beginning to have for Viggo and the expectations of her parents, the royal family and the whole of Constantinople.

'That seemed to go well,' Viggo said.

She nodded.

'Marianos listened to you. Zoe heard you.'

She bit her lip.

'So. More lessons tomorrow?'

Helena stopped and turned to face him. She couldn't. She had to put an end to this, no matter how hard that would be.

'I don't know, Viggo.'

'Don't know about what?' he said.

'I just think that, what with the quake, we should stop the lessons now.'

He halted. 'I see.' He braced his hand on the balcony and looked out over the city, over the little fires burning all around the arena and out to the Strait, where the ships bobbed about on the dark waters.

She felt the need to fill the silence. She owed him an explanation. 'I just…us spending so much time together. I'm not sure it's a good thing,' Helena said.

'In what way?'

She raised her hands. 'I don't know. It just isn't.'

'I'm confused. One moment you want my help, now

you don't?' Anger began to seep into his words. He turned around and rested his back on the balcony, crossing his arms over his chest.

'I'm confused, too,' she said.

'About what?' he asked.

'You!' she wanted to yell.

But she couldn't tell him the real reason—that she was starting to have feelings, romantic feelings, for *him* instead of the Prince. He would think she was a fool. He would surely walk away anyway.

This was for the best. She needed a little distance from him to regain perspective. For her own preservation.

'So the first sign of approval from Marianos—a spark with the Prince that you so desired—and that's it, I'm gone?' he spat.

She reared back. Spark? What spark? She hadn't felt one.

'I thought we were friends,' he continued, shaking his head.

'We are.'

He pushed off the wall and came towards her. He looked down into her eyes. 'No, I'm not sure that's what we are.'

'What's that supposed to mean?' she said, her heart pounding painfully in her chest.

'I get it. You needed my support until you got what you wanted and, now you have the Prince's attention, you don't need me any more. You're going to walk away.'

'No, that's not it.' She shook her head fiercely.

He gave a bitter laugh. 'That's exactly it, Helena.'

'You're so…so cynical! Not everyone's like your mother and father, Viggo.'

He recoiled. Stilled. His eyes turned glacial. And she knew, instantly, that she'd said the wrong thing.

'Don't talk about my parents. You know nothing about it.'

'I know they had a bad marriage. That they abandoned you. Now you think every other person will do the same.'

He stepped towards her and she backed away, her shoulders hitting the wall.

'You think you know me and my family? You're right, my mother deserted me. She left while Sofie and I were asleep one night, when I was just ten winters old. Because she didn't love us enough to stay.' He took another step towards her, so his chest was almost pressing against hers. 'But did you know that with her gone, there was no one to protect us from my father—from his drunken rages and his nightly beatings?'

The breath left her.

His eyes roamed over her face. 'No, I didn't think so. So don't tell me you know anything about my parents, Helena. Or me. You don't.'

'I'm—I'm sorry,' she said, her voice breaking, her heart splintering—for him and his sister. She didn't want to think of him suffering, ever hurting.

'You know what?' he said, suddenly moving away from her. 'I don't need to be here, wasting my time, doing this, helping you. I think you're right. I think we're finished here.'

And with a last hard look, he turned on his heel and walked away from her.

Tears threatening, Helena picked up the hem of her tunic and ran.

She didn't stop until she reached her room, her lungs burning, angrily swiping at the tears falling down her cheeks. Flinging open the door, she raced inside, slamming it shut behind her. She threw herself on to the bed and sobbed, hard, burying her face in the furs.

It had been the worst day.

She had been so afraid when she'd started to feel the tremors of the ground shaking beneath her feet and when she'd seen the buildings around her—and the people—start to fall. At first, when they'd made it back out into the arena, she'd felt dazed—in complete shock at what had happened. But she'd forced herself to rally; there were too many people in need of help. She just had to keep going.

She didn't think she could have got through the day without Viggo. Whenever she'd looked up, she'd seen he, too, was helping someone and it inspired her to carry on.

She had thought she was doing the right thing in suggesting they spent less time together—for him and for her. But in doing so she knew she had offended him. And then he had dropped that shocking reveal about his childhood—and her heart had gone out to him once more. She had wanted to reach out and comfort him, but she didn't dare. She knew he wouldn't want it.

She sat up and wiped her face and caught a glimpse of a shadow pass under the bottom of her door and she clamped a hand over her mouth to stem her hiccups. Was he outside, ensuring she had made it back to her room? She hoped he hadn't heard her cry.

The shadow moved back and forth, as if he was pacing, and then it was gone. She released the breath she was holding.

She clambered off the bed, frustrated with herself—and Viggo—and moved to the dresser. She pulled out the stool and sat down. She picked up the comb and began to run it through her hair, staring at her messy reflection.

Who was this girl staring back at her? Who was she becoming? And why was she feeling so wretched that he had put an end to their friendship, when she had been about to do the same?

Because she was falling for him. Had fallen for him.

She enjoyed his company and wanted to be around him. He consumed her thoughts. Whenever he came near, she couldn't understand it, but her pulse pounded and her body heated, yet it didn't scare her, it excited her. She wanted to get closer. And even though it was foolish, because she had promised herself to the Prince and knew it couldn't amount to anything, deep down, she had begun to hope Viggo liked her, too.

Chapter Eight

'We have arranged the witnesses for the bedding ceremony.'

'What? No!' the Prince roared. 'I do not need an audience.'

Marianos was standing on a stool in his chamber as the seamstress amended the elaborate purple robe he was to wear for his coronation and wedding ceremony. But he jerked so fiercely at his mother's words, the seamstress gasped, pricking her finger on the needle so it drew blood.

Viggo stepped forward and handed her a small rag.

'There will be men from the clergy who will witness your consummation, as is tradition, Marianos. So you will refrain from drinking too much, do you understand? At least until the deed is done.'

'Mother…' he warned.

'It will legitimise your union and reinforce your commitment to your roles. And it is imperative you produce a royal heir.'

'On the first night? Really, Mother?'

'As soon as possible. What is the problem?' Zoe asked. 'It won't be the first time you will be engaging in intimate relations with a woman now, will it? Helena is very beautiful. It can't be too much of a hardship for you…'

'Enough!' Marianos said, stepping down from the box, preventing the seamstress from progressing any further with his robe. His face had turned ashen. 'I do not wish to discuss my sexual relations with you.'

'I don't see the problem,' she continued. 'If Helena doesn't satisfy you—fine, after you have got her with child, take a mistress. But on your wedding night, things will be done right.'

'Done right? Do you even know the meaning of what's right, Mother?' he roared, his anger reaching new heights. 'Nothing about this has been right from the start!' Marianos tore off his robe, threw it to the ground at Zoe's feet and stormed out of the room.

She raised her brow. 'General Markou, what say you about it?' Zoe asked.

The General stepped forward. 'I think the council will be keen to know consummation has taken place. And the only way they can be sure is to have witnesses present. I'm certain the Prince will be up to the task on the night.'

Viggo clenched his fists as he watched the General take his leave to go after Marianos and he regretted helping the man yesterday. In fact, he wasn't entirely sure why he'd been summoned in here this morning now he'd been usurped by the General. Although he had the feeling that command to palm him off on Helena was the Prince's doing, not Zoe's. But this was the first time he hadn't wanted to be a part of the Empress Regent and Marianos's conversations. Viggo really didn't want to be here, listening to this. His stomach was churning, bile rising in his throat.

There was so much he could be doing back at the Hippodrome. They needed to continue clearing and rebuilding—

they had to make the most of the daylight. And there was still so much to be done to secure the city for the wedding.

Zoe sighed. 'Who do you agree with, Viggo?'

The thought of Marianos taking Helena to bed made him feel nauseous. And the thought of any of the male members of the clergy seeing it happen, watching her lose her innocence, it was sickening. He didn't want any part in this discussion.

Plus the fact they were already talking of Marianos taking a mistress, before he'd even married her? It made his blood simmer. The Prince didn't realise what a prize he had. Helena didn't deserve this. She was a good person. She was willing to put others before herself. She was strong yet kind, and always right…the things she'd said last night about his family, about him pushing people away, they were true.

He did do that, because if he was the one to do it, he couldn't get hurt when they abandoned him, could he? Which was why he'd lashed out, triggered by feelings of frustration and helplessness. He had been reeling from the fact she'd said she didn't want to spend time with him any more, even though he knew why she was doing it. It wasn't safe for them to continue spending time together alone. Their meetings carried an undercurrent of longing, for him at least, and if he wasn't careful, he could land himself in a lot of trouble.

Helena clearly had more sense—was stronger than him—to instigate their parting. And instead of flying off the handle, he should have told her how he felt. But what could he say? He couldn't exactly tell her he didn't want her to marry Marianos. That he did see her as a friend, but he would dearly love to be more than that if she wasn't marrying his ruler in a few days' time…

But he couldn't. His feelings weren't acceptable. They made him a traitor, testing his loyalty to the Prince. And he couldn't be sure what her thoughts were on the matter. He was convinced she wouldn't want someone like him. Someone who had blood on his hands.

'It's an outdated tradition—intrusive, don't you think? Perhaps Marianos—and his bride—might be more comfortable if they were left alone on their wedding night?' he said.

Though that didn't offer him much comfort.

'I'm not sure he can be trusted to get the task done. He is not himself, as you can see. No, I need to be certain. We all do,' Zoe said and Viggo briefly closed his eyes in despair.

He felt tense and irritable. He hadn't slept properly in days. Last night, he'd paced outside Helena's door, feeling wretched, until he'd finally heard her crying come to an end and movement inside her room cease. He hoped she had gone to sleep.

He had wanted to stay outside all night, to keep watch over her, in case she needed him, but there was something telling him that wasn't a good idea. He was concerned thoughts of her slipping between the sheets, her hair unfastened, spread out on the furs, would challenge his resolve. The need to touch her was becoming too great. So when Theodor had come along, telling him he'd come to relieve him, he had left for his own sanity.

He'd been overwhelmed with relief when he'd made it home to find Sofie in bed, unscathed. She had felt the tremors and known what they had meant, and she'd been beside herself with worry, waiting up for him to return, eager to know everyone at the palace was safe. Fortunately, there had been no damage to their home or street. He'd asked about the baby and she'd smiled, saying she'd felt it kick for the first time.

A strange elation had rippled through him, giving him hope. He was so relieved Sofie and the baby were well.

They'd talked for a while and he'd told her of all that had happened during the day—about the quake, about General Markou. And she had tried to make him feel better, as she always did, making light of what Marianos had done, until she'd succumbed to sleep. But while he'd taken himself off to bed, he'd been unable to stop thinking about the way Helena had felt in his arms, pressed up against him, clinging on to him, her delicate floral scent drifting up his nose as the ground had trembled beneath them. It had been torture holding her body so close, yet when the quake had stopped he hadn't wanted to let her go.

He was proud of her—the way she'd stood up to Zoe. The things she had said. And he'd wanted to tell her, only he hadn't got the chance. She'd started pushing him away as soon as they'd left the hall. After the first glimmer of interest from Marianos, things had quickly turned sour between them.

He had been so angry that when she'd mentioned his parents, he'd snapped back, revealing too much. He'd seen the shock on her face and instantly felt bad for his heated words. His past was his problem, not hers—and he didn't want her pity.

He heard Marianos shouting from down the hall, drawing him back to the present. He seemed to be heading towards Helena's chambers, and something about the anger lacing Marianos's voice unsettled him. *Helena...*

Helena stared at her reflection in the mirror. It was an exquisite tunic—long, with wide sleeves, made of the finest silk and decorated with intricate patterns and embroidery. Tiny little pearls adorned the top and bottom.

She turned from left to right, studying herself. Her ladies-in-waiting were all staring up at her in admiration, only she wasn't sure whether she liked what she saw. It wasn't the tunic as such, it was her in it. It didn't feel right. None of this felt right.

Could she really go ahead with this wedding and marry the Prince?

Suddenly, she caught a glimpse of Marianos storming past her chamber. 'Close the door,' she shrieked to her attendants. But it was too late. He'd already seen her and to her horror, he retreated his steps.

The Prince stood staring up at her and her hand came up across her mouth in shock. 'Marianos, you're not supposed to see me in this before the wedding,' Helena said.

The ladies bustled about.

'*Kyries*, leave us,' he said.

They picked up their skirts and began to rush out, offering her apologetic glances that they hadn't been able to shelter her from sight, until they were gone and she and the Prince were alone.

'This is a surprise,' Helena said, nervously smoothing her palms over the skirt of the tunic. And then her words dried up as she saw the puce colour of his face, the ire behind his eyes. It wasn't the way you wanted your future husband to look at you in your wedding attire. No, he was not happy. Had he been in a dark place before he'd seen her, or had stumbling across her in her bridal tunic ignited his anger?

His hands on his hips, his eyes raked over her and she didn't like the cruel light in his eyes. 'Take it off,' he said, his voice deadly.

'I can't. It's pinned in place. I need help.'

'My mother said we must wed. Now she says I must bed you,' he said, ignoring her. 'The trouble is, I'm not sure I can pluck up the enthusiasm to do so.' His voice was full of fury.

'Bed me?'

'Take it off, right now,' he said, stalking further into the room.

Panic pounded in her chest, along with confusion. Uncertainty. What was happening?

'You're right. I'm not supposed to see you in it. I don't want to see you in it. Not now. Not ever,' Marianos spat.

He gripped her arm to tug her down off the box and Helena gasped. 'Stop!'

'What's going on here?' a cold voice bellowed.

Viggo.

She and Marianos both looked up to see him in the doorway.

Helena sagged.

'Your Majesty, this woman is to be your wife,' Viggo said and she could hear the rage vibrating off his own words.

'And I am to be Emperor.'

'She deserves your respect.'

Helena whimpered and Marianos glanced down at her, immediately releasing his hard hold on her arm.

The Prince straightened and let out a deep, fake sigh. 'I've seen enough anyway. Far too much. I am wearied, done here,' he said, before he stalked out of the room.

Helena whimpered and Viggo rushed towards her.

She was unbearably humiliated. She had seen the look in Marianos's eyes. He hated her. Just like her father. There was no other explanation for it. But why?

She felt herself sway and Viggo reached out to grip her arm to steady her.

'Helena,' he whispered.

But his long fingers curling around her elbow did nothing to reassure her—instead, his touch on her bare arm sent unsettling heat rippling up her skin and she shivered.

'Are you cold?' Viggo's thick brows drew together and he pulled off his cloak and wrapped it around her shoulders. She gingerly took the material from him with trembling fingers.

A tear tumbled on to her cheek and she swiped it away.

'I know I'm not your favourite person right now, but I need to know. Are you all right?' he said, searching her eyes, her face.

'I'm not sure what I did wrong,' she whispered, her body shaking.

He hooked his thumb and forefinger under her chin and tipped her face up to look at him. 'Nothing. You did nothing wrong, Helena. The Prince is at fault.'

'My mother said the Prince is never wrong.'

He raised a brow. 'Believe me, in this instance he is.'

Was he right? Could the Prince be wrong? Was she indeed going to marry a monster, as she and that other participant had jested that day of the bride show… Perhaps this was her comeuppance for saying such a thing. All her hope now turned to despair. Sickness swirled in her stomach. Maybe a life spent in the nunnery would be better than being Marianos's bride.

'You look stunning,' Viggo said.

She was acutely aware his touch was rough, his fingers calloused, unlike the smooth skin of the Prince, yet they were strong, warm, and she sought his strength. He led her over to her bed and she sat on the edge of it.

'I will fetch some water,' he said.

She gripped hold of his hand. 'Don't leave me,' she said, her voice wobbling.

He squeezed her fingers. 'Everything will be all right. We will sort this out. I promise.'

She liked the sound of the 'we'. He released her hand and she wanted to snatch it back. She so desperately wanted more of his comfort.

When she had sensed him pace outside her door last night, she had wanted to go to him, to talk to him, to ask him more about his upbringing and reassure him. Yet, she knew that she couldn't. He was angry with her and they both needed some distance. But then, this had happened and he'd been at her side immediately, despite their quarrel. He'd stood up for her to Marianos. He was always here when she needed him—even after she'd dismissed him last night.

'I don't understand what that was all about,' she said. 'Why he was so livid to see me like this.'

Viggo sighed. 'Marianos was getting his robe altered this morning, too. He and his mother had words. I think he took his anger out on you.'

'What did they argue about?'

He rubbed the back of his neck.

'Viggo?'

'He has asked that you have privacy on your wedding night.'

Her delicate eyebrows pulled together. 'He wants to be alone with me, after disregarding me for days?'

'It would seem so.'

'And Zoe doesn't approve?' She was struggling to comprehend what Viggo was telling her. 'She doesn't want us to be alone?'

'Traditionally, you would have witnesses present.'

'Witnesses?' she said, glancing up at him. 'For what?' Nothing was making any sense.

He stalked around the room and came in front of a chair, as if he was putting some kind of barrier between them. He braced his hands on it. 'To ensure the marriage has been consummated. The Empress Regent and her officials believe confirmation of the union is paramount.'

'Consummated?' she asked, shaking her head a little.

He inclined his head. 'They want to be certain you perform the marital act.'

'I see.' She frowned. 'Actually, I don't see,' she said, pulling her legs up on to the bed and tucking them beneath her knees. 'What is the marital act?'

He raised his eyes to the ceiling, as if he was praying to God for strength. 'Perhaps that is a question for your handmaidens. Or your mother?'

'I'm asking you,' she said, pulling his cloak tighter, taking comfort from the scent of it—him—wrapping around her.

Silence reigned.

'How am I meant to perform this marital act if I don't know what it is—what is expected of me. Viggo, help me.'

'I thought you no longer wanted my help.'

Her eyes narrowed on him and he relented. He looked towards the door, as if to check no one was in the vicinity, before sighing and coming off the chair, back towards her. 'I don't understand how you have received lessons in royal etiquette, how you have been taught the Prince's favourite foods, his pastimes—everything, but not this.' He seemed annoyed—but not with her, perhaps with her mother.

She came up on her knees and reached out to grip his arms, surprising them both.

'Please, Viggo. My mother obviously left out a vital part of information in my learnings. What is it? Tell me.'

He drew a hand over his face and went and fetched the chair. He pulled it up so he was sitting beside her as she lowered herself back down on to the bed. He took a deep breath and leaned in. 'I think perhaps your mother was trying to protect your innocence and your virtue. I made that mistake with my sister—not keeping her informed. If I'd have told her, she might have made better choices.'

'Go on,' she said.

'It is called the bedding ceremony. It's what happens between a man and a woman on their wedding night. To make the marriage official.'

'I thought the wedding ceremony in the church made it official.'

'This adds to that. It confirms the arrangement, makes it legitimate.'

'All right…so what am I meant to do?'

He swallowed and for the first time since she'd met him, she thought he seemed uncomfortable. He stood again and began to pace. 'After the wedding feast, you will come here to be undressed and helped into your night tunic by your handmaidens. Then you will be escorted to the Emperor's bedchamber. There, you will…lie together.' His voice sounded strained, as if it was an effort to get the words out.

'On the bed?'

'Yes.'

'And people—'

'Men of the clergy,' he clarified.

'Watch us lie on the bed?' It sounded absurd.

He sat down again, and groaned, burying his face in his hands.

She took his arm and pulled his hand away from his face. 'Viggo! What's the matter?'

He looked at her, his eyes full of emotion, as if willing her to understand.

'That's not everything?' she said. 'Is it?' There was more.

'No. That's not everything.'

'Tell me.'

He took a breath. 'As your husband, Marianos will remove the rest of your clothes. He will want to look at you, kiss you…touch you.'

Her frown deepened. 'Where?'

'Everywhere. He will touch you with his hands. And his body.' She saw him swallow. 'Your bodies will press against one another to become one. And this…breach of your body…is what they call consummation. When this happens, your marriage will be official.'

She looked at him, wide-eyed. Perplexed. 'Why? Why is this done?'

'It is what is done to create a child. How you will produce an heir for the throne.'

Her fingers came up to her mouth, aghast. How had she not known that? She had thought…oh, she was such a fool. How had her mother kept her so uneducated? So underprepared?

She glanced up at him. 'Will it hurt?'

He struggled. 'If done right, if Marianos is gentle, the act should be pleasurable—for both of you.'

Would Marianos be gentle? She couldn't imagine it. Not after the way he had stormed in here and spouted ugly words at her today.

Viggo must have seen the fear enter her eyes, for he lowered his voice.

'Helena, you don't have to do this,' he whispered. 'You could—'

'The need is greater than ever for me to do this,' she interrupted him. She didn't have a choice. Marianos was a ruthless man. And she was too trapped by circumstance. But she also couldn't abandon the people now. They needed someone to look out for them. She might just be able to make a difference. He knew that and so did she. She knew she didn't have a choice—her parents were counting on her, too. So what point was there in pretending otherwise? It was futile. 'You were saying? How should it feel?'

He sighed and stood again. She could tell he was finding this difficult. She imagined this wasn't deemed proper—for him to be telling her, speaking of such things. He put his hands on his hips. 'He should make you feel warm, feverish...sensual...'

'Perhaps a little breathless?' she said, realisation dawning. 'A sudden, erratic beating of my heart?' The way she felt when Viggo came near her, touched her?

'Exactly.'

'I thought it might be wrong to feel that way.'

His eyebrows raised. 'You've...experienced those feelings?'

She nodded. 'Yes.' All those feelings and more. 'Is it normal?'

'Yes. Don't worry, yes. It is not wrong to feel that way. It is what desire feels like.'

Desire.

Only, she had not felt it with Marianos. Not once. Nothing had passed between the two of them—no bolt of lightning when he had looked at her, no tremble when he'd taken her hand. His touch left her cold.

Yet with Viggo…

She had such strong reactions to him. The yearning to have him take her in his arms again was great, and as for the aching, pulsing heat between her legs—it had been building, terrifying her, all week.

'I feel so naive. I always thought children were born out of love.' She gave a bitter laugh. 'I should have known there was more to it—I often wondered how I could have been created as I'm not sure my mother ever cared for my father. And I wondered how Marianos and I could have a child if he didn't care for me.'

'It is *meant* to be an act of love,' Viggo said, inclining his head. 'Done by two people who care about each other.'

She considered him for a moment. 'Do unmarried people do this?'

He lowered his voice. 'It tends to be frowned upon, but some do, yes.' She instantly thought of his sister and her predicament. And as if he was following her thoughts, he added, 'It is, for some reason, deemed acceptable for a man to do this out of wedlock, but not a woman. Which is why I am keen to keep my sister's situation private. I do not wish to cause a scandal.'

She nodded. 'Was Sofie all right, after the quake yesterday?'

'Yes.'

'Thank goodness,' she said, her hand coming up over her chest in relief.

'Helena, about last night—' he said, coming to sit down opposite her again.

But before he could go any further, a thought struck her. 'Have you ever done this?' she interrupted, gesturing to the bed. She didn't like the thought of it. Of him kissing another woman. Of him touching another woman's body.

His eyes widened and he reared back a little.

She brought her hands over her cheeks in flustered dismay. 'I'm sorry. Forgive me. I had no right to ask…' And yet, the thought burned, consumed her. If he'd done this—this act of love—who had he done it with?

She came off the bed and began to pace, tugging his cloak around her again.

'You said priests will watch me and Marianos do this?' she asked, trying to distract herself from the images in her head, going over her old questions, her fears returning to the surface.

'It is a strange custom, I know, but historically, members of the clergy escort the royal couple to their chamber to make sure this act takes place—only for the first night. After that you'll be left alone.'

'First night. Do you mean to say this happens every night?' she said, swinging round to look at him, aghast.

'Yes. After the first time you may do it as often as you'd both like.'

She couldn't imagine doing this with Marianos even once—exposing her body, letting him put his hands on her. She couldn't envision enjoying it. She couldn't picture being intimate with a man who had been so cruel. He didn't even seem to like her, let alone want to touch her. What had he said? *I'm not sure I can pluck up the enthusiasm to bed you.*

They heard the ladies in waiting coming down the corridor, and Viggo swiftly moved the chair back to its rightful position. The women entered the room with a tray of treats and he stepped back, giving them room to place it on the table.

'I'll leave you now to finish the final adjustments to your tunic. I'm sure it'll be ready in no time,' he said, giving her one last look.

She hoped so. But what of her? After everything that had happened, she felt like a broken mess. And she had a feeling her predicament could not be so easily fixed.

Chapter Nine

Viggo was glad of the physical work, taking his frustration out on the stone as he heaved rubble. He was furious with Marianos.

When he had entered Helena's chamber and seen her standing there looking so beautiful in that exquisite bridal tunic, for a moment he'd been stunned. For the first time in his life, he wondered if it would really be so bad to take a wife. To be tied to Helena for life. Somehow, he couldn't see them hurling abuse at each other like his own mother and father had. Even after their fight last night, he still wanted to protect her.

Then, as he'd realised what was happening, he'd been horrified. Marianos was yelling at her, telling her to take it off—that he never wanted to see her in it. She had looked shocked, afraid and devastated all at once.

A fierce rage blazed in his stomach that any man would treat her in such a way and it had him speaking out against Marianos in her defence.

He was bound by his position—to go against the Prince was insubordination. Punishable by death. But there was not a chance he could have stood by and watched such unpalatable behaviour and not have done anything about it.

So he'd intervened, protecting Helena, preventing Marianos from causing her any greater humiliation.

Thank goodness he'd got there when he had.

The Prince really couldn't like her at all, to treat her in such a way. Viggo couldn't understand it. It was disturbing that, despite this, they would soon be wed.

Even more disturbing still was that the thought of anyone touching Helena—apart from himself—sent a shaft of fury through him. He'd felt possession dart through his blood. He wanted her to be his.

She deserved someone who would take care of her, someone who would go out of his way to get to know her—and appreciate her. He had the strong desire to wipe those memories from her mind, to show her a man's words—and touch—could be gentle, pleasurable, but he knew he mustn't, *couldn't.* His loyalty to Marianos would never allow it.

He shouldn't have sat Helena down and informed her about a man and woman's intimate relations. It had been inappropriate of him to discuss it. He knew that kind of information was not openly shared. Only, he'd felt oddly compelled to do so. Someone had to prepare her, didn't they? He'd never felt able to discuss such intimate things with anyone before. He'd never previously wanted to share anything about himself either. But with Helena…he could speak to her, tell her anything.

But *helvete*! The thought of Marianos kissing her, touching her, breaching her innocent body—as men of the clergy stood over them and watched—made him heave. He couldn't bear the thought of it. Yet, when she had asked what desire felt like and he had begun to explain, she had told him she had experienced those sensations—that awareness—and a fist had clenched around his heart. The thought of her having those feelings for Marianos tore him up inside.

Frustration rippled through him. So she was attracted to her future husband's looks, even if she didn't like his character. The fact had no right to bother him, but it did. It really, really did. The idea of her with Marianos made wrath boil over in his stomach.

No matter how hard he hauled the rocks, no matter how much he dug or chiselled away, lifting remnants of the arena, trying to fix what had been broken, the image of her was still there. Her huge green eyes staring up at him, the silk of her tunic wrapped around her perfect breasts and hips.

How had he let this happen? How had he started to have feelings for a woman who could never be his? He needed to control himself and fast. He needed to stop yearning for something that could never be.

He couldn't believe he'd told her she could still turn down Marianos's offer of marriage—almost encouraged her to do so, suggesting that he would help her find a way to escape the Prince's clutches. What did he think he was going to do? There was no way out. No one could save her from this. She could only leave this place now if Marianos told her to, or with her head indeed in a basket, as Zoe had said.

Besides, Helena had made it clear she still wanted to go ahead. *The need is greater than ever before.* Her needs? Or the people's need? He couldn't be sure.

He heard the chanting of her name, people stamping their feet in a unified show of support, as if they were echoing the beat of his heart—and he swung round, astounded to see her making her way towards him, stepping out on to the track of the arena.

He hadn't known she'd intended to come out here today. He'd thought she was safely tucked up in her room, busy with wedding tasks, with Theodor standing guard at her door. He'd given him strict instructions no one could enter but her handmaidens. Yet once more, the young soldier was scrambling after her, looking concerned that he couldn't get her under control. That she wouldn't listen.

Viggo couldn't help but give a wry smile. She was so stubborn!

He wiped his hand on a rag, his view of the surroundings changing immediately to scout out any potential threat, and he scanned the grounds, the crowd, for danger. He was at her side in an instant, before anyone else could reach her.

'What are you doing here?'

'I came to show my support, to see how the wounded were doing, to encourage the soldiers with their efforts.'

'That is good of you, but some warning might have been nice,' he said.

'I didn't know I was meant to ask your permission,' she said.

He raised a single brow. They both knew full well she was defying Zoe's rules. And his own.

Despite the intimate topic of their conversation earlier, he was excruciatingly aware that they still hadn't smoothed over their disagreement last night. He knew he should apologise for his outburst, but now wasn't the time, not with crowds of people gathering all around.

'I didn't mean to stop the work. I just wanted to go round and say a few words, to keep up people's spirits, then I'll leave you in peace,' she said.

'I'll accompany you.' He had no choice.

She approached a family and asked them about their night. She had a unique ability to converse with anyone, he thought, getting down to the children's height and engaging with them. She moved on to the next group and incredibly she told them about her own injury to her knee, sharing in the trauma they had all suffered, making her more relatable to them. The people drew closer, wanting to get a better look at her, wanting to reach out and touch her. The fact she was willing to spend her time talking with them, to hold their hands and show compassion endeared her to many.

In such a short space of time, she seemed to have become a symbol of hope. Someone in the palace who would listen to them, who wanted to help. She had done the monarchy a world of good. If only Marianos could see her now…

He saw what she was trying to do—she was attempting to build a bridge between the people and the palace, and it appeared to be working. A fragile peace seemed to have befallen upon the city after yesterday's event—tragedy, and her show of kindness, was bringing people together.

She hadn't married Marianos yet, but it didn't seem to matter—in these people's eyes, she was their Princess and she had their support. If anything were to happen to her, it would spell disaster, so Viggo kept close to her, his one hand on his sword, his other hovering near her elbow. If she minded his touch, she didn't show it.

Had a peace been agreed between the two of them as well? Had they forgiven each other for last night? He knew he would need to find the opportunity to explain the things he'd said to her, about his past, to smooth things over. Because there was one thing was becoming increasingly clear—she was adored by the people, but most of all by him.

* * *

Helena swirled the contents of her chalice round and round, before taking another sip. For once, she enjoyed the feeling of the velvety liquid burning her throat—the taste of the grapes and cloves, and the way it was helping to dull her emotions.

The events of today played over and over in her mind.

Her mood had been brightened by going outside and talking to the people, assessing the situation at the Hippodrome. She had felt she'd done something positive amid all the tragedy of late. But once she'd returned to her chambers, thoughts about how Marianos had behaved kept coming back to her, making her feel vulnerable. How could she ever trust the Prince to speak kindly to her now? He hadn't physically hurt her, but she had been defenceless against his cruel onslaught. He had hauled hateful words at her once again, making her feel degraded.

Now she was angry, but also fearful of their future interactions after everything Viggo had told her. Were she and Marianos really going to have to lie together on their wedding night, after he'd treated her like that? She had been apprehensive before, but now she was afraid. The thought of him undressing her, touching her, being intimate—when she didn't even like him, or he her—and with strangers watching made her shudder.

She knew she was building up the marital act to be this big, horrific thing in her mind, but how could she not? It meant someone touching her against her will. It sounded barbaric.

At least what had happened today had given Viggo a chance to tell her about the bedding ceremony and what was expected of her. If Marianos had approached her on her wedding night, and started doing all those things to her, with no warning, with others watching on, she would have been in shock—she might have put up a fight. It could have been even more traumatising. She had seen the way Viggo had struggled when she'd asked him if it would hurt.

She was so glad Viggo had been the one to tell her—it felt right, somehow, that it was him. He'd opened her eyes, educating her again.

But she was still reeling from her own naivety. How had she not known? She was mortified. He must think her such a fool.

She took another gulp of her wine. Perhaps she should have accepted his offer when he'd suggested she didn't go ahead with the wedding. Maybe he could find her a way out of this situation, one she couldn't think of. Only, surely if Zoe and Marianos—and her parents—said she had to marry the Prince, she had to marry him? What other option did she have? Her choices hadn't changed—she could spend a lonely life confined to the convent or trapped in a loveless marriage, forced to bear Marianos's children.

Marianos had said her sole purpose was to bear him a son. Now she knew what she'd have to do to achieve that and her stomach roiled. He sounded as if he intended to use her like an object, to play with as and when he needed her, but she'd be cast aside the rest of the time. Was that to be her lot in life? It couldn't be. She would have to make sure there was more to it than that.

If she was going to marry a man she didn't love, then she would at least use her position to better the lives of her people. She would endure Marianos's nightly visits for them after seeing how they were suffering. It was more important than ever that they had someone in the palace looking out for them, swaying decisions so that they benefitted them.

And Viggo would be here. She would still be able to talk to him and enjoy his company. If he was here, she could do anything. Viggo, and being away from her parents' watchful gaze for the first time in her life, had opened her eyes to so much.

At least as Empress she had an opportunity, this chance, to do something good, to carve out a role for herself. She would enjoy those responsibilities, if not the others. She would make it worth it. Worth marrying a brute for.

A knock at her door made her jump. Would she always be on alert now, worried Marianos had come down the corridor, seeking her out?

She teetered to the door. 'Who is it?'

'It's me.'

Viggo.

Her heart clamoured.

Instinctively, she hid the chalice behind her back before pulling open the door in haste. She was pleased to see his face, but that didn't mean she wanted him to know she'd been drinking wine. She didn't think he'd approve.

'I'm heading home for the night, Theodor's on his way back, but I wanted to check you were all right, after today?' He looked tired. She had seen how hard he'd been working. She knew she wasn't the only one trying to make a difference. And he and his men had made great progress already.

He was a good man. He had been her rock this week. She felt more courageous, more determined, more everything with him at her side.

All day she had been wondering if he had experience of being with a woman—he had avoided answering her question earlier. She couldn't believe she'd asked! It wasn't her place. She shouldn't care. But she did. Too much. She couldn't help it.

She looked down and noticed he was holding what appeared to be a branch in his hand. When he saw her staring, he held it up.

'I actually came to apologise,' he said, inclining his head. 'It's an olive branch. From the tree. A symbol of peace.'

She couldn't help but smile.

'I never meant to get cross with you last night, Helena,' he said. 'Let me explain?'

She was touched by the gesture. She looked up at him and knew he deserved to be heard out, especially after he'd come to her rescue today.

She opened the door a little wider.

'You were right. I am cynical. Distrustful. I do tend to push people away.'

She shook her head. 'I should never have said that…'

'And I should never have said I was wasting my time helping you. I didn't mean it.'

He offered the branch to her and she went to take it with her free hand, but she fumbled, her movements clumsy. She'd barely had anything to eat today—she hadn't felt hungry after Marianos's visit to her room. Perhaps she'd had more wine than she'd intended to on an empty stomach.

'Does that mean you accept my apology?' he asked, when she took it off him.

'Yes.'

'Good. I didn't want to go home for the night without us clearing the air,' he said.

She took an unsteady step back and his brow darkened. Concern filled his gaze.

'Helena, are you sure you're all right?'

'Yes.'

'What's behind your back?'

'Nothing,' she said, defensive.

He moved closer and her breath halted.

'What do you have in your other hand?' He slowly reached out, his hand curving round her body, grabbing her by the wrist, and she gasped. 'What are you hiding?' he asked, as he slowly brought the cup between them, wine spilling over the side.

He looked down at the chalice between them.

'Have you been drinking?' he asked. His voice was like acid.

She licked her lips, suddenly feeling parched. She needed water.

He peered past her into her room and she knew he would see the half-empty carafe on the table. His spine straightened. 'How much have you had?'

He released her and stalked past her, shocking her as he barged into her room, heading for the tray.

'Do you mind?' she asked.

She moved nearer to him, but was aware she was wavering. Come to think of it, she did feel a bit woozy. Was that the effects of the drink? She put the branch down on the chair.

He picked up the other chalice, empty and lying on its side. He brought it up to his face and sniffed it, his nose wrinkling. And when he turned and lanced her with an ice-cold, disgusted look, she pressed her lips together.

'If anyone sees you like this…' he said, shaking his head.

'It was just a goblet with dinner. There's no rule against that, is there?' she said. But she heard the guilt in her voice and winced. She was talking too quickly, downplaying the situation, as if she had to explain herself. But she knew he was right—she'd had far too much. She'd wanted to drown her sorrows. She wanted to block out all thoughts of Marianos and their imminent nuptials.

'Why are you drinking in here, alone?' She heard the condemnation in his voice and she didn't like it. What right did he have to judge her?

'Who else was I going to drink with, you? In case you hadn't noticed, I'm all alone here. I have no one to speak to.'

The look he sent her made her wither. She watched as he took the chalice from her hand and picked up the carafe from the table, stalking out of the room with them.

'Where are you going?' For a moment, she panicked, wondering what he was going to do—was he going to fetch someone, tell someone? And then she realised. When he reached the balcony, he began to empty the burgundy liquid in the carafe over the side of the portico. Then he did the same with the chalice, all while his eyes bored into her. They didn't move from hers until both vessels were dry.

Her own anger burned. He had come here to apologise, but one moment he had been saying sorry, the next he was chastising her, making her feel like a naughty child. He was meant to be her friend, on her side. He had been encouraging her to make her own decisions all week—yet now he was taking the control away? He was such a hypocrite!

'Well, that was a waste,' she said, tossing her hair over her shoulder, flashing her eyes at him, defiant.

'A waste?' He laughed, but the sound was brittle. 'Really?' And she shivered, his dark, dangerous mood sobering her just a little.

He strode towards her and she backed away into her room. 'That's what my father used to say when I threw away his ale.'

Just before he beat him.

She raked in a breath. He didn't need to say the words. She knew already.

She could feel the wrath vibrating off him and knew she'd caused it. She had known how he'd felt about people drinking—he had hinted at it before. Sofie had told her his father had always turned to ale.

'I used to hide it, you know,' he said, 'the ale. Because I knew if it was available, he would drink it. And I knew if he drank it, he would turn into a monster before my eyes. I didn't just have myself to worry about. There was my mother. My sister, too.'

'Viggo—'

'No, you will hear this!' he said, silencing her. 'My mother soon had enough of it. I woke one morning to find her gone. And without her, there was no one to protect us and he got a whole lot worse. It was all I had to look forward to every night—his angry words and a beating. For five years.'

'Viggo, I'm sorry,' she said. She wished she hadn't touched a drop. She wished she hadn't reminded him of it. She didn't like herself very much right now. She wasn't sure she could bear to hear any more. 'Please…'

But he didn't stop. It was as if he needed her to hear it, to vent it, or to punish her. To put her off drinking for ever. 'Do you know what was worse than him hurting me? It was that he'd have no memory of it the next day, the aftereffects of the ale clouding his thoughts. So there was never any remorse. It just kept happening, over and again. There was no reprieve. And one night? He did this.' He pointed to his face and the nasty knot of scars that met in the middle of his cheek.

Her breath halted, her stomach churned.

'To think I had thought I was winning,' he said, giving

that harsh, bitter laugh again. 'I'd smashed his drinking horn. It had splintered to the ground. But it sent him into an even deeper rage. He pushed me, shoving me down on the floor alongside it, wanting to break me in return. He pressed his boot to my jaw as the shards of horn bit into my cheek, the pain of a hundred knives splintering into my skin.'

She flinched, horrified. She couldn't bear to think of it. She stood on shaking legs, holding on to the bedpost, and shook her head, trying to rid herself of the images of him being held down, being hurt, by his own father. It was unbearable. She could only imagine what damage that had done—yes, she had seen the scars, but to him as a person. How had Viggo ever been able to trust anyone after that? After his mother had abandoned him. After his father had beaten him?

How would he trust her if she drank—and hid it from him?

'It was after that I knew I had to get Sofie away from there. That we couldn't put up with it any more. That no one was coming to save us. We had to make it on our own. My sister has always been the most important thing in my life. That is why I plan to take her away from here,' he said, lowering his voice. 'After the coronation and the wedding, we intend to leave the city.'

Pain lanced her chest, swift and brutal. 'You're leaving?' she gasped. He was abandoning her.

'We plan to start a new life somewhere no one knows us, so Sofie can have her child and raise it without judgement.'

No! She didn't want him to go. He was her only friend here. She had only survived these past few days because he had been here to support her. She couldn't imagine living here and him not being around. It had been the only thing that had made this remotely bearable. That she would see his fascinating face every day.

'I would never say anything about your sister, Viggo.'

She could understand why he wanted to take his sister away. He had good reason. She didn't begrudge him that. He was trying to help. But still, she wanted him to stay. She needed him to. She suddenly felt desperate.

'Do you really have to go?'

'We must.' He closed the distance between them, his hard chest almost pressing against hers. 'So don't ever talk to me about this being a waste, Helena,' he said, nodding to the empty chalices. 'Not when I've seen what it can do to people. How it can destroy lives. My life.'

She looked up at him, at a loss as to what to say, unsure words could make it better. Her heart was breaking, for his terrible childhood—and that soon he would have to leave his home for a second time. He would have to leave her. Instead, she reached up, invading his space. She didn't know what had come over her, but she just knew she wanted to comfort him, to let him know she was here for him. That she cared. She wanted to run her fingers over his scars, to make everything better.

As her fingertips trailed over the silvery lines, following their path, his eyes filled with consternation at the intimate touch and he gripped her wrist, hard. 'Don't,' he said.

He released her and then he was gone, turning his back on her and pulling the door to behind him, leaving it rattling in its frame.

Chapter Ten

Viggo stood by the altar in the Hagia Sophia, the grand cathedral in the centre of the city, suffering the monotony of the wedding rehearsal. The afternoon dragged by as he watched the Patriarch of Constantinople tell Helena and Marianos where they should stand and what they would need to say on the morrow. Viggo's hands kept bunching into fists at the man's words, his stomach hardening as the Bishop explained the meaning behind every ritual.

'You will exchange rings. These represent your commitment to each other,' the Patriarch said. 'And you will be crowned, signifying family. Finally, you will share a chalice of wine.'

Helena cast Viggo a worried look, before instantly glancing away again, and his chest squeezed.

He felt like such a beast for his behaviour last night.

When he'd gone to see her before leaving the palace, he'd been concerned to discover she'd been drinking—tottering slightly as she stood in the doorway, her eyes glassy and unfocused. As he'd watched her run her tongue over her lips while they'd been talking, drawing his attention to the red-wine stains around her mouth, his blood had iced over.

He had overreacted, he knew that. It stemmed from an old fear that had reared its head. It was irrational—of course she was allowed to have a drink with her dinner. He had no right to criticise her. God, she must think him so overbearing. Controlling. Sofie had often called him such when they'd argued. And yet, he hadn't been able to help himself. He hadn't liked seeing her in such an inebriated state—she wasn't herself and he especially hadn't liked watching her denial.

It had scared him—to see her turn to wine to make herself feel better. It was irresponsible and he'd wanted to lash out and reprimand her, and shock her into never doing it again.

So he'd told her about his father. It had all come pouring out, shocking her and alarming himself that he had been so loose-lipped. He'd never told anyone about it before, or how he'd got his scars.

He didn't know why he'd done that. He guessed the fear, and frustration, had made him. He wondered what she'd thought. At least he hadn't told her the worst part. At least he'd kept that back. Thank God…

He had been stunned when she had raised her hand to his cheek, her fingers lightly trailing over his scars. No one had ever done anything so personal before. No one had ever looked at him in that way, her eyes full of compassion. He couldn't be sure if it was the drink that had made her do it, or if she really cared. Either way, the private, inappropriate touch had disturbed him and he'd known he had to get out of there, fast, before he did something reckless—like gather her to him and touch her in return.

'You will circle the gospel book,' the high-ranking Bishop was saying now, drawing back his attention. 'Come on, circle the book!' he said, gesturing with his hand. And Marianos and Helena reluctantly began to walk around the holy book, doing as they were told. 'Rejoice, O Isaiah! A Virgin is with child and shall bear a son,' he said.

Marianos faltered and came to a stop, the Bishop's words seeming to displease him.

'Next, I will announce you may kiss the bride, and—'

'I can't do this,' the Prince said, pulling the elaborate headwear off his head.

'Marianos,' Zoe said sternly. 'Listen to what the Patriarch has to say.'

'No,' he said. 'No, Mother, I can't. I won't.' He turned and stormed down the aisle, half-running out of the church as his guards followed after him, bringing a halt to the rehearsal.

'I think someone must be nervous about the ceremony,' Zoe said, making light of it. 'Perhaps we'll stop there for the day.'

'There's not much to it. Everything will go smoothly, I am sure,' the Bishop said kindly to Helena. Then he turned to Zoe. 'Shall I walk you out?'

Viggo watched them retreat, thinking this whole situation was absurd. Anyone would think a funeral was about to take place, not a wedding. No one seemed happy about it apart from the Empress Regent.

What was wrong with the Prince? Was Marianos concerned about the ceremony, like Zoe had said, or was there more to it?

He glanced up at the columns holding up the vast dome, the walls decorated with shimmering mosaics. He imagined anyone would be uneasy to be getting married in such a place, knowing the whole city would be watching.

All alone in the quiet of the spiritual space, he glanced

over at Helena. She looked forlorn and was pressing her fingertips to her temples.

'Feeling all right?' he asked her, coming towards her.

'Regretting my choices,' she said.

'Oh?' His heart lifted in hope.

'You were right, I shouldn't have drunk last night. My head is pounding.'

'Ah,' he said, disappointment crashing through him.

While he was glad she was admitting she wished she hadn't drunk so much wine, he had hoped she'd been talking about her decision to marry Marianos.

He offered her his flask and she gratefully took it from him, their fingers brushing. She took a large swig of water and he watched her throat work as she swallowed the liquid.

'I just wanted to forget everything for a while.' She shrugged, handing the vessel back.

'Alcohol is never the answer.'

'I know that,' she sighed. 'So what do we think happened there—why did Marianos storm out?' she said, lifting her hands up in exasperation, before slumping down on to the three carpeted steps.

'I have no idea,' Viggo said. 'I swear he's getting stranger by the day.'

His comment drew a smile.

'Mind if I sit?' he said, gesturing to her side.

When she shook her head, he lowered himself down next to her.

'I had no right to get cross with you last night. I'm sorry,' he said, wiping his palms on his thighs.

'Again,' she said.

'Again.' He inclined his head.

'Or judge me?' she said, quirking an eyebrow.

'Or judge you,' he said, agreeing with her. 'It's not up to me what you do.'

She looked across at him.

'I had no right to come down so hard on you. To try to control you like that,' he said.

'So why did you?'

He looked down at his feet, scuffing them across the marble floor a little. 'I guess I don't want anyone else I care about to succumb to the clutches of alcohol.'

She nodded, seeming to take that in.

Had he just told her he cared about her?

'I understand. I'm so sorry about your mother leaving—and about your father, Viggo. What he did…' She shuddered. 'I can't stop thinking about it.'

Had she really listened to him and remembered everything he'd told her about his childhood, even in her inebriated state? It made him think perhaps she cared, too, just a little.

He swallowed down the lump in his throat. 'It was a long time ago.'

But however many years passed, he would never be able to forget it. It never eased the pain. He was reminded of it every time he looked at his reflection.

'Do you ever wish to return to Norway, to see him again? See if he's changed?'

'No,' he said. 'There's nothing to go back for.' He had made sure of it. But he could never tell her about that. What was at the heart of him. It was a reminder he should really stay away from her. She would never be able to look at him in the same way if she knew what he'd done. So he had determined to keep quiet about it, always.

'You don't want to show him the man you've become, all you've achieved?'

'No. Why would I? He had no part in it.'

'I wish I could be more like you,' she said, surprising him. 'I always cared far too much what my father thought. It ate away at me and I was so determined to prove him wrong.'

'I think you've done that, don't you? Look how much you've achieved this week.' He bumped her arm. 'When the Bishop pronounces you man and wife in the Hagia Sophia, in front of the entire aristocracy of Constantinople, your father will be proud.'

She gave him a weak smile. 'Do you think the wedding will actually happen?'

'It's on the morrow. We've just had the rehearsal. I'd say so.' His heart clenched.

'And look how well that turned out,' she said. 'The very idea of having to kiss his bride sent Marianos running from the church.'

Viggo grimaced. 'I don't know what the matter is with him. I'm sorry, Helena. I tried to talk with him…'

'I know.'

And he had. But he'd got no answers. Marianos had just dismissed him, without giving an explanation for his actions yesterday.

'How are you feeling about the ceremony?' he asked.

'I'm worried I'll trip on my veil, fall on my face…'

'Your maids of honour will hold up your veil,' Viggo said. 'And I won't let you fall.'

'I know that, too,' she said. 'But I'm still afraid I will get the words wrong, or that I'll mumble or stutter.'

'You just need to repeat what the Bishop says,' Viggo reassured her.

'And if I get to the altar and Marianos refuses to marry me, in front of all those people?'

'He'd be a fool.'

She gave him a shy smile.

Helena got to her feet and took a breath, as if she was preparing herself once more. 'So I will stand tall, I'll speak loudly and Marianos will come round,' she said determinedly.

Viggo stood, encouraging her on, not wanting her to feel worried. 'Exactly. He will place the ring on your finger and you will do the same to his.'

'The Bishop will do the blessing, the crowning, the sipping of the cup, the dancing round the book,' she said, gesturing with her hand to where they had just pranced around, moments before Marianos had stormed out. 'And then he'll tell the newly crowned Emperor he can kiss his bride and he'll…'

'Kiss you,' Viggo said and then frowned.

'I don't know that part.'

'Just…follow his lead,' he said, his eyes dipping helplessly to her plump lips.

She looked up into his eyes. 'I'm frightened, Viggo.'

'I know,' he said, stepping towards her, lifting his hand to stroke her cheek.

So was he—of the traitorous feelings rushing through him. Of the force of his feelings for this woman. Of how much he absolutely didn't want her to go through with this.

'Viggo,' she whispered. 'Will you…kiss me? Show me what to do?'

The breath left him.

He had spent years in the Prince's service, serving him loyally. To kiss his bride in the very cathedral where they were to be married tomorrow would be an act of betrayal. She was forbidden. And yet he could already be deemed a traitor, for his body had unexpectedly hardened in reaction to her request, his heart hammering in his chest with desperation to fulfil her plea.

The flickering pulse beating fast in her throat intrigued him and he wanted to reach out and run his thumb gently over it. Her lips parted, her green eyes held him in their snare. But he mustn't succumb. He must remember his oath. He had to stay away from her, to protect her—and himself—from certain death.

So he pulled back.

Viggo dropped his hand from her face and Helena felt him step away.

'I can't,' he said, his voice gruff, his eyes still focused on her lips.

She wrinkled her nose, feeling vulnerable about her request—hurt that he was rejecting her. She tipped her head to one side. 'Do you want me to look like a fool in front of all those people?'

'Helena...' His voice sounded desperate. 'You are Marianos's bride.'

'And you said you cared about me. That you would help me.'

He gave a sharp shake of his head. 'Not with this.'

'Why not?'

'Because it wouldn't be right. It would be treason to kiss you.'

'It would be a betrayal not to. How can you send me out

there, in front of the enormous congregation, not knowing what to do? I'll bump his nose, or knock his teeth.' She tried to smile, but it crumbled.

He softened and stepped back towards her, raising his hand again, smoothing his thumb over the corner of her lips, and she felt her breathing quicken. 'You won't, Helena. You can't get this wrong. Besides, you're in a place of worship, it will be brief.'

'How brief?' she said, looking up at him. 'So brief no one will notice? Or ever know?'

His eyes narrowed on her and something passed between them, a mutual understanding. He glanced towards the door, the need for discretion, to avoid detection, imperative, before turning back to her. He stared down at her, his ebony eyes searing hers, and her breath hitched.

As if his decision was made, his fingers slowly stole round her neck and twisted into her hair, making her shiver. Then gently, unbelievably, he drew her face towards his. She stopped breathing altogether. Her eyes fluttered shut as she waited for the touch of his skin and she gasped at the contact as their lips brushed, his mouth carefully pressing against hers.

She felt sudden heat. It was as if time stood still and she leaned in, wanting to linger, tender feelings rushing through her, needing to get closer, and then he abruptly pulled away. He dropped his hand from her jaw and she opened her eyes, feeling unsteady as she stood there looking up at him.

'There,' he said, moving briskly away from her. 'You'll be fine.'

'Good,' she whispered, nodding, reaching out to hold on to the altar rail, shocked at the disturbing feelings rushing through her. 'Thank you. You were right. There really is nothing to it.'

He swung back to look at her.

'I don't know what I was worried about. To think I was concerned about a little kiss.'

Fire blazed in his eyes. The same fire that had erupted inside her—like a burning, desperate need. She knew it was destructive, that it threatened to destroy everything, but right now, in this moment, she didn't care. And when he gripped her wrist, pulling her back towards him, bringing her up against his chest, hard, she gasped, thinking neither, it seemed, did he.

'Did I disappoint you?' he said.

And before she had chance to answer, he took her face between his hands and the impact of his mouth on hers again was explosive. This time, his lips were firm, moving with purpose, and he opened her mouth with his to kiss her fully. His hot silky tongue swept inside and she gasped at the erotic invasion of his tongue. She felt a frisson of heat ripple through her and her whole body trembled.

She thought about pulling back, thinking that she ought to, concerned someone might see them, but she couldn't. She didn't want to. She was lost to him. And instead, her fingers splayed out against his chest as she sank into him, allowing his hands to move slowly over her shoulders and down the curve of her back, to press her closer, crushing her breasts against him and deepening the caress of his kiss.

Her entire body was in flames. Untameable fire. She needed more. She wanted to eradicate any space between them, needing to feel his muscles pressed against her, and she wriggled nearer, her hips grinding against his. The reaction in his lower half was instant. She felt him harden.

Thinking she knew now what it meant, how things worked between a man and a woman after he'd enlightened her, she drew in a sharp breath, shocked, excited, all at once. But her sharp inhale had him lifting his head, pulling back urgently. He stared down at her and then with a violent curse she was cast from his arms, so suddenly it made her reel.

She stumbled, grabbing hold of a pew.

His back was turned away from her, his head bowed, as he leaned over the altar.

'That should not have happened,' he said finally.

'Shouldn't it?'

He whirled around. 'No!' He raked a hand through his hair. 'I shouldn't have done that. It was wrong of me.'

Wrong? She wasn't sure.

There were many things that had happened this week that had felt wrong, but his kiss certainly hadn't been one of them. It had been significant, yes. But definitely not wrong.

She realised this was what he had been talking about the other day. This was what desire felt like, what she should feel like on her wedding night—to want a man to put his hands on her, to want to press up against him and create more of those delicious, tingling feelings, yet she had never experienced this with the Prince, only with his Varangian Commander.

It was as if that one kiss had turned her life upside down, altering everything she'd thought to be true, everything she'd ever been told about how she should behave and how she should feel. It was as if she had been stirring from a hazy dream all week and now she was wide awake. Because no one had ever told her it was possible to feel like that. And now she knew that it was, how could she go back?

'Helena, I'm sorry,' Viggo said again, stalking back towards her. 'I took things too far. I behaved badly. Forgive me.'

She raised her gaze and their eyes clashed. 'I don't want you to be sorry, Viggo,' she said. 'I asked you to do it.'

He inclined his head. 'Not quite like that,' he said wryly.

She smiled, the tension easing a little between them. 'No, I don't think it will happen quite like that at the wedding.'

They both sobered at the thought.

Because despite that earth-shattering kiss, there was still going to be a wedding. Viggo could hold her, touch her, kiss her and make her feel alive, but tomorrow she would still have to marry Marianos.

Chapter Eleven

As they stepped into the afternoon sun and headed down the steps outside the cathedral, Helena raised her hand, sheltering her eyes from the light.

'Viggo, please can we not return to the palace just yet? Will you take me somewhere—just for a while? Somewhere I've never been? I'd love to walk, to see a little of the city.'

He drew a hand over his beard. 'I don't know, Helena. They'll be missing you. It's the eve of your wedding.'

'Exactly. It's my last night of freedom. I don't want to spend it locked away in my room. Please? I will wear my veil, so no one recognises me. I promise I will behave and do as you say. It doesn't have to be for long. I'm just not ready to go back. Not yet.'

He wavered. He felt the same. He didn't particularly want to feel those walls closing in on them again, to watch the daylight hours fading away, to spend the dark hours tossing and turning, waiting until the sun would come up and she would have to be wed. It felt good to be out of the confinement of the palace for a while, just the two of them.

Plus, he wasn't ready to face anyone after what he'd just done.

Looking down into her pleading big green eyes, he knew he couldn't say no to her. And he ought to make amends for taking liberties with her inside the cathedral. He felt like such a swine.

He was the person she was depending on to help her, who she had put her trust in more than anyone else—and look what he'd gone and done. But when she'd pleaded with him to kiss her, asking for the schooling, implying no one would know, he had relented. Caved in. He had discovered his weakness and she was it.

It was hard to say no to something you wanted so badly.

His first kiss had been brief, soft and chaste—he had made sure of it. It was meant to be anyway, but just the mere touch of their lips had set off a cataclysmic shift in his body…like the moving of the ground beneath his feet during the quake the day before…and he'd pulled away, knowing the power of its destruction, realising he had to protect himself from the devastation it could cause.

He should have stopped there and walked away. Imagine if someone had seen them! His life would be over. But when she'd said that there was nothing to it, her eyes defiantly blazing into his, he'd thought that he had disappointed her and it was more than he could bear. She was challenging him, he realised, and suddenly all reasoning was lost. He just…wanted, regardless of the outcome.

It had him reaching out for her, hauling her back to him once more, wanting to satisfy her—and himself. He had taken her in his arms and left no part of her mouth undiscovered, pushing his tongue deep inside. He could still taste her now. And incredibly, she had responded, her full, lush lips moving against his, and the impact was disturbing. He had felt something he'd never felt before—a burning, all-consuming need that he knew only she could sate.

Dear God, but he'd wanted more, to press her closer,

to feel their bodies touching, everywhere. Her hands had come up to grip on to his shoulders and he'd tugged her waist towards him, holding her fast. When she'd writhed against him, he'd felt his groin harden, heard her innocent gasp and then the inevitable guilt had come. He had almost lost control—in the cathedral! Finally, he'd cast her off, appalled with himself, and he'd had to turn his body away from her to get himself in check.

She had never been kissed before and there he was, pressing his mouth down on hers, putting his hands on her, tugging her into his body and wanting to do a hell of a lot more—when she wasn't even his to touch.

He felt a bitterness burn his throat, a pain in his chest.

It was so unfair. Marianos didn't even seem to want her, he wasn't treating her right, yet Viggo still couldn't have her for himself.

But he wanted her to be happy, above everything else. And if she thought marrying Marianos would make her so, no matter how much it bothered him, ate him up inside, he would try to be happy for her.

'Where do you want to go?' he relented.

'Anywhere,' she whispered. 'Just away from here.'

'The market? The water?'

'Both.' She smiled.

He'd informed the coachman to return to the palace without them. He told a white lie, saying Helen wanted to see her parents before the wedding, before they headed in the other direction, to the market. The sights and smells of the multitude of stalls bombarded their senses as they wandered through the hectic, humid streets. Helena's eyes were wide beneath her veil and Viggo knew she had never seen anything like it before. The stalls were bustling as people haggled with the traders who were selling their wares—spices, silks and precious metals.

He led her through the vibrant maze, keeping her close, not wanting to lose her among the crowds, their arms and hands brushing. They stopped every now and again to admire the woven baskets and rugs. He pointed out the skilled craftsmen busy in their workshops and the dazzling array of pots, and her lips rose up in delight. There was an abundance of food on offer, the steam and spices tickling their noses, and he delighted in showing Helena a whole pomegranate, insisting on buying her one, making her laugh.

They came upon a man who had a gathering of people around him, and as they peered closer, they saw he had an exotic bird in a cage with bright blue-and-green plumage. The animal was making amusing noises from its curved beak.

'*Κοίτα την όμορφη κυρία.* Look at the pretty lady!' a boy said to his mother.

'*Κοίτα την όμορφη κυρία.* Look at the pretty lady!' the bird mimicked and Helena gasped. Viggo saw her cheeks turn a beautiful pink shade beneath her veil and she laughed in surprise. It was a delightful sound. He wished to make her laugh more often.

He thought perhaps he and Helena were causing more interest than they'd intended—more so than the gaudy bird—when the boy glanced up at him, noticed his sheathed sword and cowered behind his mother's legs.

Viggo crouched down to his level. 'Come out from behind there,' he said. 'I'm not going to hurt you. There's nothing to fear here.'

The woman pushed her son forward.

'Are you a Varangian warrior?' the boy asked.

'Yes.'

'What happened to your face?' he asked.

Viggo flinched. The mother hushed the child, flustered, and for a moment, he hesitated, too. He hadn't been expecting such open scrutiny and not in front of Helena. The humiliation was great.

But amazingly, she stepped in. She crouched down beside him. 'They're battle wounds,' she said to the boy. 'Great marks of honour—a sign that he defended and protected others.'

Viggo turned to look at her and their eyes met. He was grateful to her, for coming to his rescue, for finding the words to explain. He always found it difficult. He liked that she was defensive of him, it meant a lot.

The boy stepped closer. 'I want to be just like you when I'm older. A soldier in the Emperor's palace.'

'We'll be sure to keep a space open for you, then.' Viggo winked. But when he looked back at Helena, she wasn't listening. Something had caught her eye in the distance. He followed her gaze and saw she was staring at a group of Markou's men at the end of the street. He bristled.

The General was nowhere to be seen, but he could tell she was alarmed.

'I'm not ready to go back yet,' she said, panicked, placing a hand on his arm.

'Come on then, let's go,' he said, leading her in the opposite direction, out of the soldiers' sight. 'This way.'

As they raced down an aisle, he broke out into a run, dragging her with him, making her yelp at the excitement of it. They startled the crowds, who gasped at their approach, breaking apart to make a pathway for them. On they charged, leaping over chickens who seemed to have escaped their pens and through a group of people readying to pray. As they turned a corner, they stopped to catch their breaths, laughing, and he reluctantly released her hand.

'Do you think they're looking for me?' Helena asked, bent double, her hand over her chest.

'Let's hope not. Not yet anyway. But perhaps we should get out of the market.'

They walked the rest of the way to the strait, this time avoiding the dark alleyways and unsavoury neighbourhoods he had foolishly taken her through the other night. When they reached his street, instead of heading towards his residence, he led her down to the gently lapping shore. He was pleased to see there was no one around—the little stretch of sand was deserted.

'Want to sit for a while?' he asked.

She nodded and lowered herself down on to the ground.

'It's beautiful here. You're lucky to live so close to the water.'

'You have views of the strait, too,' he countered.

She glanced behind her, looking back at the palace looming over the city on the hill in the distance. 'Yes, but it's so far away. You're close enough to smell it. To taste it,' she said, turning back, closing her eyes and drawing in a deep breath. 'I envy you. To feel the breeze on your face.' She opened them again. 'You'll be far away, too. Will we still be friends when I'm married, Viggo?' she asked.

'Of course,' he said, his voice sounding peculiar.

'But will I still see you?'

'Maybe some day. Perhaps we will come back and visit.'

'I can't bear the thought of being there, at the palace, and you not being around. You're my best friend.'

His gut twisted. He didn't want to just be her friend.

'I couldn't have got through any of this without you. Every moment I've spent with you, I've found my confidence increasing. In just a few short days, I feel as if you've taught me more than anyone. Mainly, who I am and how to be myself. To believe my opinions matter and I will be forever grateful.'

His jaw clenched. He didn't want her to be grateful, he just...wanted her to be his. Yet it sounded as if she was preparing to say goodbye. 'You're stronger than you think,' he said.

'When do you plan to leave?'

'The day after the wedding.'

'That soon?' she gasped, pulling her knees up to her chest and wrapping her arms around them. 'Where will you go?'

'Nicomedia. There's a military centre there. I should still like to be useful. But perhaps I won't need to be so busy. I can be with Sofie more, help her with the child.'

'Of course, you'll be an uncle,' she said. 'How do you feel about that?'

'I'm coming round to the idea. And you? It might not be long before you become a mother.' His gut twisted. He didn't like the thought of it—her laying with Marianos and her body changing as she carried the Prince's child.

She released her hands and began raking her fingers through the sand. 'You know, no one has ever asked me if I actually want children, it's just a given. Expected.'

'Don't you?'

'I don't know. I just wonder how I could possibly be a good mother, when I still feel like I have so much to learn myself. I have begun to resent my own mother—I realise now I spent so much time training to be the Prince's wife, I barely had a childhood myself.'

He could identify with that. His sister was always calling him controlling and he knew he struggled to relax. He thought it was because he had never been able to enjoy himself as a boy. He'd had to take care of Sofie. Life had always been so serious.

'I resented some of the other boys I grew up with, for their lack of responsibilities. Their freedom. I had no patience for frivolity. It could be why my sister behaves so recklessly sometimes. Maybe I've been too strict with her. Perhaps I should try to behave more freely from now on.'

'You?' she asked, offering him a wry grin.

'Yes, *me*,' he said, adding emphasis to the words, making her smile wider. 'I can engage in playful endeavours when I want to.'

'Really?' she said. And there it was. That challenge in her eyes again.

He curled himself up on to his feet. 'All right. So let's do something neither of us got to do growing up.' This was her last night before she became Empress, before her responsibilities would be great. She deserved to have some fun. Perhaps he did, too.

'Like what?' she said, her eyes lighting up.

He looked all around him before he leaned down and unlaced his boots. He kicked them off, his toes curling into the sand. He rolled his breeches up a little, before he waded into the cold water.

Helena's eyes widened. 'Is it cold?'

'Freezing.'

When he turned round to face her, he saw she'd got to her feet, watching him, wondering what he was going to do.

'Want to come in?' he asked.

She bit her lip. 'Is that allowed?'

With a wink, he kicked the water with his foot, splashing her.

She shrieked, laughing, as the spray covered her. 'Viggo!'

'What?' he asked, putting his hands on his hips.

She slipped off her own boots, smiling. 'I'm going to get you for that!'

She raced into the shallow water, gasping, slowing her steps as the cold hit her, making her draw in a breath, but she still scooped up a handful and threw it at him, delighted when he got wet. Her eyes glinted with mischief.

'Oh, you're in big trouble now,' he laughed.

He moved towards her in the water and she tried to wade backwards, quickly, squealing. 'Viggo, no,' she said as he launched another handful in her direction.

She tried to escape the onslaught, but in attempting to get away, she fell backwards, landing on her back, fully in the water, and she clambered back up, spluttering, shocked by the cold, but still laughing.

'Are you all right?' he asked, grinning, too, reaching for her. He held out his hand to pull her up and she took it gratefully.

'Yes,' she said, nodding. 'Yes, I'm fine.'

And then she tugged him hard, with all her might, and he stumbled, trying to avoid falling on her, hurting her, instead tumbling into the water, getting completely soaked, too.

They looked at each other and both fell about.

When she stood, the wet material of her tunic was clinging to her skin, the peaks of her nipples peeking through, and his mouth dried.

He saw a man walking along the river towards them. Perhaps the fun should be over. They couldn't be spotted here, behaving like this.

'We'd better get you dry,' he said. 'Come on, the house is just over there. Let's get you inside.'

They picked up their boots and raced across the sand, then up the pathway that meandered through some gardens that led into the back of Viggo's residence. He pushed open the door for her to go in, but as they stepped inside, he heard muffled voices and he stopped dead. He put his hand against Helena's lips to shush her, to still her from going any further.

Through the gap in the doorway, he saw Markou's soldiers surrounding the front of the house and a prickling feeling of unease spread through him.

Had they realised he'd lied—that they hadn't gone to see her parents after all? Had they come for him—and her?

And then he realised—someone was inside the house. Someone was talking with his sister. His pregnant sister. Her secret would be out.

He looked down into Helena's wide eyes, his mind racing with what he should do.

But as he strained to listen, he realised that he knew that voice.

Sofie was speaking to the Prince. No, whispering with the Prince. Marianos was here, in his home. Why?

And then, the noises changed. He heard gentle gasps and murmurs, a rustle as clothing began to be removed, accompanied by soft sighs and heavy breathing.

Through the slit in the doorway, he saw them—the Prince's mouth to his sister's throat, his hands touching her half-undressed, pink, swollen body, and Viggo's stomach rolled.

Comprehension came thick and fast.

They must have met at the palace, when Sofie was Zoe's lady-in-waiting.

They were having an affair.

Marianos was the father of Sofie's child.

And betrayal burned.

Had this been going on all this time—right under his nose? He tried to swallow down his fury, his hands suddenly shaking with rage.

No wonder Marianos had swapped his duties with Markou's. He would have wanted to keep Viggo occupied, to draw him away so Marianos could come here and continue his seduction of Viggo's sister. He felt sick.

How could Sofie not have told him? Was she complicit in this? Did she want him touching her? Anger had him launching forward. He moved to open the door, but Helena stepped in his way, stopping him.

'No!' she mouthed, shaking her head, as she gripped his arm tightly.

Helena was reeling just as much as Viggo from this discovery, but if he opened that door and made their presence known, they would all be ruined. Marianos might panic. They couldn't be sure how he would react. He might have them executed just for being together, outside of the palace, and for seeing what they'd seen. It could put Sofie's life at risk, too.

Viggo stared down at her, his eyes flaming, his chest heavily rising and falling, his feelings no doubt springing between anger and hurt and confusion. She knew because she, too, felt all of the above. But her hand on his arm at least had some effect, halting him, calming him, just a little, and she pleaded with him with her eyes not to do anything foolish.

He seemed conflicted, but behind them shadows crossed the door and they saw some of Markou's men filter into the garden, supposedly to guard the back of the property. Her heart was in her mouth. They were trapped. Any moment now, they would surely be seen.

It forced Viggo's decision. Brusquely, he tugged her with him, bundling her into a small larder. She could feel the waves of emotion rolling off him, yet at least he now seemed to be thinking of their safety.

He drew a hand over his beard, thinking, and then he moved across the room and lifted up a trapdoor in the ground. Lighting an oil lamp, he silently gestured for her to take the steps down. She did so, but halted a few stairs in, waiting for him to join her with the light. She couldn't see a thing. When he did so, he pulled the door down above them.

Where were they?

As her eyes adjusted to the soft glow of the lamp, she saw they were in some kind of cellar where oil and grains were stacked up against a wall. It was cool down here and she shivered.

Viggo placed the lamp on the floor and slumped down on to some kind of crate. He buried his head in his hands. She was worried about him. Had he seen as much as her—Marianos's lips locked with Sofie's, before his mouth had moved down her neck, their bodies entwined? It was good Viggo had told her about these things, had shown her, otherwise she might have wondered what was going on—it had looked like some kind of frantic tussle.

Was Viggo in shock? She knew she was. She had not been expecting to see that today. The day before she and Marianos were due to wed.

She knelt down in front of him. 'Viggo?' she whispered.

'I'm going to kill him,' he said, lowering his hands. He stared at her. 'I should have killed him right there and then, for daring to lay a hand on her.'

'And then we'd both be dead. You did the right thing to stay back.'

'I can't believe this,' he said, shaking his head. He launched himself to his feet, starting to pace. 'Maybe I should go up there.'

'No.'

'But what if he's hurting her—or the baby?'

'It didn't look like it. She seemed to be enjoying it,' she offered. 'She wasn't protesting. From what I could see, she was encouraging him.'

Viggo winced, the thought of his sister doing the things she was doing clearly disturbing him.

'Do you think he's the father of her child?' she asked.

His fingers curled into fists. 'I don't know. It looks to be that way, doesn't it?' He shook his head. 'I've failed her, haven't I?' he said, coming back towards her and lowering himself down again.

'You haven't,' she said, resting a reassuring hand on his knee. 'You're too hard on yourself. This isn't your doing, Viggo. They're both adults. Let's not make excuses for them. You can't be responsible for all the choices she makes. You have done so much for her. You took on your parents' responsibilities—even though it meant sacrificing your own childhood. You brought her here and gave her a better life. But like you told me, we all have to make our own choices. She's making her own decision right now, choosing to do this, with him.'

'Well, she's naive,' he said. 'She must know he's using her to satisfy a need.' And then he looked up at her, forlorn.

'Oh God, I'm so sorry, Helena. I shouldn't be saying these things. You must be in terrible shock, too. You must be...'

'Relieved,' she said, finishing his sentence for him, leaning back to kneel on her feet.

His brow furrowed.

'This explains everything, don't you think? At least now I know why he has behaved the way he has this week. Why he doesn't want me. I was starting to think there was something wrong with me,' she said.

He shook his head. 'There's not. He's a fool.'

'A fool for liking your sister?' she said, raising her brows.

He couldn't answer that. Instead, he just raked a hand over his face, still in disbelief.

'I'm sorry for her part, too,' he said.

'I don't understand, though,' Helena said. 'If he cares for Sofie, if he left the rehearsal to see her, if he wants to be doing that with her, why isn't he marrying her? He is the Prince—he can do what he wants. Why did he go through with the bride show? Why is he marrying me?'

'No matter what his feelings are for Sofie, my sister wouldn't be deemed suitable to be a royal bride. Not in Zoe's or his council's eyes. She's a nobody from Norway.'

'She's not a nobody. *You're* her brother.'

'Zoe still would have said no.'

'But if he knows about the baby...' she said.

'Lots of emperors before him have taken a mistress, many mistresses, and had children with them. What he needs is a royal bride—someone of noble birth—to make a legitimate heir.'

'Poor Sofie,' she said. 'Poor me,' she added wryly and then shivered. The wet material of her tunic was making her dither, the cold seeping through her bones.

'We should get you out of those clothes,' Viggo said. 'You'll freeze to death down here.'

She gestured towards the ceiling. 'How long do you think they'll be doing that for?' she asked.

Viggo grimaced. 'I have no idea. I don't want to think about it.'

He stood and began to rummage around, looking through boxes, until he found a few blankets and brought them over to her.

'Here, are these any good? We could hang up your tunic for a while and hope that it dries out.'

She took the blanket from him and wondered how she was going to be able to wrap it round her and keep it secure, while getting her garments off at the same time.

'Actually, can you hold it for me?' she asked.

He gave a curt not and held it up like a screen, so she could undress behind it. It felt strange, peeling off her clothes when she was just a whisper away from him. As she lowered her tunic, her skin erupted in goosebumps, prickling in reaction to the cool air—and to her awareness of him. As she stepped out of the garment, the wet material fell to the floor and she snatched the blanket from him, wrapping it around her naked body as quickly as possible.

He picked up her tunic and hung it up on a hook on the wall.

'What about you?' she said, peering at him and the way the sleeves of his tunic were sticking to the muscles in his arms. 'Aren't you wet, too?'

'I'll make do.'

'You could catch your death as well, you know. Isn't it uncomfortable?'

'Oh, all right,' he said and tore off his mail coat, before

tugging his tunic up over his taut stomach and sculpted chest, pulling it over his head. Her breath hitched at the sight of his beautiful bare chest again. She wanted to ask him about the scars, the dragon ink, but her words had dried up on her tongue. He flung his things on another hook and picked up the second blanket, roughly drying his body with it.

When he caught her staring, she glanced away. 'Better?' she asked.

'I'll be better when they've left here,' he said. He threw down his blanket on the floor and sat on it, stretching his long legs out and leaning his head back against the wall, closing his eyes.

'Will you say anything to her? Or to him?' Helena asked.

He opened his eyes.

'Come over here,' he said. 'I can hardly see you all the way over there in the dark and you're still shivering.'

She came to sit beside him on the blanket, seeking his warmth.

'I will have to speak to Sofie about it. I can't believe she never told me. All those men upstairs, they know what's been going on in my home, behind my back, and I feel as if she and Marianos have made me out to look like…' He shook his head, his words trailing off.

'I'm also not sure she realises what danger she could be in. The implications of her actions. It's disturbing. I mean, if she's having the Prince's child, did she really think we could just leave this place and there would be no consequences? How can we go now? I mean, would Marianos even let us?' He turned to look at her. 'What will you do?' he said. 'Now you know about this.'

She shook her head. 'I don't know. What can I do? The choice has never exactly been mine to make, has it?'

He brought his arm around her shoulder, pulling her in, perhaps to offer her reassurance, knowing she must be despairing. 'Helena, if I'd have known…'

She gathered the blanket closer and hesitantly rested her head in the curve of his shoulder. 'It's hardly your fault, Viggo.'

She was so aware of his large arm curved around her back, his hand holding her. His hip was pressing against the side of her bottom. She liked being this close to him, her cheek nestled against his bare skin. Seeing his magnificent chest again had made her feel all achy inside. She wanted him to pull her closer, to take her face in his hands and kiss her again, and she suddenly felt hysterical.

She was meant to be getting married tomorrow, yet her fiancé was half-naked, seducing another woman upstairs, and she couldn't stop thinking about another man—*this* man, a formidable warrior whose solid arms were curled around her, comforting her, keeping her warm.

'Still. I'm sorry you had to see that.' The tips of his fingers grazed her shoulders.

'I'm not.'

His fingers stilled and he pulled away a little. 'What do you mean, you're not?' he said.

She raised her head and turned to face him.

'I thought you liked him—felt things for him. Has seeing them together, doing that, not upset you?' Viggo asked.

'No, not at all.'

He stared at her. 'You don't care for him?'

'I barely know him. And what I've seen hasn't been entirely pleasant.'

'But you said, when we were talking about your wedding night yesterday, you said you had felt all those things I described. You said you knew what desire felt like.'

She tried to steady her erratic heartbeat. It felt like a great moment of truth between them. A huge question hanging in the air that she knew she had to answer.

'I wasn't talking about Marianos.' She wanted to be brave. She had to be. This was her last chance. 'I meant I felt all those things with you, Viggo.'

She sensed his breathing falter, but he didn't reply. He just continued to stare, his black gaze assessing her, and she twisted her hands in her lap. She couldn't bear it. She came up on her knees before him.

'You don't like Marianos in that way?'

'No,' she said, shaking her head, biting her lip. 'He leaves me cold. But you…' She gestured towards him. She felt her cheeks burn.

His eyes raked over her face, as if he couldn't believe what she was saying. As if he was searching for the proof of her feelings.

'Viggo?' she whispered. 'Say something.'

'You…like me?' he asked.

'Isn't it obvious?' she said, giving a short laugh, suddenly feeling shy—and vulnerable. She'd let down her guard, expressed how she felt—she was exposed.

He shook his head. 'Not to me.' He swallowed. 'Why? Why do you like me?'

'Why wouldn't I?' But when he didn't respond, she carried on. 'You're a good man.'

He shook his head. 'I'm not.'

'You are. You're strong. Kind. You're my closest friend. I feel as if I can speak to you, tell you anything. You understand me. You're always there for me. And you make me feel—'

He leaned in closer. 'What do I make you feel?'

'Everything,' she whispered.

He brought his hand up to cover his cheek. 'But these,' he said.

She reached up to place her hand over his. 'Knowing how you got them, protecting your sister, only makes them more attractive to me,' she said, entwining his fingers with hers and pulling his hand down, away from his face. She rose up and placed a kiss on the marks instead.

He closed his eyes briefly, before opening them again. 'Helena… I'm not who you think I am.'

'You are.'

'No. I'm not.' He released her fingers and held his palms out in front of him. And she suddenly got the feeling he was about to tell her something. Something huge. Something he thought would put her off him. 'If I'm such a good man, like you say,' he said slowly, his voice strained, 'why do I have my father's blood on my hands?' It was as if he could see the stains on his skin that he was talking about.

Her breath halted.

'I took his life, Helena. And I can't forgive myself for it.'

She swallowed, taking in his words, staring into his desolate face. But she was careful not to move away. She wanted to hear him out. She had the feeling he needed her to.

'What happened?' she asked him, taking one of his hands in hers and giving it a squeeze, encouraging him on.

'It was one night, not long after he did this,' he said, gesturing to his scars. 'He was wild, out of control, and he was determined to hurt Sofie.'

Her heart broke for him all over again, for what his childhood was like. She couldn't bear to think about him ever suffering.

'I stood between them and picked up a knife from

the kitchen, threatening him. And he laughed, saying I wouldn't do it. But then he charged, trying to tackle me, and the knife cut into his skin. It all happened so fast. The wound was deep and he fell… And then, he just went still. And I knew, I knew he had stopped breathing. That I had caused it.' He shook his head. 'The worst part is, in that moment, I didn't feel any guilt. I just felt relief. Relief that it was over. That I'd stopped him. That I'd saved us.'

He drew a hand over his face. 'We left that night, before I could get in trouble in our settlement. We had no choice. But it still haunts me, what I did. I killed my own father, Helena. That's the kind of man I am. I've wanted to tell you, so many times, before now. But I was worried you'd think differently of me. Yet I can't let you continue saying any of this, about how you feel, about what a good person I am, without you knowing the worst of what's inside me. It wouldn't be fair.'

She moved closer towards him. 'You were just protecting yourself—and your sister. I can't imagine any of the people in your settlement would have thought ill of you. They must have known what he was like. You're not to blame, Viggo. You're not.' She wrapped her arms around his shoulders and held him tight. 'It's natural to feel guilt, but you were justified in what you did. You were just a child and he was hurting you. Hurting Sofie. It would have only carried on. Got worse. He gave you no choice. If you hadn't fought back, you might not be here now. Or Sofie and her unborn baby.'

His hands came up in a rush to grip her arms, his body rigid. 'Helena.' She wasn't sure whether he was going to haul her to him or push her away. But then his fingers tightened around her and he buried his head in her shoulder.

She understood now that he struggled to forgive himself. He saw himself as evil after what had happened. He hated himself for it, but she didn't. She was glad he'd fought back. If he hadn't, it would have been him lying there dead instead of his brute of a father.

They sat like that for a while, holding each other, until Helena finally pulled away to look at him. 'Thank you for telling me. But this doesn't change anything. I know what kind of man you are, Viggo.'

He searched her eyes, as if he couldn't believe what she was saying.

She felt dizzy being so close to him, drinking in the musky male scent of him. And she was desperate to know if he liked her back. 'Do you feel the same way about me?'

He drew her closer, so their faces were just a breath away.

'Isn't it obvious?' he said, repeating her words.

'Not to me,' she said. 'Show me.'

His fingers came up her arms to brush her cheeks. He brought her head towards him and his lips found hers. Her eyelids fluttered shut as she allowed him to take possession of her mouth, his tongue tenderly stroking hers, and it felt glorious to know this time he wasn't kissing her because she'd asked him to, but because he wanted to.

Viggo moaned and dragged his mouth away.

'Helena—this is serious,' he said, resting his forehead against hers. 'Treacherous.'

'I know. It is. But I want this. I want this with you.'

She bravely took his jaw in her hands and pressed her mouth against his, showing him she meant it, and he gave in to the feel of their tongues gliding against each other in a slow, sensual caress. Heat flared throughout her body, and she slid her hands down over his chest, exploring the feel of his skin beneath her fingertips.

She felt as if she had wasted too much time in her life already. If she was going to be forced to give up her freedom tomorrow, she wanted to make every moment she had with Viggo count.

When his mouth came down on hers again, there was a desperate seeking urgency to his kiss and the world began to fall away. All her responsibilities, duties, were forgotten as he gently lowered her down, so they were lying side by side on the blanket and her hands began to roam all over him—greedy. They slid over his shoulders, up into the base of his silky hair, and around his muscled back, holding him close to her, before her fingertips trailed over the vast expanse of his chest. Over his ink. Over his scars.

'Are these—?'

'Mostly battle wounds,' he said. 'Others are from my father.'

She ducked her head and pressed a soft kiss to the centre of his chest.

She wanted to kiss them all better, everywhere.

'And the ink? It's incredible. Why a dragon?' she whispered. 'Is it because you're a Varangian?'

'Partly. And partly to cover up the scars. A dragon is also a symbol of rebirth and transformation. I wanted to turn the scars into something positive.'

She ran her fingers along the dark lines, wanting to explore him. And going by the way his hands were behaving, the feeling was mutual. He rolled her on to her back and his body hovered over hers, his lips hunted out her jaw and throat, his tongue lightly flicking over her skin. She tipped her head back, hoping that he'd move his hot mouth lower, to taste and discover her body further. Now she knew what these maddening feelings he was creating were, and what they meant, she only wanted more.

And as if all her wishes were coming true, his slow, gentle hand skated up her ribcage on top of the blanket, to curve over one of her breasts. He moulded her into the palm of his hand and she felt the peak harden through the material. He caressed her with his thumb, tweaking and toying with her, while still kissing her, his tongue teasing hers and sending a spasm of shocking heat coiling down low in her belly, blossoming between her legs. Her excitement soared and she arched into his body, wanting him to get closer.

As if he could sense that, with one deliberate swipe of his hand he eased the blanket that was covering her away, letting it fall from her body until she was naked in his arms, and she gasped at the sudden exposure.

'Is this all right?' he asked and she nodded.

His eyes raked down over her body and the cool air combined with his heated perusal had her growing restless, pressing her thighs together.

'You are the most beautiful woman I've ever seen,' he whispered, his hand drifting across her stomach, then back up to trail over her breasts, to knead her and feel the weight of her. She shivered. 'I want to discover every part of you.'

The sight of her pale breast cupped in his large, tanned hand made her desire hitch and, when he dipped his head to take her thrusting pink nipple in his mouth, teasing the tip with his tongue, she threw her head back, unable to help a moan escaping her lips.

'Sshh,' he whispered. 'Is that nice?'

'Yes.' She nodded. 'More.'

She pulled him back down on top of her, to cover her up,

but also wanting to feel his nearness. He kissed her again, slowly, and she liked being sprawled out beneath him like this, feeling his large body on top of her. Her hands slid over the taut muscles in his shoulders and down, securing him tighter to her, and the sensation of his warm, solid skin pressing against her own was thrilling. He pushed one of his knees between her legs, parting her thighs, and when she felt the hard length of him straining against his breeches, pressing into her thigh, she was fascinated. Had she caused that reaction?

His hand smoothed down over the side of her waist, grazing over her hip, and swirled over the tops of her legs, giving her time to get used to all these new sensations his fingers were creating. She wriggled against the solid thigh he'd placed between her legs, frustrated and craving a satisfaction she didn't fully understand.

But he did, of course he did—he seemed to know exactly what she wanted. He raised his body a little, allowing room for his fingers to trail back up to the sensitive skin beneath her stomach, and she shuddered. His hands were so close to where she was desperate for him to roam and her breath was suspended as she opened her eyes and met his black heated gaze.

'Do you want me to touch you?'

She nodded, unsure she was able to speak. And then his fingers threaded through her intimate curls on their dizzying descent and she stilled in anticipation of the first personal caress.

Wonder rushed through her as his large steady hand moved between her legs and she gasped as his fingers pressed against her slick skin, exactly where all her feelings had been mounting. He curved lower and pushed one long finger inside her, making her cry out in shocked pleasure.

He kissed her, to muffle her cries, smiling against her mouth. 'Is that good?'

It felt glorious and she clung on to him, whimpering, giving him his answer.

She writhed against him, demanding more, and his slow, masterful, gentle strokes made her head spin and her body soar, pleasure strumming through her body as a restless wave began to take hold. It was building, rising, threatening to roll over and shatter, and she wondered if this was normal, or if she should tell him to stop. If he carried on, she felt as if she might shatter into a million little pieces.

'Viggo?' She panicked, looking up at him, still needing his tuition.

'Give in to it,' he said.

And there was nothing she could do but let it happen. She let his touch tip her over the edge and as his finger slid inside her again, she came apart, and he kissed her as soft exquisite explosions rippled all around her body.

He raised his head and stared down at her, and she opened her eyes.

'Did you like that?' he asked.

'Very much.' She smiled.

Rolling on to his side, he pulled her towards him and trailed his hand down her back, stroking her.

'You know, you could have just done that yesterday, instead of trying to explain it,' she said, looking up at him.

He laughed and she liked the feel of the low rumble against her cheek. 'I agree. It might have been a great deal easier.'

Chapter Twelve

Viggo couldn't believe the Prince's men were upstairs, Marianos himself was in his home and here he was, holding Helena—naked—in his arms. She'd allowed him to kiss her and touch her—and when she woke from her slumber, he intended to do it all over again. It would be worth losing his head over.

After seeing Marianos with his sister, his oath of devotion to the Prince had crumbled, as if it was no longer relevant. Seeing them in a state of undress, their bodies entwined, had rocked him to the core. Everything he'd believed had been cast into doubt—he'd obviously been lied to and deceived. It was as if his loyalty to Marianos was being tested.

And now this…with Helena.

He couldn't believe he'd told her about his father—what he'd done. He had never told anyone before. His sister didn't even know the truth. How would she feel if she knew he'd taken her father from her?

He was astounded at how easily Helena had accepted what he saw as the worst part of himself. That she had told him he wasn't to blame. Could that be true? He wasn't sure he believed her, yet he wanted to. It was everything he'd needed to hear. That she didn't think him evil. That he had just acted in defence. Helena's absolute faith in his character had made resisting her even harder and he hadn't been able to refrain from touching her any longer. He'd kissed her and lost all restraint.

Now she was tucked into his shoulder and he was stroking her beautiful hair, the perfect golden skin of her back, and it felt so good to be able to hold her, to breathe in the sweet scent of her at last.

As for Sofie, he didn't know what to think. Was she curled up in the Prince's arms in a room above them? Did she love Marianos? He thought she must. He kept going over their past conversations and, now that he knew, he wondered how he had missed the signs—like on the day of the bride show when she had wanted to know every detail. And when he'd told her someone had tried to assassinate the Prince, she had paled.

It made sense now why she didn't want to tell him who the father of her child was. She couldn't. And Marianos—it explained his strange behaviour of late. Why he was so angry about the bride show and his upcoming nuptials. Why he'd been so eager for Viggo to return home after the quake—to check on Sofie. Did the Prince love his sister? What did it mean for the baby?

And he wondered…was that why he was being given a reward? An incentive to see Marianos wed, in case he knew about the child—to keep him quiet? No, he couldn't believe that. He guessed they knew he was in the dark.

Did Zoe know about the baby? He didn't think she'd let it stand and he suddenly feared for his sister's safety more than ever.

Did Sofie still intend to leave with him? Could they, now, after all this?

And what did all of it mean for him and Helena?

The questions whirled around in his mind, threatening to overwhelm him.

'Viggo, have you touched a woman like that before?' Helena said, speaking into his chest, breaking into his thoughts. She was awake.

His hands stilled and he pulled away from her so he could look into her eyes. He knew he couldn't lie.

'Yes.'

His fingers began to trail over her lower back again.

'Who was she?'

He paused. 'They.'

She reared back.

'There's been more than one?' she asked, her eyes wide. 'How many? You said the things a man and woman do together was an act of love. Have you *loved* lots of women?'

'I said it's *meant* to be. Not that it ever has been for me.'

Until now?

'So you do this kind of thing with just anyone?' She went to move, reaching for the blanket, to cover herself up—presumably to put a barrier between them, but he was faster, stopping her, gripping her wrist in his hand, holding it at her side.

'What are you doing?' he asked her.

'Am I just another to add to your list, then?' she said, her eyes flashing, struggling against his hold, still trying to get away from him.

'No, this is different.'

'How is it?' she bit out.

'Do you think I'd put our lives at risk if it wasn't? You know it is.'

He kissed her, hard. He couldn't not.

When she stopped fighting him, he released her hand, moving his own to curve over her bottom and pull her closer towards him, and her body softened, giving in to him.

'Who were they?' she asked. 'These women.' She still wasn't ready to let him off the hook.

'They were strangers, really. Someone to find comfort with on a lonely night. It was never more than that… I never wanted it to be. You were right the other day. I had seen from my mother and father how relationships could be damaging, so I avoided them, defending myself against ever getting hurt.' He had built up barriers around his heart to protect himself, but Helena, she had come into his life, shaking him up, making them crumble, just like the arena walls.

He reared back a little. 'Are you jealous, Helena?' He liked that she cared enough to be bothered, but he had been suffering gut-wrenching envy about her and Marianos for days and he knew it wasn't a pleasant feeling. It could tie you up in knots. He didn't want his past to trouble her. He saw a crease had appeared in her forehead and he leaned in and kissed it away. He'd been wanting to do that all week. 'There's no need,' he said, kissing her neck, her shoulder, the top of her breasts. 'There are many, many things I haven't done with other women. Things I want to do with you…'

He couldn't resist her. Because this was all that he desired. He wanted to show her the way she deserved to be touched. And if this was going to be the one and only night they could ever spend together, he had to seize it with both hands.

He rolled her on to her back and his lips roamed down, nipping their way over her stomach, kissing away her worries. She writhed beneath him. 'What? What haven't you done?' she whispered.

He broke away from her and sat up on his knees, between her legs, staring down at her, and her body twisted, as if she was trying to get away from his thorough perusal, but he gripped her arms, holding them either side of her body.

'Let me look at you,' he said.

'Is this what you've never done?' she said, still wriggling, raising herself up on her elbows.

'No…' He ran his hands down her ribs, over her hips, and smoothed his palms over her thighs. She raised her knees a little, and he caught sight of the bruise from the quake the other day. It distracted him momentarily.

'How's your knee?' he asked.

'A little sore but it's fine.'

He ran his hand down her calf, and she shivered. He liked that he had that effect on her.

He raised her ankle, forcing her to lean back, and her eyes widened as he placed little kisses to the inside of her leg and over her bad knee.

'You seem intent on tormenting me.'

'Is that what I'm doing?' He grinned.

He began kissing her inner thigh and she giggled, his beard tickling her sensitive skin.

'You'll have to be quiet,' he warned.

And as his tongue traced higher, his kisses becoming more indecent, her breathing changed. And he knew she was lost when she helplessly parted her legs in submission, giving in to the burning intimacy.

'This is the something I've never done before,' he whispered, as his mouth reached the junction of her thighs.

She tipped her head back and moaned, and his cock

soared. He loved that he was causing such a fierce reaction. She bucked in disbelief at the tender caress of his tongue and then the world disappeared. He ravaged her and nothing mattered, but this, his mouth on her, between her legs, tasting her, giving her pleasure.

'Viggo,' she groaned. A breathless, hectic whisper.

She came in a rush against his lips, his mouth pressed hard against her, before he pulled himself up her body until he was lying on top of her, smoothing her damp hair and settling her shocked, choking cries, soothing her with kisses.

'I never imagined such a thing was possible,' she whispered. He pulled her into his arms. He held her until her body stopped trembling with emotion from the explicit things he had done to her.

She placed her hand over his heart on his chest. 'Viggo, should I, am I meant to, touch you?' she asked shyly. And his breath halted. 'Is it possible for me to make you feel like that?'

Need lanced him and he groaned, resting his forehead against hers.

'Yes, very, very possible,' he said.

He was so hard, straining against his breeches. He wanted her to push down the material and release him, to set him free. He wanted to spread her legs wide, to thrust deep inside her and take her innocence, making her his, at last.

But he couldn't.

She wasn't just some woman he'd met in a tavern one night and would never see again. And he didn't want to take her innocence on the floor of his cellar, with Marianos's guards above them. This would be her first time. It should be special. And they weren't even married. If he was going to make her his, he would do it properly.

The thought brought him up short.

He had made a vow to himself he would never wed.

She was meant to be marrying the Prince—not him. Tomorrow.

And yet the moment he'd kissed her, touched her, both of those promises had been torn to shreds. Hadn't they? He knew now what this was between them, was different to what his parents had. His feelings were so strong for her, he knew he would marry her if he could. He wanted her to be his, for ever.

But she hadn't said she was going to break off her engagement. She hadn't told him she was going to cancel the wedding. So what was he doing, putting his hands on her, kissing her, everywhere, before she had even uttered her intentions? He certainly couldn't claim her body until he knew for sure he was what she wanted.

The thought helped to cool his body, just a little.

As did the sound of a door slamming somewhere above them.

She flinched.

'But not here, not now,' he said, forcing himself to shift his focus.

'Have they gone, do you think?' she asked.

'It sounds like it.'

It took every ounce of his resolve to roll off her and cover her back up with the blanket. He sat up, tilting his head, listening for any sound of movement upstairs. There was none.

'We need to get back, don't we?' she said, coming to sit up beside him. 'Before someone realises we're missing.'

He turned to look at her. 'I think so.'

He was driven to move by concern, suddenly realising the danger they were in—how long they had been gone. He quickly put his tunic back on, passing Helena her own, and they both fumbled reservedly with their garments.

Viggo felt his way over to the stairs and quietly lifted the trapdoor, listening once more. Nothing.

And then light flooded the cellar as he pushed the door up fully.

'Have you got everything?' he asked, his voice taking on a hint of urgency.

'Yes.' She joined him on the stairs.

He allowed himself to pause, for just a moment. 'What are you going to do, Helena?'

She shook her head. 'I really don't know.'

It was her wedding day. The whole of Constantinople would soon be waking at first light to prepare for the ceremony and feast, yet Helena didn't want to marry the Prince. She had known that from the moment she had met him, so how had she continued down this path and let it get to this point? She hadn't looked up into his eyes and been enchanted that day…instead, it was this man, the Varangian Commander, who was ushering her through the quiet streets in silence, who had stared down at her at the bride show, making her feel things. She hadn't realised what it meant then, but she did now.

And yet, she had no more choice about her impending nuptials than she did a week ago. Everyone expected her to marry the Prince, to go ahead with this forced marriage.

Every fibre of her body was telling her to run, yet, they were heading back to the palace. Because it went without saying, if she and Viggo tried to escape, Zoe and Marianos would never let the treason lie. They'd be hunted, for the rest of their days, always looking over their shoulders.

Looking up at Viggo, before she'd nodded in agreement, giving him permission to do those incredible things to her body, she had known he was the one and only man who would ever stir her heart and her body. He made her feel feverish and cherished all at once. He was both soft and strong. He was good. No man could ever compare to him. She loved him, she'd realised. Only being with him meant putting his life at risk. If they were caught, it would mean certain death and she could not let that happen.

Besides, Viggo would never leave here without Sofie.

So she had to conform and do what was expected of her—didn't she? And yet she didn't want to. Not any more.

Last night, she and Viggo had opened up to each other, and the way he had touched her had changed her. Changed everything. She felt exhilarated. Liberated. That for once she had done something for herself. And having embraced a little independence, having discovered all these incredible new feelings with Viggo, she was filled with a fresh determination. Over the past few days he had helped her to accept she deserved to be happy. To feel valued and heard, and have an opinion. But she knew he couldn't fix her situation for her.

He had been quiet since they left the cellar—perhaps because he wanted to minimise drawing any attention to them, but she was worried her answer on the stairs had disappointed him. But she really didn't know how to solve this.

He was walking with purpose, but his body was rigid, his face stern. He was concerned for their safety, she knew that. The closer they got to the city centre, the busier the streets became. The sun was only just beginning to rise, but crowds were already gathering to secure a spot to watch the royal procession to the coronation and wedding celebrations. All the people were hoping to catch a glimpse of the Prince and Princess—and Helena and Viggo both knew, if she were to be seen here now, all hell would break loose. It would cause a scandal—anarchy. That the bride was out with the Commander, in the middle of the city, looking dishevelled, on the morning of her wedding.

She didn't know what was going to happen when they arrived back at the palace, but she wanted to tell him, to reassure him, that she would endeavour to speak to Marianos. She would attempt to appeal to his better judgement. She had to at least try, didn't she? She had to fight for the future she wanted. And she knew now that what she wanted was Viggo.

But she couldn't tell Viggo what about her intentions right now, not with all these people around. A tense but celebratory atmosphere filled the air. She pulled up her hood further while tugging her veil down, checking it was in place, avoiding meeting anyone's gaze for fear of being recognised. The route her carriage would later make to the cathedral was well guarded—she could see Viggo's men all about. But he evaded them, too. He used the crowds strategically, the hordes providing opportunities for them to blend in. And finally, they were back at the palace by dawn. As soon as they entered the gates, there was a commotion, with Markou's men surrounding them.

'They've been looking for you,' the General said. 'You're in a whole world of trouble.'

Helena sent Viggo a glance as she shivered.

'Thanks for the warning,' Viggo replied, inclining his

head in acknowledgement. There seemed to be an unspoken truce between the two men since the day of the quake—perhaps even a newfound respect from the General's side.

They were ushered into the great hall, where Marianos and his mother were waiting. Everyone turned to look at them as they walked across the vast space. Helena's tongue felt dry, her body racked with tension. Despite her years of training, she didn't know where to place her hands. She felt exposed.

'Where on earth have you been?' Zoe demanded, as they drew nearer, disapproval lacing her cool, controlled voice.

'Helena couldn't sleep. She asked if she could take a walk to ease her wedding nerves,' Viggo said. 'I apologise if we caused any concern.'

Zoe's eyes gleamed in sharp suspicion, looking between the two of them, like a dangerous spider ready to pounce on its prey. Helena could tell the shrewd woman didn't believe the lie.

'You're wet,' the woman observed.

'I tripped. Fell in some water,' Helena muttered. 'It was quite foolish of me really.'

Helena wondered if she looked different. She certainly felt different, after last night.

'What does it matter where they've been, Mother? They're back now,' Marianos said cheerlessly, from his position on the throne behind her. Helena imagined he was disappointed to see she had returned at all.

'Actually, I was hoping to have a word with the Prince alone,' Helena said.

'On your wedding day? No. We cannot allow that,' Zoe said with cold authority. 'You shouldn't even be seeing each other, let alone speaking before the ceremony. Now that you're back, you must go and get dressed. Immediately. Your *cubicularii* are waiting for you.' She wasn't going to let anything get in the way of her perfectly laid out plans.

'But it's important,' Helena insisted, wringing her hands—which may as well have been tied. Her mouth might as well have been gagged. She was certainly not being heard.

'Nothing is as important as being on time for Marianos's coronation ceremony. Whatever it is you have to say, it can wait till after the wedding. We won't have you making us late. We are behind schedule and you've caused enough concern already.' She turned towards her son. 'Marianos, you, too. Go and get ready.' And as Helena watched him stalk off, his brows pulled together, his shoulders slumped, she suddenly felt desperate.

But before she could call him back, try to halt him, to put a stop to all of this, the Empress Regent placed her hand on Viggo's arm. 'Thank you, Viggo. For looking after Helena's safety. You're worth every coin of that reward I owe you.' She sent Helena a knowing look.

'Reward?' Helena asked, her attention suddenly sidetracked. The woman was an expert in manipulation, she realised. But when she saw Viggo move his hand away from the woman's touch and run it around the back of his neck, her blood iced. Was there something in what Zoe had said—an element of truth? She shook her head a little, feeling uncertain, taking the dangled bait. 'What reward?'

'Didn't he tell you?' Zoe continued, her voice lined with condescension. 'Viggo assured us he would protect the Prince until his coronation. That he would see him safely wed. He has doubled his efforts and the guards, he has undertaken extra training and more hours. In return, we offered him a reward. A bonus, if you will. Once the wedding takes place, he will be a very wealthy man.' She shrugged. 'Isn't that right, Viggo?'

Helena's pulse was pounding heavily in trepidation. No! Surely it couldn't be true.

She looked up at Viggo but he didn't meet her gaze and his admission, or lack of one, left her stunned. Surely Viggo wouldn't want to make coin out of her situation? It was hateful, despicable. She had thought he had been helping her to win over Marianos out of the goodness of his heart. But he'd had an ulterior motive all along. He had his own goals he wanted to achieve. Great riches.

'So you see, it's within everyone's best interests that the wedding goes ahead as smoothly as possible,' Zoe finished.

Helena's heart erupted in pain. She felt utterly betrayed.

It wasn't that it bothered her so much that he would get a reward if she wed—she knew the Varangians were paid well, and often, to maintain their loyalty. It wasn't even that he hadn't told her about it. It was the fact that she had thought—no, hoped—that he didn't want her to go through with the wedding.

But he did. He must.

Despite their physical intimacy last night, he had made no verbal commitment to her. Thinking about it now, she had practically begged him to kiss her, to touch her, but had he ever had any intention of it being more than a one-night thing?

What had he said about Sofie and Marianos? *She must know he's using her to satisfy a need.* Had he done the same?

When she had asked him about it being an act of love, he had answered with the words: *It has never been for me.*

An icy claw of realisation gripped her heart. She had wanted to touch him in return. She would have taken things further, but he had stopped her. Was that because he knew she still had to marry Marianos, so her innocence needed to be intact? She felt sick that he might have had such a calculated thought.

They should have talked about it, discussed their future. She should have asked him what his intentions were, before she had let anything happen. If he ever told anyone, her reputation—her life—would be in tatters.

Oh God, she was such a fool.

A completely devastated fool.

And the one person she wanted to tell about it was him. But she couldn't. Because he was the culprit. Viggo and his cruel deceit.

Tears pooled in her eyes and she willed them not to spill over. Her pride would not allow one salty drop to fall. She would not give Zoe the satisfaction of seeing her cry.

'I want you dressed and ready to leave within the hour,' Zoe said, finally stalking away from them, now that she'd dealt her fatal blow. The woman left the hall, followed by her entourage.

Helena felt numb. Wounded.

'Helena—'

She shrank back from his voice. 'So, you were using me,' she said, her voice flat. 'To get a reward.'

'What? No,' Viggo said, stepping towards her.

'No?' Another wave of hurt thrashed through her. Her voice took on an accusatory tone. 'You agreed to help me win Marianos's affections so you could receive the coin Zoe promised you.'

He reared. 'That's not fair. You came to me, remember?' He placed his hands on his hips, but she couldn't bring herself to look up at him. 'You followed me to my home and begged me for my help. I was just doing what you asked of me.'

'I thought you agreed to help me because you wanted to, because you cared about my predicament. I didn't know there was something in it for you.' She felt the emotion rise thick in her throat. He was the only person she thought she could trust and his duplicity felt so disloyal. 'But there is. Silver.'

'So?'

'How much silver, Viggo?'

'I was doing it because I thought it was what you wanted. Because I thought it would make you happy. Will you just listen? Let me explain...'

But she was too distraught to hear him out. She stumbled back. Her eyes narrowed on him. 'I thought you were different. I thought you were my friend,' she said, shaking her head.

So much more than a friend.

'I am.'

'No. You're just like my mother. My father. Zoe, and everyone else in my life who seeks to control me, to use me for their own gain.' Well, she'd had enough. She was sick of people making decisions for her. Livid, in fact. What about what she wanted—did that not matter? This past week she had begun to believe she deserved to live her life on her own terms.

'Helena, about last night...'

'It doesn't matter now,' she said, slashing the air between them. 'It's forgotten.'

He reached out to touch her but she sprang back. 'No,

don't,' she said, holding up her hand. She could not allow him to touch her. Never again. Because the awful truth was she still wanted him. She still craved his touch, even though she knew she shouldn't. She mustn't. 'Don't say anything more. I've heard enough.' She knew she must withdraw from him. 'After all, I have my wedding to get to. I don't want to keep the Prince waiting. And once I'm married, well, then we'll both have everything we want, won't we?'

Chapter Thirteen

Helena stepped out of the palace into the sunlight in her bridal tunic and Viggo's hopes and dreams shattered around him. She was a vision of beauty in her regal purple silk tunic—so stunning, she took his breath away. She looked ready to be Empress.

She wore an elaborate headdress and a veil that indicated her purity. Could she still be deemed pure, after the things they had done together last night? He clenched his fists. He was a goddamn fool. What must she think of him? What kind of man seduced a woman on the eve of her wedding to another—to the Prince, no less?

He should have made her promise not to marry Marianos before he'd taken her in his arms, kissing her everywhere. Instead, he'd touched her, tasted her, yet he had proposed no ulterior plan. But had the intimacy they'd shared not moved her as it had him? It couldn't have.

The waft of her familiar floral scent as she brushed past him made his body harden.

He could tell she was determined to ignore him, to punish him. And he deserved it.

He should have told her about the reward before he'd laid a hand on her…but it hadn't even occurred to him to do so, or that she would find out, and he hadn't realised it would look so bad that he'd kept it a secret. *Helvete!* He was a short-sighted fool.

He no longer even wanted the reward—he'd find another way to help his sister—he just wanted Helena. Instead, he'd ruined her trust. Everyone in her life had let her down, including him, and he felt like such a brute. He was infuriated with himself. But he was infuriated with her, too, for believing the worst in him, for not hearing him out.

He was desperate for her to at least know why he had agreed to accept the reward from Zoe in the first place. He couldn't bear the fact she thought ill of him. He wanted to make amends before she went ahead with today, yet Zoe had insisted Viggo return to his duties as Marianos's right-hand man for the duration of the coronation and wedding, and he was overwhelmingly frustrated. Knowing Marianos had seduced his sister, and not being able to say anything about it, was one thing, but the Prince—and his mother—preventing him from speaking to Helena on the journey to the cathedral was almost too much to bear. It was as if they were intentionally keeping them apart.

If he could just talk to Helena, plead with her… But what would he say? He was too late.

As they'd made their way back to the palace this morning, there had been a huge part of him that had wanted to ask her to make a run for it with him, but he'd known they couldn't do that to Sofie. And he wasn't sure it was what Helena wanted.

He'd thought it unfair—to ask her to turn her back on her life's training, her duty, her people, and put her family at risk. Her father's debts wouldn't be paid. She would destroy her parents' reputation and her own. And why would she suffer all of that—for him?

The truth was, he'd been afraid. He had been afraid that if he'd asked her to stay with him, to choose him, she might have said no. So he hadn't. He'd been a coward. And now the worst was happening anyway.

Helena was doing what she had to do—what she thought was necessary—and she was walking away from him in the process. It confirmed his long-held fear—that love always led to pain.

Love.

Was that what this was? This awful, gnawing ache in his heart?

Yet the only woman he had ever felt this way about was readying herself to start the procession from the palace to the Hagia Sofia, embarking on the journey that would end with her becoming Marianos's wife.

But Viggo would not ruin her special day. What right did he have to intervene now? She had made her decision. She was going ahead with the wedding. Of course she was. She had never told him otherwise.

And it seemed Marianos had resigned himself to it, too. The marriage would be legalised and the bedding ceremony would soon follow—and there was not a thing in the world Viggo could do to stop it from taking place.

Mutiny struck up inside him at the thought of Marianos touching Helena.

He wanted to kill someone—not that he would, no matter how angry he was. And the realisation jolted him, stopping him in his tracks. He was no murderer. He wasn't like his father. He would never hurt someone intentionally, unless it was on the battlefield, during a fair fight. But the tussle between him and his father hadn't been fair—a grown man against his son. All he had been able to do was raise the knife and defend himself.

Helena had made him see that. Helena seeing the good in him had broken through his guilt and made him see that perhaps he wasn't to blame. Now he was more concerned she thought he was someone who had taken advantage of her situation for financial gain.

As he escorted Marianos through the busy streets, Viggo and Markou's men kept the crowd under control, but he felt as if he was wading through mud, as if every movement was an effort, as if he was Jesus carrying the cross on his way to his crucifixion. Suffering enormously. He just wanted to be put out of his misery, for this to be over.

It felt as if everything was ending and he guessed in a way it was. Helena had chosen another man over him and he would be leaving the city and the life he knew tomorrow. He would never see her again.

He thought about Sofie. He wondered if her heart was breaking just as his was right now, knowing that the person she had been intimate with, whom she loved, was about to marry another. Had all her hopes and dreams crumbled to dust, too?

He should have checked on her this morning before they left for the palace. He was regretting that now. But he'd been angry with her at the time—and consumed with getting Helena back before she got into irredeemable trouble. He hoped she was all right.

The royal party finally reached the cathedral and the cool, reverent interior was filled with the scent of old wooden pews, the melting wax of the candles and fragrant, fresh flowers. Once everyone was seated, a solemn hush descended and the coronation ceremony began. The Patriarch's words drifted over him, but Viggo couldn't focus on a single one. Instead, he stared at Helena, willing her to turn his way and look at him, but she would not. She stubbornly stared straight ahead throughout the entire service. It was the longest morning of Viggo's life.

He watched as the crown was placed on Marianos's head and the Emperor received acclamations from all the aristocrats who stepped forward, confirming their support. And then it was time. Time for the worst part of all—the marriage ceremony. He had been hoping it would never come.

He saw Helena's seat was empty—she must have slipped out during the acclamations. Beautiful singing drifted through the cathedral, signalling the bride's arrival, and sickness swirled in his stomach. It was happening.

As Helena began to walk serenely up the aisle in front of the packed congregation, towards Marianos, towards him, Viggo felt as if someone was reaching into his chest and ripping out his heart.

And frustratingly, she still evaded his gaze.

The Patriarch began with one of the rituals they had practised at the rehearsal, before launching into the service. When he asked the couple and the congregation if anyone knew of any reason why the marriage should not proceed, Viggo's heart lifted in hope, but a deathly stillness settled around the cathedral.

Every muscle in Viggo's body was urging him to rush forward and put a stop this. To pronounce his deep affection for this woman. But what difference would it make? No one cared about his feelings. And how could he do it, if it wasn't what Helena wanted? Even though she'd chosen the Emperor over him, he would still put her happiness above his own, because if you loved someone, you'd do anything for them. Even keep your screams to yourself when you were in so much pain.

'I do.' A voice suddenly spoke out.

His head shot up.

Helena. Helena had spoken.

Whispers and mutterings echoed around the grand cathedral. Viggo's heart began to pound.

He looked between her and Marianos and realised the Emperor had turned deathly pale. Helena stepped forward and took the Emperor's hand in hers and Marianos let her. It was the first time Viggo had ever seen any real connection between the two of them and he struggled to understand what was happening.

Helena turned to speak to the Patriarch. 'I think, as a prince, Marianos was forced into agreeing to this union, and, in truth, now he is Emperor, he would rather it didn't happen.'

Gasps reverberated around the cathedral. Zoe leapt out of her seat.

'I don't believe he cares for me in this way, but in fact is in love with someone else,' Helena continued.

Zoe was at their side in an instant, trying to shush her.

'Commander, General, if my mother takes another step, please restrain her,' the Emperor said, turning to Viggo and Markou, and Zoe halted, humiliated, her eyes going wide.

Viggo couldn't believe what he was hearing. Was Marianos standing up to his mother?

'Helena, you were saying...?' Marianos said, a little braver now, as if he wanted Helena to continue to speak out about him.

'The Prince was too kind, too good a man to let me

down, willing to go through with this union,' she continued. 'He wanted to do the right thing by his people. But as Emperor, he should no longer have to do what others want of him. As Emperor, he can decide what his future will look like.'

She squeezed Marianos's hand, offering him her strength, and Viggo wondered, was it possible the two of them had discussed this before? Perhaps this morning, after he and Helena had parted ways in the hall? That this had been their plan when they'd entered the church today? To wait until Marianos had become Emperor, until he had complete control.

The Patriarch stepped in, deeply concerned about all that was being said. 'Is this true, *Basileus*? Do you have feelings for another woman?'

Helena inclined her head, offering Marianos encouragement, and the Emperor looked up at the holy man. 'It is true.'

There was instant pandemonium in the cathedral, as the guests turned to each other, protesting their shock and outrage. The council were out of their seats, in uproar. The din was deafening.

Viggo's own head was spinning, his heart lightened with hope and possibility.

'The other woman is here and she will be taking my place as the Emperor's bride,' Helena asserted. 'Marianos and I are in agreement—that would be the best course of action for all.'

'I cannot allow this,' Zoe raged. 'The council will not allow it.'

'Control yourself, Mother,' Marianos said. 'If you would

like me to marry, it will be to Sofie, or no one else. Now I am your Emperor, you will listen.'

The rumble of voices in the congregation grew louder as they saw Marianos assert his authority in his new role. Finally, he seemed to have grown into a man.

To Viggo's astonishment, Helena gestured to a woman to step out from the pew she was sitting in and Sofie rose and came forward. He reeled that his sister was here. He had thought she was safe, hidden behind their four walls at home. But now, everyone could see her…and her swollen stomach.

Ripples of shock spread around the congregation as the scandal soared.

He wondered if he should do something, put a stop to this, but it was too late. Sofie was removing her veil, revealing her face—her beauty—for all to see and she was smiling up at Marianos, giddy with happiness.

Helena slipped her fingers out of the Emperor's grip and placed Sofie's hand in his instead.

'Will you marry me, Sofie?' Marianos asked her.

'Yes,' Sofie said, tears filling her eyes. And then she sent a nervous look Viggo's way. 'If my brother will allow it—and forgive me for my deceit. His blessing would mean everything to me.'

Viggo swallowed down an enormous lump in his throat.

'Will you give me away, Viggo?'

His heart hammered. Sofie had been his responsibility for so long. He had taken care of her his whole life. He didn't want to give her away to anyone. And yet, when he saw the love she felt for Marianos and that it was reciprocated in the Emperor's eyes, he knew he could not deny their contentment. No one would ever be good enough for her, but if she wanted this man, then who was he to stop the union?

'You both have my blessing,' he said.

'Marianos, you cannot do this,' Zoe said through gritted teeth. 'I forbid it.'

'Actually, Mother, I can.'

With Sofie by his side, he seemed to have found his kindness and his courage that had been lacking of late. He turned and addressed the congregation.

'Today, I intend to marry the woman I love. The woman who is carrying my child. The future heir to the Byzantine throne.'

What could anyone say or do? No one would go against the Emperor's word.

'Marry us,' Marianos said, turning back to the Patriarch.

'Please,' Sofie added and smiled.

Viggo swung to look at Helena, but she was already moving. She picked up the hem of her tunic and began to walk away from Sofie and Marianos, Zoe—and him—without as much as a backwards glance. She walked past her mother and her father, past all the people in the congregation, her chin tipped up, before she disappeared out of the cathedral, stepping out into the sun.

One evening spent in the convent was like an entire winter in the outside world and Helena wondered how she would bear a second.

Her worst fear had come true. She was back where she had started.

Sitting in the saloon of her parents' residence on her ruined wedding night, her life in tatters, she listened, her hands clenched together in her lap, as they hurled angry words at her.

'You foolish girl,' her mother berated her. 'You had everything in the palm of your hand. You were just moments from marrying him, from becoming Empress—and you threw it all away.'

'I knew this would happen,' her father raged, pacing up and down. 'I knew you would never amount to anything. Well, you had your chance. There'll be no more talk of marriage now. You'll spend your life in the convent, praying for our forgiveness.'

There was no kindness, no attempt to understand. Her beautiful bridal tunic was taken away and she was handed a drab habit, the scratchy material already irritating her skin.

They were right. She had given up everything—including her chance to make her parents proud. She had defied their wishes and they would probably never forgive her. They blamed her for not keeping the Prince's interest. But didn't they realise she'd never had it? He had been in love with Sofie well before she had even come along. So she didn't regret it—in fact, she was proud she'd brought them together. At least they would be happy.

When she had left Viggo that morning in the hall and gone to see Marianos, she had been in despair. But despite her devastation at Viggo's betrayal, she'd still known she couldn't go ahead with the marriage. She had come to a decision. She had lived her whole life for her mother and father, and she had determined to live the rest of it for herself.

She'd searched her mind to come up with a way to speak with Marianos—something important enough that he would agree to speak with her alone. It had to be discreet, so Zoe wouldn't find out and prevent them from meeting.

She'd settled on the only thing she knew he cared about—Sofie.

She had sent him a last-minute wedding gift, via one of

her handmaidens, praying he'd open it. Thinking quickly, she had inserted a letter inside a trinket box, which she had wrapped in silk. It asked him to meet her, telling him it regarded Sofie.

He had appeared at her room not long afterwards, with General Markou at his side. Her ladies-in-waiting were shocked to see the groom at the bride's doorway again.

She hadn't really known where to start. How to reach him. There had never been any connection between them; they were strangers. But she knew she couldn't waste any time.

'What is this about?' he'd said, holding up the parchment with her handwriting on. 'Where did you hear this name?'

'She loves you,' Helena had said, going straight for her target—his heart. There was no point in drawing this out. 'Are you really going to go ahead with this wedding, knowing that? Even though she is carrying your child?'

'Everybody out,' he'd roared. 'Even you, General.'

When the last of his entourage had shuffled out of her chamber, he'd turned to her.

'How do you know about Sofie?' he'd said, his blue eyes burning with intensity.

'Never mind about that. But if you love her back... Marianos, why are you marrying me? Why did you go through with the bride show?'

'Because my mother said I had to!' he spat, but his voice cracked and she knew his emotions were bubbling beneath the surface, threatening to be unleashed, just as hers were. She thought perhaps he wanted to let them out. And she needed to give him permission to do so. 'She said no one would ever accept Sofie as my bride. That she was unsuitable and I could have her as a mistress, but nothing more.'

'But what about the baby? Don't you want to be a father to your child?'

That broke him.

He'd slumped down on to the bed and put his head in his hands. 'More than you could know.'

It was what Helena wanted to hear, as it reinstalled her belief in him. Perhaps he did have some redeeming qualities after all.

Yes, he had treated her unkindly, but it was because he was in love with another. He hadn't wanted to kiss her, bed her or marry her all because he'd wanted Sofie. It had made him lash out at her and understanding why he'd behaved this way had redeemed him, just a little, because she knew just how desperate he felt.

When she had realised she was in love with someone else, the thought of marrying Marianos had become so awful to her, she hadn't been able to bear it. Really, their positions weren't too dissimilar—they were just a son and a daughter who were expected to fulfil the duties their parents demanded of them, against their own wishes.

'I've made such a mess of everything. I never meant to hurt anyone. Not her—and not you,' he'd said, his eyes filling with tears. 'I'm sorry for the way I've treated you, Helena. I was just so angry with my mother, and frustrated with you for not being Sofie.'

Helena had lowered herself down next to him on the bed. 'I think the person you're hurting most is yourself and you need to stop. You're about to be Emperor, which means you have to make your own decisions. You have to know your own mind. You have to make choices that are true to who you are.'

He'd looked up at her. 'What are you saying?'

'A very wise man told me this week that if you loathe your life, you have to change it. No one else will do it for you. I don't think either of us like our lives very much right now, but we do have the power to change them.'

'What are you suggesting?'

'I don't think it would do either of us any good to be trapped in a loveless marriage. After the coronation today, I think the first thing you should do, as Emperor, is to choose love. I believe you will be a better man, a better ruler and will make better choices for your people, with a heart filled with joy. With the woman you love at your side.'

And so, they had come up with their plan. For the first time, they had become allies, working together towards a common goal, and it had been a success. Things had turned out well—for Marianos at least.

Only it didn't feel as if Helena had been quite so triumphant, not while she was being shouted at, as if she were a child.

She knew her parents' words were meant to wound her. They were ashamed of her and it hurt, but she was shocked to discover their anger and rejection wasn't as painful as she had expected it to be—because she had at least stayed true to herself.

And frankly, nothing could be more excruciating than walking away from Viggo.

He was the man who had made her the woman she had become. All her life, she'd been taught her only reason for being was to make the Prince happy, but it was Viggo who had turned the tide and had taught her to think of her own needs.

She had been grappling between duty and personal fulfilment since she'd met him. She knew what the union to

Marianos meant to her family. Their security. But she'd had to consider her own future happiness. She had only one life and she didn't want to spend it tied to a man who loved another. She didn't want to settle.

She still wanted the love she'd always longed for. She knew now there would never be anyone for her but Viggo. But he had been clear from the start—he never wanted to marry and she had been foolish and fallen for him anyway.

A small part of her had hoped that after Marianos had taken Sofie's hand in his and asked the Patriarch to marry them, that Viggo would turn to her and say the same. That he'd beg her to be his wife. But he hadn't, of course he hadn't.

Viggo's words kept swirling round in her mind. *I've seen what bad marriages can do... I've seen how relationships can be damaging. I avoided them, protecting myself against ever getting hurt.*

Had she just been—what were his words?—*someone he could find comfort with on a lonely night*? And yet, even now, doubts plaguing her, she couldn't bring herself to regret it. She would not confess to the priest. Now that she would be forced to renounce all worldly pleasures in the convent, she might need those memories to cling on to. But the thought of never experiencing Viggo's touch again, never seeing him again, made her throat ache and her heart bleed.

She wondered if she had scuppered his chances of getting his reward, as the wedding hadn't taken place—not the one Zoe wanted, anyway—and if he was very angry with her. What did he want the coin for anyway? Knowing Viggo, he would have given it to his sister to help her. Yes, that's exactly the kind of thing Viggo would do.

Suddenly, she felt a pang of remorse. In her anger, she had thought the worst of him, the way she had done that night when they'd come across those bloodied bodies and the way he had done about himself his whole life. But he didn't deserve it. She wished she had heard him out this morning. He had never given her reason to doubt him before. Yet she had been too stubborn. So now here she was, back at the convent.

She still wanted to serve the people. She would not give up on them. She just needed to find a way to support them. She intended to speak to her father about opening up the nunnery as a place of refuge to help the poor and care for the sick. That would be something. But she would have to wait until he had calmed down.

'We could have been feasting in the palace tonight, but instead you'll dine with the nuns,' her mother was saying.

'You'll sleep in the dormitory. No more special treatment,' her father vowed.

And as Helena finally crawled into bed, curling up against the cold wall, she didn't mind. She was only relieved that the consummation of her marriage wouldn't take place tonight, in front of all the clergy, because she had determined if she were ever to perform such an intimate act, it would be with the man she loved.

Chapter Fourteen

Helena hadn't married Marianos, but she was still gone.

Viggo had searched for her after the wedding ceremony, but she was nowhere to be found. And there had been no sign of her or her parents at the feast, either. But of course there hadn't been—they wouldn't have wanted to wait around and face the scrutiny of all the guests, would they?

But every moment in the three days since she had walked out of the cathedral had been torture.

While Viggo had smiled and pretended to be happy throughout the celebrations—for the sake of his sister and Marianos—all he could think about was Helena.

The fact she had left him.

And it hurt.

It hurt too much.

His hand came over his heart and he slumped down on to the steps of the arena. He and his men had made good progress the past few days. He was trying to keep busy, hoping that would help distract him from his sombre thoughts and quiet yearning. But nothing seemed to ease the terrible ache and emptiness he was carrying in his chest.

His mind kept drifting to the moments he and Helena had shared together, her stubborn ways and her beautiful smile, which lit up a room and brightened his days. Now the light had gone out.

He felt lost.

Sofie was happy with Marianos and he had barely seen her. They had retreated to a private residence to celebrate their marriage away from public life for a week or so and it felt strange to not be needed by his little sister.

He had been overwhelmed when Helena had put a stop to her wedding and secured Sofie's future happiness instead. It was an incredibly selfless thing to do. He had fallen in love with her even more. He had felt a glimmer of hope that Helena might want him after all, but then she had walked out of his life, crushing his dreams all over again. Just like his mother. She'd caused as much damage as the quake, leaving total destruction in her path.

He felt like that battered and broken boy lying on the floor in his home in Norway, abandoned and in pieces.

An old fear mocked him and he tried to crush it, push it down, but it was demanding to be heard. *What did you expect?* it said. *Of course she left you. It's what people do.*

His own mother had forsaken him when he was just a boy. His father had never cared for him, choosing ale and violence over love. Why would Helena stay? Why would she want him? He was a nobody, with an ugly, scarred face. What could he offer her?

Of course she would reject him. She would be a fool not to.

But it didn't mean it didn't cut deep.

He reached out and gripped the wall. He welcomed the anger flooding his blood—with her, for doing this, for deserting him, but he was even more furious with himself for putting himself in this position. He had vowed never to feel anything, for anyone, for fear of this very thing happening. But he had opened his heart to her, fallen for her and she had wounded it, beyond repair.

A figure walking towards him caught his eye and for a moment he thought it was Helena, come to find him in the arena just as she had the other day. His heart imploded.

But when he raised his hand to shelter his eyes from the sun, he saw it was Sofie walking towards him. He couldn't believe he was seeing things now.

'What are you doing here?' he asked her. 'Shouldn't you be enjoying the first days of your marriage?'

'I asked Marianos if we could return early. I was missing you. I wanted to see you.'

A lump rose in his throat. 'You didn't need to do that.'

'We barely had chance to speak after the wedding. Not since all this happened.' She waved her hand in the direction of the palace.

'I'm really happy for you, Sofie.'

She came to sit beside him on the stone step. 'I'm sorry I kept the truth from you, Viggo,' she said, bumping his arm. 'Are you very angry with me?'

'I admit I was a little furious with you at first,' he said, then he smiled at her. 'But I've never been able to stay cross with you for long. I'm glad you're content. That's all I ever wanted for you.'

'I know.'

He stretched out his legs and leaned back a little. 'I always wanted you to have the best life.'

She nodded. 'You certainly made that happen. Look where we've ended up.' She laughed.

'Who knew you'd be ruler of the empire?' Viggo said.

'I know, a little girl from Norway. If only Mother and Father could see us now. They'd be sorry.'

He sat up, turning pensive. 'There's something I need to tell you, Sofie. About our father. About why we left. I should have told you a long time ago.'

'I know why, Viggo.'

He reared, swinging his head to look at her. 'You do?'

'Yes. I was only young, but I remember it. What he was like. I remember the things he did. I know things would have been a lot worse for me if it hadn't been for you.'

Had she really known the truth for all these years?

'You know what I did?' he asked her, looking into her eyes.

'He was going to hurt me—and would have hurt you, too—if you hadn't intervened. I know you've never been able to forgive yourself for what happened. But you did nothing wrong, Viggo. It was all on him. He wasn't a nice man. You were protecting me, *did* protect me, and have been doing so ever since. And I'm so grateful you took us away from there. You're the best of men. The best brother a sister could ever hope for.'

Emotion threatened to choke him.

'Thank you, Sofie,' he whispered.

'I want you to be just as happy as I am. It seems only fair.'

'Who says I'm not?' he said, attempting a smile, only it didn't quite reach the sides.

'You know, Helena made all my dreams come true when she spoke to Marianos the morning of the wedding, when she came up with the idea to swap places at the ceremony. When Marianos sent for me, I knew I would never be able to repay her for her kindness…but over the past few days, I've had time to think, and I'm starting to wonder if that is true. Perhaps there is something I can do to make it up to her.'

Viggo turned to look at her.

'Helena had everything every woman ever dreams of—and she gave it all up, for me.' She shook her head. 'It's been going round and round in my head. I've been wondering—why would she do that?'

'I don't know.'

'Really? You have no idea?' she said, her perceptive gaze studying him.

He swallowed.

'The only conclusion I can come up with is that she didn't have everything she wanted. She didn't have everything she wanted, because, in fact, what she wanted was you.'

He shook his head. 'I don't think—'

'You love her,' she said, interrupting him. 'It's so obvious to me now. I don't know why I didn't see it before. And she loves you back.'

He stared at her, astounded.

'I saw the way you looked at each other that day she appeared at our home and the way you were looking at her in the cathedral, during the service. You couldn't take your eyes off her. It's the same way I look at Marianos and I hope the way he looks at me. So why did you let her go?'

'I didn't! She left, remember?'

'She would have had no choice but to return home with her parents. You have seen what it's been like for me these past months—women have little say in these things.' Sofie tilted her head to one side. 'Did she know you wanted her to stay? Did she know that was an option?'

No. He hadn't asked her to stay because he didn't want to be the reason she gave everything up. And because he'd been so afraid she would say no. In the end, she'd been the brave one, calling off the wedding, facing Zoe and her parents' wrath. And he'd left her to deal with it all alone. He wondered how she was faring, back at the convent. She had said it would suffocate her. He couldn't bear the thought of her suffering.

And then a thought struck him. Had he made her feel unlovable, as her father always had? He hoped not. He launched himself to his feet and raked a hand through his hair, agitated.

'Please don't tell me you told her your long-held beliefs about marriage?'

He stared down at Sofie, dreadful realisation dawning. All he'd ever done was tell Helena he'd never take a bride—since the moment they'd first met. But wasn't that for the best? What if she did want him and they married—and things turned sour, as they had for his parents?

'I know you've never believed in marriage after seeing what our own mother and father were like together, but you and I, we're different people. We've learned not to be like them. Don't ruin this chance of being happy, of having love in your life, because of a fear, a fear that stems from the past.'

He drew in a deep breath and sighed.

'Did you even get to tell her how you felt?' Sofie pressed gently. 'Before she left?'

He might have shown Helena how much he cared with his hands, with his kisses, but he had never said the words. And he'd given her no guarantees.

He shook his head. 'I told her about what happened—back in Norway. About what I did,' he said, his voice gruff. 'Like you, she said it didn't change anything. But I wondered if my confession had begun to play on her mind, making her think twice about being with me. That, and the fact she discovered I would get coin if her wedding to Marianos went ahead.' He buried his head in his hands. 'Oh God, I really let her down, didn't I?'

Sofie stood and put her hand on his arms and pulled them down, so she could see his face. 'I'm sure she knows what kind of man you are, Viggo. Even if you still don't see it yourself. But you need to go to her. You need to speak to her, to explain about the reward. You need to fight for her, just like you fought for me all those years ago.'

He nodded. 'Thank you for coming back. For talking sense into me.'

'You're welcome.' And then she gasped.

'What is it?'

'It's the baby. It's kicking. Feel!'

She placed his hand on her tunic, over her swollen stomach, and he waited. And sure enough, he felt the little jab of a tiny limb against his hand.

'I felt it!' He grinned. 'That's incredible.'

'He's giving you a nudge,' she said.

'He or *she*.'

'Whichever, I don't mind.' She laughed. 'I think they're reacting to my excitement that their uncle might finally be about to settle down.'

And he laughed with her. 'Let's not get too carried away. Helena hasn't said yes yet.' But for the first time since the wedding, he felt hope rushing through his veins.

It had been days and neither of Helena's parents would speak to her—apart from telling her she had ruined their life's work.

The hours dragged.

Each morning was spent in prayer, before she would have a chance to weave, although she wasn't wonderful at it and her interest would wane quickly, at which point she might go outside and tend to the garden. She had thrown herself into digging a vegetable patch as a distraction, to take her mind off everything that had happened over the past week—and since the wedding. More prayer and contemplation followed in the afternoons, and she could not abide it. She couldn't contemplate her life any longer. The mistakes she had made.

She was desperately missing the freedom of life beyond these walls and the people she had met. But mainly, she was missing Viggo. She could not stop thinking about him and it was torture. Was he now oceans away from here, or had he stayed?

She might be in a spiritual sanctuary, but she absolutely wasn't at peace. Her heart felt as if it was at war—with herself, with everyone. She couldn't sleep. Or eat—not even the pomegranate that had been served last night, reminding her of happier times.

She dragged her feet along the convent halls on her way to the morning service. As she prayed alongside the fellow novices, her shoulders hunched over her chest as she wallowed in her misery. She tried to focus on the priest's words about God always being there for her, how he would never abandon her, and she tilted her head to the ceiling and let out a sigh.

But the priest's words struck a chord. The words Viggo had said about his mother came into her head. *She hadn't loved us enough to stay.*

She had abandoned Viggo that morning of the wedding. In leaving him without speaking to him, had she hurt him, as he had hurt her?

The thought caused her heart to pound.

She could just picture him searching for her after the ceremony and discovering she'd gone. He would have thought she'd left him, just like his mother. He would have thought she didn't want him. Now she could only imagine what memories that might have stirred.

But surely he realised she'd given everything up to be with him.

Maybe not. And now she'd spend the rest of her life not knowing if he knew how she really felt. Because he didn't think she cared.

It was more than she could bear. She hung her head, feeling utterly wretched.

The rumblings of a commotion at the back of the church stole her attention. Casting a quick glance over her shoulder, she tried to see what was going on, but there were too many nuns' coifs in the way.

The sound of people talking over the priest grew louder and the nuns started to jostle, unhappy that their peace and tranquillity were being disrupted.

Helena turned back again to see her father and mother there—and all of a sudden, a tall, dark warrior pushed past them. Helena's breath caught. Her heart leapt.

Viggo. Viggo was here!

Could it really be him?

She watched as he strode determinedly up the aisle, as appalled gasps reverberated around the congregation at his formidable presence. There were strict procedures—men weren't allowed in the convent, it broke all the rules of enclosure. But right now, it didn't look as if he cared.

'Helena?' he shouted, looking all around.

She brightened immediately and rose to her feet on trembling legs, as everyone turned to stare.

'I'm here,' she said, projecting her voice, and his dark eyes turned and met hers across the room.

The world stopped turning.

'Helena, you will stay where you are!' her father barked.

No! She absolutely would not.

She pushed past the other women in the pew, making her apologies, urgent to get to Viggo, and eventually stepped out into the aisle—she was at his side in a heartbeat. She had thought she'd never see him again and she drank in his handsome features as if she'd been deprived. She looked up at him in wonder. He seemed darker, more dangerous, more attractive than ever.

'What are you doing here?' she asked, breathless.

His eyes raked over her and he took her hand in his, hauling her up against his chest. All the nuns began to protest—the whole church was in uproar—and yet she didn't care. Her elation soared.

'I never meant to keep the truth from you about the reward, Helena,' he said. 'I didn't know you when Zoe promised it to me. It was my intention to use the coin to take my sister away from here,' he said, lowering his voice.

'I came to think as much,' she said.

'When I met you, all thoughts of the silver went out of my head. That's why I didn't mention it. It wasn't even important to me. Not like you were. *Are.* And then you left me…'

She shook her head. 'I wasn't sure you cared. You never said—'

'I was a fool,' he admitted, tugging her closer. 'I should have told you that night in the cellar not to marry him. That I wanted you for myself. I guess I was afraid you might say no.'

'I wouldn't have.'

He pulled right up against him, his arm coming around her waist, causing outrage from their audience. 'So marry me,' he said.

'I thought you were against marriage?' she gasped, searching his face. Did he really mean it?

'That was before I met you. The past few days have shown me I can't live without you. I've been so miserable. I want to spend the rest of my life with you. I know we could make each other happy.'

It was everything she wanted to hear.

He was so close she could breathe in his intoxicating, familiar spicy scent, making her feel giddy. She had always said if she was going to marry, she would marry the best. In the beginning, she had thought that meant the Prince, but she'd been so wrong. This man, standing in front of her, was the best man she had ever known. The man she loved with all her heart.

'I came to tell you I love you,' he said.

'Well, it's about time!' She smiled. 'Yes, I'll marry you, Viggo.'

'She will not!' her father said, suddenly appearing by her side.

'*Despotes*, Husband, do not argue with the Commander. Do you know who he is?' Helena's mother hissed. 'He's a Varangian. The Emperor's bodyguard. The Empress's brother.'

Viggo turned to stare at her mother, then her father, his gaze unamused.

'I know who he is. But our daughter will remain here, in the convent.'

'If this is about the dowry, I don't want any coin. Just her,' Viggo said.

Her father reared, surprised. He shook his head. 'I don't understand. She's worthless to you.'

Viggo looked back at Helena. 'That's where we will never agree.' He glanced back at the Bishop and lowered his voice. 'I have paid off your debts—all of them.'

The man stumbled back in shock.

'And I will provide for Helena from now on,' Viggo continued. 'She will no longer be your concern. I only ask that you or your priest marry us immediately. I'm not leaving here without her. After that, we will never ask you for anything again.'

Helena grabbed the bible off the pulpit and practically threw it into her father's hands. And what had been a normal service turned into a wedding, with one hundred nuns as witnesses. She never thought she'd marry in a habit, but it didn't matter, she just wanted to make it official—that she belonged to this Varangian warrior and he to her.

She felt dizzy with happiness.

He had come for her. He wanted her. For ever.

As the priest concluded the ceremony, he told Viggo he could kiss his bride. He was so desperate to kiss her again that he pulled her towards him so urgently it made her gasp. He claimed her mouth with his, shocking the audience with a full, proprietary kiss. She never wanted it to end, but when it did, he grinned down at her, whispering in her ear that there was more of that to come, before swinging her up into his arms and carrying her down the aisle.

They walked past her speechless mother and father, past all the nuns, most of whom looked on in shocked silence, though some of her closer novices couldn't help but let out a little clap and cheer, until they stepped beyond the convent walls.

Chapter Fifteen

Viggo took his wife's hand and led her through the city streets.

'Where are we going?' Helena asked.

'Somewhere I can kiss you again, but properly,' he said.

She laughed and he loved to hear it.

He was in agony—he couldn't wait to have her in his arms again. He knew he couldn't kiss her in the middle of the busy street, in broad daylight, though he desperately wanted to. And yet, he had just got married—something he thought he'd never do—and he was feeling reckless.

He tugged her down a side passageway, stealing away from the crowds. He pressed her up against the stone wall and bent his head to capture her lips with his. It had been five days and he hungered for her touch, the taste of her. It felt so good to see her, to feel her again and knowing she was now his—for all time. He started slowly, his tongue sensually stroking hers, but it quickly deepened to a frantic, fiery full-mouth kiss as their bodies moulded together, leaving them both breathless.

'Are you happy we're married?' he whispered, pulling just a whisper away.

'Yes. Very. Though I had given up hope of you coming.'

'Did they treat you all right?'

'They were angry—it was to be expected. But it didn't seem to bother me as much as I thought it would. Perhaps it's my rebellious streak. I was a little gleeful that they hadn't got their way.'

He grinned. 'I'm sorry it took me so long. I had some things to sort out before I came for you. I will explain...' He took her hand in his and they began to walk again. 'I wanted to come after you, straight away. I wanted to follow you down that aisle, but doubts plagued me. I wasn't sure I was what you wanted. After you left...it knocked me.'

'I know,' she said, seemingly appalled with herself. 'You must have thought I'd abandoned you,' she said, shaking her head. 'I'm sorry, Viggo.'

He stopped and turned to look at her. Would they ever make it home? 'Why didn't you talk to me in the hall? Why didn't you tell me what you had planned? It might have saved me a lot of pain.'

'I'm sorry,' she said again, raising his hand to her mouth and kissing it. His eyes focused on her lips. 'I was despairing. I just didn't think you wanted me either. You hadn't said. And doubts started to set in for me, too.'

'I have wanted you since the moment I laid eyes on you, Helena.' He squeezed her hand. 'I couldn't believe it when I heard you speak out at the wedding, when I realised what you were doing. What you did for Sofie...' He shook his head. 'Thank you. She is so deliriously happy, it's preposterous.'

'She can't possibly be as happy as me,' she said and he smiled. 'Don't thank me, though, Viggo. I'm glad they are finally together. But what I did, I didn't do for her, but for myself. Since I met you, you have taught me to realise my own happiness is important. I decided I wouldn't—I couldn't—compromise on it.'

He ducked down to look directly in her eyes. 'I'm very glad about that.'

'So, what happened—after I left?' she said, as they continued to walk.

'Well, the wedding took place, and Zoe and some of the members of the council were livid, but there was nothing they could do about it. Afterwards, they went back to the palace and everything went to plan, just as it would have if you had been his bride.'

'Only Marianos was more jovial?'

'Yes,' he said. 'Thanks to you.' He inclined his head. 'I wanted to come—that night. I wanted to come and find you. But I started to doubt myself—everything, thinking maybe if you'd returned to the convent, you would perhaps start regretting all you had given up. Of not being Empress, giving up all that wealth... That you'd begin to resent me. I convinced myself you didn't want me. Or if you did, some time from now, you'd change your mind. That things would end badly. Until Sofie made me see sense. That we're not my parents and I had to at least talk to you, ask you...'

'I know you've been uncertain about marriage, because of the past...'

He stopped her again. 'I'm not uncertain about this. You. Us.'

She nodded, her eyes filling with emotion. 'Nor me. But as for the riches, I never cared about that,' she said. They were coming out of the city now, heading for the water where they'd splashed each other and fallen into the water that day, and she felt so free, to be back out here with him.

'About that,' he said. 'I received the reward I was promised.'

Her brows shot up in surprise. 'Zoe gave it to you, even though Marianos married a different woman?'

'Marianos insisted she give it to me. And as Zoe wanted people to think Sofie had at least come from a wealthy family, making her a more suitable match, she conceded.'

'You deserve it.'

'We,' he said. 'Sofie no longer needs that coin, so I used some of it to pay off your father's debt…'

'It was incredibly good of you.'

'…and I thought we could do with a new home. Something of our own. Something that suits our status as a married couple. What do you think?'

They'd stopped outside an enormous mansion—it was white marble, with striking colonnades and beautiful balconies, with views of the Bosphorus and a garden leading down to the shore.

'Viggo!' she gasped, overwhelmed.

'Want to take a look inside?' he said. 'I just picked up the key. It's taken me a day or so to get it organised.'

A tear slipped down her cheek. 'I was so worried you'd left and gone away…'

He led her up the path. 'No, there was no way I was going anywhere without you, Helena. Not when I realised you might want me, too.'

'What made you finally realise?' she said.

'It was something Sofie said. She told me how you'd gone to speak to Marianos. She said there was something that you'd told him.'

'What?'

'That you had wanted to find love like in the fables, but had started to doubt it was real. But now you knew that it was—that true love wasn't some silly ideal and Marianos should hold on to it, if he'd been lucky enough to find it.' He grinned.

They'd reached the door to their new home and he looked down at her. 'Did you mean it?'

'Every word. I love you, Viggo.'

'And I love you.'

The house was incredible. Not as big as the palace, but far grander than the home Helena had been brought up in. Better, all round.

She could barely contain her excitement as Viggo pushed open the door and led her inside.

'We can get some staff… I just thought we might like to be alone for our first few days first.'

'Alone is good,' she said, a frisson of anticipation running down her spine as he closed the door behind them, shutting the world out.

And the moment the wood filled the frame, they were in each other's arms. She had been starved of his touch and it was clear he felt the same. Viggo pulled her up against him, pressing her against the door, the full length of his body coming up against her as he drove his lips down on to hers. His hands stole into her hair, holding her face, their tongues caressing, clinging, as her hands slid around his waist, holding him close. The kiss went on and on, deepening to become so unrestrained, so desperate, she almost cried out when he pulled away.

'Do you want me to give you the tour?' he asked.

She stared up at him, breathless. She tried to compose herself, but he'd left her achingly incomplete. She wanted him to take a tour of her body, not the house. She wanted more of his hot, hard kisses.

'Please,' she said politely.

He tugged her into a large hall, the walls covered in intricate mosaics. 'Reception halls,' he said, his voice strained, as if he was trying to cling on to his own sanity. Next to it were the private chambers, organised around an interior courtyard, where an olive tree sat in the middle.

'Nice touch,' she said, still trying to get her breathing under control.

'I thought so.'

He whisked her through other ground-floor rooms, all empty. 'You can do what you like with these,' he said. 'And in here is the kitchen.' It was a lovely, huge space, with a jug full of hyacinths on the worktop.

'My favourites,' she said.

'I remember. Hungry?' he asked her.

For him, yes. Food, no. She shook her head.

She looked through another door at the back of the kitchen, before turning back to look at him over her shoulder. 'Is there a cellar?' she asked mischievously and he grinned, following the line of her thoughts.

'Of course,' he said, coming up beside her, gathering her by the waist. He dipped his lips to her ear. 'There is a private bathhouse too,' he whispered.

She shivered. 'Really?'

'But I want to show you upstairs,' he said, turning her around in his arms, the need on his face reflecting her own.

'I'd like that,' she said, her pulse pounding.

And suddenly his lips were back on her mouth, her neck, his hands roaming everywhere—down her back, and lower, to cup her bottom. And so were hers, as she kissed him wherever she could see skin, her fingers running over his shoulders.

He pushed his solid thigh between her legs and began to half-walk and half-carry her backwards, through into the hallway, still kissing her, tugging at her gown, attempting to smooth the habit from her shoulders, seemingly as eager as she was.

Viggo was all she'd thought about since she'd left the cathedral. She wasn't actually sure how she'd got through the past few days. She grappled with his own tunic, managing to lift the material up, raising it off his shoulders, stripping it away, her fingers fumbling. They were both in a rush to be naked in each other's arms again and they fell against the wall and each other, laughing, at their own desperation.

'You know, I never thought I'd find a nun so alluring, but this…this is…' He shook his head.

She giggled and it helped to relieve some of the tension. She was nervous, she realised. Really nervous.

He managed to get one breast free from the material and he was greedy to have it in his hot mouth. He couldn't seem to get enough of her nipple and flesh as he ravaged her, holding her hands in his, behind her arching back as she thrust her chest towards him, urging him on.

He raised his head. 'Do you want me to touch you again?' he growled.

'So much,' she said, her whole body shaking.

Rucking up her tunic to her waist, bunching it up into his hands, moving it out of the way, his fingers stole between her legs and she gasped. She knew she was wet, her excitement coating her thighs.

'I'm not sure we're going to make it up the stairs,' he said, as he toppled her backwards on to the steps and she lay back, sprawled against them. His head moved lower and he looked up at her, smiling, making clear his intent. He lavished her with kisses, his mouth on her stomach, moving over her thighs.

She succumbed, throwing her arms up above her head—he was exactly where she wanted him. She had been dreaming of him doing this to her again all week, having his mouth between her legs. She let him bring her knees up over his shoulders, and he cupped her bottom, hauling her against his mouth, binding her to him, and she cried out.

She gave in to his onslaught, her hands coming back down to curl into his hair, needing something to hold on to, fixing him in place as he plundered her. He seemed to be savouring the taste of her as he kissed her slowly, explicitly, intimately. She began to come apart, raising herself towards him on trembling legs, her desperate whimpers growing louder, more urgent, until she threw her head back and let herself go, crying out his name, over and over.

He grinned at her as he tugged her down the steps, into his lap, holding her, stroking her hair and kissing her temple as her breathing settled.

'I take it you missed me,' he said.

'Every moment we were apart,' she said, breathless from the pleasure he'd given her.

Facing each other on the cool marble floor of the hallway, her hands smoothed up over his chest, and then down to fumble with the waistband of his breeches.

'Helena,' he said, stalling her hands. 'I want you so badly, but I'm determined our first time won't be on the cold marble of our new hallway floor. Let's go upstairs.'

He held out his hand for her to take and their fingers entwined. They slowly climbed the steps that wound round the inside of the building, before he led her across the landing to a doorway.

'This will be our room,' he said and flutters of excitement erupted low in her stomach.

'Our room?' she asked. So they would share? No separate chambers? No separate beds? Good. She was glad.

'There are others, but this one is the best. Take a look at the view.'

She crossed the room, aware her legs were still trembling, her heart still pounding, and peeked out of the window. There was a balcony with seating that overlooked the glistening waters of the strait. It was stunning.

He pushed open the doors, letting in a gentle wisp of breeze from the Bosphorus. It was a welcome respite in the cloying heat of the afternoon. It helped to cool her cheeks that felt flushed after the things he had just done to her.

She glanced back at the sumptuous, canopied bed, dressed with soft, silk curtains that drifted in the gentle gusts of air.

The knowledge that this was their wedding night hung heavily in the space between them. They were finally going to do this. Her legs felt so weak, shaking with desire, she didn't think she could stand. And he was too far away.

'Viggo,' she breathed and he met her in the middle of the room, grasping her to him, gathering her up in his arms, knowing what she wanted, what she needed, because he did, too. He bent his head, catching her mouth with his, his tongue urgently seeking out hers once more. Her hands came up to curl over his shoulders and clasp around his neck as he tugged her closer.

'Can we take this hideous thing off now?' he whispered. A desperate plea.

She bit her lip, nodding.

He brought her hands up in the air, outstretched above her head, and, gripping the woollen material, he drew the tunic slowly, gently, up over her body, peeling it away, and discarded it on the floor. She shivered under his gaze as a waft of summer air whispered across her skin. There was no dim glow of lamplight, no dark to hide in today, instead the soft afternoon sun illuminated her skin.

He held her round the waist and pulled her to him, gently drawing her over to the bed, tugging her down with him, so they were lying side by side.

'You're so beautiful,' he murmured against her skin. 'From the moment I saw you I knew I wanted to make you mine. I never imagined it would be possible.'

He curved his hands over her hips, stroking her body, trailing his fingers up and down her back, making her melt against him, their breath mingling. Her fingers began to explore the solid muscles of his chest, wanting to feel his skin against hers again. She pressed herself closer, crushing her breasts against him.

He kissed her deeply, toying with the curve of her bottom, before one hand came up to cup her breast, his thumbs circling her nipple, and she arched into him, wanting more, whimpering softly.

He ran his hands up into her hair, his fingertips making her tingle, and he released the band, her silk tresses cascading around her shoulders. His lips moved down her throat, before prowling lower, taking the hard bud of her breast into his mouth properly now, free from restraint of all clothing, his beard brushing against her sensitive skin, and she tipped her head back, sighing in surrender, giving in to all the delicious sensations his lingering caresses were causing.

He blazed a trail down between their bodies with his expert fingers and she felt liquid desire gather between her legs again. She had never imagined she could feel this way. That she could want, over and again. He lifted her thigh over his hip, opening her up, allowing him better access to all her secret places, before reaching between her thighs, moving lower, and she gasped in anticipation of the touch she now knew would come. His fingers threaded through her triangle of hair and touched her as he stared into her eyes.

'I missed you,' he said.

He slid his finger inside her before she could answer, and she moaned softly, burying her head into his shoulder, tugging him closer, letting him know she'd missed him, too. 'What are you doing to me?' she whispered.

'Making sure you're ready for me,' he said. He stroked her slowly, excruciatingly slowly, seeming to take note of her reactions, tormenting her.

'Open your eyes. Look at me,' he whispered.

She raised her head to look into his ebony gaze as he slipped his fingers inside her more deeply. It was so intimate, she almost couldn't bear it, and she lowered her leg, pressing her thighs together, gripping his hand, wanting to keep him there forever.

'Can I touch you, too?' she asked him.

And he groaned, resting his forehead against hers.

'Yes, you can touch me, Helena.'

'How?' she asked.

He took her hand and placed her palm on his chest, then moved it down, sliding over his taut stomach, down the thin line of hair to the top of his breeches and lower, and her fingers curved over his length, straining against the material.

He drew in a sharp breath.

'Does that hurt?' she asked.

'No,' he laughed. 'It definitely doesn't hurt.'

Her fingertips stole beneath his waistband and his laughter dried up. His breathing halted. She reached down to take hold him in her hand, her fingers curling round his huge length, and he pushed down his breeches, finally freeing himself from restraint.

'Viggo?'

His fingers came down to curl around hers, around himself, and he showed her how to move her hands to please him. When she became more acquainted with the feel of him, her movements more confident, he released her, letting her take control, his hands coming up to hold her jaw, to capture her mouth again as she stroked him. She liked that she was making his breathing a little erratic, his hands touching her more urgently, his kisses becoming more explicit.

'You're good at that,' he whispered. 'A little too good.' And he moved his hand back down to still her. 'If you carry on, this will be over far too quickly. And I haven't even begun to do all the things I want to do with you yet.'

He rolled her over on to her back, bringing his body over her, coming down between her legs, and his knees pushed her thighs apart. He kissed her again as his fingers roamed back down between their slick bodies, touching her once more, and she whimpered. The feel of his shaft pressing into her thigh, the fact she wasn't able to close her legs—it excited her. He was offering her no mercy and she wasn't sure how much more of his pleasure she could take. And he wasn't stopping.

He kissed her mouth, her cheeks, her jaw—he smothered her in his kisses and then withdrew his hand and she felt him, right there, his hard, silky tip poised, ready to take possession of her body, pressing against her folds—and suddenly, her body rebelled and she froze. Her eyes flew open. He must have felt her stiffen, as his eyes seared down into hers.

'Wait.' She panicked.

'Helena?'

He moved off her immediately, coming down to lie by her side, and she instantly missed his weight, guilt rushing through her. He stroked his hand over her hip, soothing her.

'Are you all right?'

She bit her lip. Her breathing was coming in bursts and she felt her emotions rise up. Tears welled in her eyes. Had she ruined everything? She brought her hands up to cover her face.

His fingers immediately came over hers and he pulled her hands down.

'Don't hide from me. What's going on? What are you thinking?'

She shook her head.

'Helena…'

'I want to do this. So much. It's all I've thought about for days.'

'Thank God for that,' he said, offering her a half-smile. 'So what is it?'

'It's just all the voices in my head, telling me bad things.'

'What are they saying?' he asked, his fingers moving back down to graze over her stomach.

'I think, maybe, I've built this up to be a big, scary thing,' she said. 'After everything that happened at the palace—how Marianos treated me. Maybe because it was kept from me, like a terrible secret… The thought of people watching it happen. It frightened me. And what Zoe said…'

'What did Zoe say?' he asked, suddenly frowning, his fingers stalling.

'She said during the bedding ceremony I should lie on my back and pretend to enjoy it.'

He cursed softly, gathering her closer. 'I don't want you

to pretend to enjoy anything. Forget everything everyone has said. There are no rules here, Helena,' he said, offering her a steady gaze. 'No witnesses. It's just you and me. And we can take our time. There's no rush. We don't have to do anything else until you're ready. We can just lie here a while. Or not. We can go downstairs, outside…'

She shook her head. 'I want to be here, with you, like this.' He was a wonderful man.

His fingers ran over her back, over her bottom, trailing the crevice of her buttocks, lighting another fire inside of her. 'Tell me, have I ever done anything you didn't like?' he asked.

She shook her head.

'Everything I do, the way I touch you, it's because I want to give you pleasure. I'm not going to hurt you, Helena.'

'I know that.' She swallowed. 'It's just…you've also done this before…maybe I'll disappoint you.'

'You could never, ever, disappoint me.'

'And…and you're so big! It's intimidating,' she babbled.

He grinned at that and lay back, looking up at the ceiling, taking a breath. 'Well, what can I say?'

She laughed at his arrogance and gave him a gentle thump on his arm.'There's not much I can do about that. But I promise you, when the time comes, it will feel nice.' He pulled her into the curve of his shoulder. 'Let's just lie here a while. Talk,' he said, grazing his fingers up and down her arm. 'It's been an emotional few days.'

She nestled her chin against him, enjoying the feel of his skin beneath her, the sound of his heartbeat. His patience was astounding, she thought. And his control. She had always admired that about him. It was what made him so trustworthy.

They spoke about the arena and the rebuild, and Sofie—

and his face lit up when he told her about the baby kicking. She asked what Marianos and Sofie had said about him coming after her.

'After I'd told Sofie, she wanted to tell Marianos—she thought he'd take the news better coming from her. And she said it made her feel a little less guilty about her deceit these past few months, doing something for me,' Viggo said. 'When Marianos found out, he called me to the hall and I was prepared to give up my role in his service, but he refused it, instead giving me the official title of *The Akolouthos*.'

Helena gasped. It meant he was the Emperor's highest-ranking official, the Chief Commander, a position that carried significant prestige and responsibility. 'That's wonderful, Viggo.'

'Marianos said he wanted to reward my loyalty. That I had remained true to him despite wanting you for myself. Sofie had said she could tell there was something between us the night you followed me home.'

His sister was right, there had been. It was why she'd gone to Viggo. She'd known she could trust him, even then.

As she lay beside him, she took the opportunity to allow her gaze to drift over his incredible body, on show in all its glory, and she ran her hand over his scars, his ink, learning the lines of him. He was so beautiful, always gentle, she knew he was nothing to be afraid of.

He had taught her to be brave. To fight for what she wanted. And she wanted him, all of him. She was ready now.

She traced the thin line of dark hair that descended from his stomach and then took him in her hand again, revelling in feeling the weight of him. She felt his breathing change, and unbelievably, he grew beneath her fingers.

'Helena?' he asked.

She wrapped her hand around the huge length and looked up at him. 'I'm ready now. I want you.'

She rolled over on to her back and reached for him.

She saw his throat work as he looked at her with burning intensity.

'You know, you don't have to lie on your back, like Zoe said,' he whispered, coming up on to his knees. 'We can do this however we want. No rules, remember?' And in one swift motion, he tugged her up, bringing her thighs over his own, so she was straddling his lap, and his hands drifted over her back, his fingers curling round her bottom, pressing her against him. They stroked lower and his slow hands built up her trust and her excitement once more.

He eased his fingers inside her, giving her a taste of what he was about to do with his body, before he wrapped her hand around the base of him, guiding him to her entrance together.

'You're in control,' he whispered, holding her gaze.

She pressed against him and he gave the gentlest of thrusts, pushing against her skin, the tip of him bulging inside her. She felt sudden heat, a rush of need at the breach, and she gasped as Viggo groaned, his forehead resting against hers.

'All right?' he managed to say, his voice unsteady, and she nodded. She was. It felt good, better than she could have imagined, and she wanted more of him. She wanted this so badly.

She gave an experimental wiggle as she gripped his shoulders, and she sank lower, needing him deeper, and as if he understood, he thrust again, edging further inside her. Little by little, she felt her body give in to his onslaught, accepting his gentle invasion, and as he held her buttocks securely, he finally slid fully inside her tight, slick body.

'Viggo,' she moaned. It felt glorious. She clung to him, staring wildly into his eyes.

'I'm inside you,' he whispered in wonder. They were locked together. 'But I don't dare move. I'm trying to keep a grip on myself, not wanting this to be over too quickly. You feel too good.'

'So do you. If it is over too soon, we'll just have to do it again.'

'And again,' he whispered.

'I'm so glad I'm doing this with you.'

'Me, too.' He grinned. He kissed her slowly, letting her get used to the feel of him filling her up. 'I think I'm ready to continue. Are you?'

'Yes.'

'Shall I take over now?'

She nodded and in a swift movement he gathered her to him so they couldn't be parted. He lifted her, before laying her down on to her back, pushing her legs apart with his knees as he came down on top of her.

'Is this all right?' he asked, his elbows supporting his weight.

'Yes,' she said, bringing her legs up around his thighs, her hands exploring his back, gliding down to feel the curve of his bottom, tugging him closer. 'Keep going.'

He laughed and gripped her hips, moving her slightly, angling her better, and with his next long, sure thrust he took possession of her body with his, making her cry out in pleasure. His movements were powerful, slow and steady—he was always so controlled, even now—intent on driving her wild with his intimate strokes.

He pulled her knees up higher, sinking deeper, wrapping

her legs around his waist, and as he thrust again, claiming her completely, she came quickly, thrashing beneath him, tears dampening her cheeks. Her soft sobs of ecstasy tipped him over the edge, yelling out her name at his own fierce rush of release inside her.

As he lay on top of her, his head buried into her shoulder, she tried to come to terms with what had happened, how incredible it had been, and how much she couldn't wait to do it again, until he lifted his head to look down at her. His arms trembled.

'Now *that* was an act of love,' he said.

She smiled. 'I'm very glad the clergymen weren't here to watch it.' She laughed.

'I think they might have been shocked.' He grinned, then kissed her tenderly. 'Do you know how much I love you, Helena?' he whispered.

'I'm beginning to understand. But I might need you to show me again very soon.'

'As often as you want.'

'I love you, too,' she said, kissing his cheek.

'You really do?'

'I really, really do,' she said, kissing his other cheek.

'Tell me again.'

'I love you, Viggo.' And she kissed him fully on the mouth.

'Do you want me to move—am I heavy?' he asked.

She shook her head. 'Never leave me.'

'Or you, me.'

And so they lay like that, with Viggo still inside her, as they fell asleep, neither of them wanting to be parted.

Chapter Sixteen

Married life had started well, Viggo thought. Too well, because he couldn't concentrate on anything but getting home to his wife at the end of each day. All he wanted was to be with her, to talk to her, make love to her—all of the time.

He'd just arrived home and he was delighted to find her waiting for him in the bathhouse. He began to tug off his uniform, ready to join her. It had been a month since he'd gone to fetch her from the convent. A month of them being husband and wife. Of them living together. He was so glad she liked the residence he had chosen for them and, in just a few days, she had made it feel like a home. They had shopped at the market together and cooked in their new kitchen, feeding each other before one thing led to another… He thought they might just have christened every room, every surface, in the house. Not these baths yet though…

Everything was coming together—and not just for them. His sister was happy and Zoe had stepped aside, withdrawing from court life to allow Marianos to rule independently. Viggo had thought Marianos might send her to a monastery, but he had kept her in a life of luxury, in a private residence in the country, and with her gone, Marianos was becoming a better ruler by the day. He was making more considered decisions, and the city was healing. Just like Viggo's heart, his memories, with Helena by his side.

He'd just kicked off his boots and chainmail when there was a loud knock at the door.

'Wait a moment,' he said to Helena.

Reluctantly, he went to see who it was.

It was a messenger from the palace.

'Who is it?' Helena asked, coming up beside him wrapped in her silk robe.

'Our presence is required at the palace,' Viggo said, his brow furrowing. He'd only just got home. They looked at each other.

'Sofie,' they gasped in unison.

Helena raced to get changed and Viggo pulled on his armour and boots once more, before they raced out into the streets where a carriage from the palace was waiting. It carried them through the city as quickly as possible.

When they arrived, they were ushered into the Great Hall to wait.

Viggo paced. 'Do you think she's all right? What if something's happened?'

Helena took his hand and gave it a reassuring squeeze. 'I'm sure she will be well. Have faith.'

Finally, when the door opened, they were led out into the portico that took them to the Empress's chamber, and there, propped up in bed, was Sofie—a beautiful baby in her arms. Marianos had his arm around them both. When they entered, he looked up and smiled. Pride emanated from his face.

Viggo stared at the happy scene, relief overwhelming him, and Helena clasped her hands together, delighted.

Viggo moved closer towards the bed, his throat thick with emotion. 'How are you?' he asked his sister. 'I'm so pleased to see you looking well. I thought something might have happened.'

She shook her head. 'Something did happen. Something wonderful. We're parents. A family, at last,' she said. 'Thanks to you both.'

'It's a boy,' Marianos said. 'We have an heir.'

'We've decided to name him Leo Viggo,' Sofie added. 'After you. The best man we know.'

Helena put a hand on Viggo's arm—she must have known his feelings were about to bubble over.

'Thank you,' he said, his voice raw.

'Do you want to hold him?' Sofie asked.

Viggo nodded and Marianos moved away to make room for him as he came to sit down on the bed. Sofie passed him the tiny bundle and he stared down at the baby. 'He's handsome,' he said.

'Like his uncle.' Helena smiled, placing a hand on his shoulder.

'He's so tiny, so precious,' he said in awe. His heart felt as if it was expanding. It would be a moment that stayed with him for ever. He felt an immediate connection to the child and a responsibility for him, just like he did for the boy's mother. He would never let anything happen to either of them. He would continue to protect them both until the end of his days.

A cough behind Helena drew her attention away from the happy scene.

'Helena, could I have a word?' Marianos asked. 'Let's leave these two to have a moment to themselves,' he said.

She sent Viggo a look and he inclined his head, telling her she should go.

'Shall we take a walk?' the Emperor said. 'It's a lovely day.'

Apprehension prickled in her stomach—what was this about?

They took a stroll along the portico, and down the steps, into the garden. It had always been her favourite place here, yet it had never felt like home. Not like her house with Viggo.

'You must be very proud, Marianos. Your son is incredible.'

'And thanks to you, I got to see his birth. I'll get to be in his life and help raise him.'

Helena inclined her head in acknowledgement.

As they came to the roses, Marianos's favourite spot in the garden, he halted. He kept touching his hair and rubbing his arms, and Helena thought he must be nervous.

'I wanted to ask you if you'd consider returning to the palace,' he blurted, and her chest squeezed. She had not been expecting him to say that.

She really hoped he didn't mean to wait on Sofie. While she adored Viggo's sister, she thought that would be somewhat degrading. It had been strange enough to be back in that chamber where she had spent the week preparing to be Empress herself. She wasn't envious of her sister-in-law, not one bit, but still, she didn't think she would want to come back here to be Sofie's aide.

He stopped and turned to look at her. 'Helena, I am well aware it is because of your honesty that I am happy. It was because of your courage that I made and am still making better choices. That period where I thought I'd lost Sofie,

I was so angry with the world. I took it out on you and my people. I feel such guilt for allowing my General to be so harsh to them. I will spend the rest of my days making amends. You have changed me, Helena, and I have decided I need you by my side in the palace.'

She was pleased she had made such a difference, as she had hoped. Viggo had told her how Marianos had reduced the taxes and had sent food and clothing out to the poorer neighbourhoods. But what did he mean about her coming to the palace? In what capacity?

'I want you to have a seat on my council—my *Comitatus*,' he announced and she gasped. It was his inner circle of trusted advisors. 'I know up until now it has been all men, your husband and General Markou included—apart from my mother, of course. But she is no longer here and we could do with a woman's perspective on things. I have seen and admired the way you handle the officials and I feel we could do with your assistance in governing the empire.'

The breath left her. She couldn't help but wonder what her father would make of that. Perhaps her parents would be proud of her after all. Not that she cared much for their judgement. Only Viggo's opinion mattered to her now.

'But most of all, I'm doing this for the people,' Marianos continued. 'It is what they want, what they have been asking for. They adore you. I didn't want to see it before, but I cannot ignore it now.'

Her heart began to flood with joy.

'They love Sofie, too, of course,' he said in a rush, not wishing to be disloyal. 'Who wouldn't? But they call for you at every event. They stamp their feet and chant your name. If you could perhaps be around a little more, a public figure if you will, an ambassador for Constantinople, as well as an advisor on my council, we could continue the good work you started.'

She smiled up at him, for the first time feeling a connection to him, understanding why Viggo had always supported him, fought for him. He had a good heart after all. 'I would be honoured,' she said.

He gave a triumphant little stamp of his foot. 'That is wonderful,' he said, his face filling with relief. 'This is turning out to be a very good day indeed. So that's settled then. You will join us for our first council next week?'

'I will.'

As they made their way back to Sofie and Viggo, Marianos insisted they stay for the celebration feast.

It was late by the time the carriage dropped them home, but she had the feeling something was wrong. Viggo was quieter than usual.

He had listened as she'd filled him in on all Marianos had said and he had seemed happy for her, pulling her in for an embrace to congratulate her, as they closed the door behind them now.

'You said yes, of course?' he asked.

'Yes, but only so I can see you at the palace every day,' she jested.

He smiled, but it didn't reach his eyes. Her stomach clenched.

'You deserve this, Helena,' he said. 'I'm proud of you.'

'I hope you're going to show me just how proud of me you are,' she said, wriggling her eyebrows. 'We could still take that bath...'

But when he ran a hand around the back of his neck, she knew she was in trouble.

'What's wrong?' she asked.

'Nothing. I'm just tired. Would you mind if we went straight to bed?'

She shook her head.

It was the first evening since they'd been married that when they got under the furs he didn't pull her to him. The first time he hadn't begun kissing and stroking her. The first time he hadn't wanted her. Instead, he rolled away, turning his back on her, and she felt hurt.

Her mind raced. Had she done something wrong? Did he not want her to have a position in the palace? Or was something else bothering him?

Her thoughts ran over the events of the day. He had been overwhelmed seeing Sofie with her child—she had seen it in the tears shimming in his eyes, his clenched jaw as he had held the boy tenderly in his arms. Did that have something to do with this? A pain seared through her. Was he worried that she wasn't yet with child—after all, it had been a month since she'd become his wife. An old fear reared its ugly head. Did he think she wasn't fulfilling her duty? She never wanted to disappoint him.

Eventually, she fell into a restless sleep.

When she woke in the night, he wasn't there and she sat bolt upright in the bed. She felt the breeze waft through the window and saw him sitting out on the balcony, dressed in just his breeches, his chest and feet bare. He looked beautiful in the moonlight, as he stared out at the night sky.

She threw off the furs and padded over to him. She hated this distance between them. She needed to eradicate it. She would have to insist he told her what she'd done wrong, so she could fix it.

She saw his eyes widen at the appearance of her naked body walking his way, his muscles tighten at the sight of her, and she was glad—at least he wasn't totally resistant to her. She lowered herself into his lap, curling up in his arms, giving him no choice. At first, he didn't move, then his arms came slowly around her, pulling her close.

'Won't you come back to bed?' she whispered.

'In a moment.'

'Viggo, have I done something wrong?' she asked.

'No. Never,' he said, shaking his head.

'But something is the matter. Won't you tell me what it is?'

He shrugged. 'It's nothing.'

'Don't do that, Viggo. Don't shut me out. I want to understand. Just sharing something that's weighing on your mind can make you feel better, even if I can't solve it… If something was bothering me, you'd want me to tell you, wouldn't you? That is what a marriage is.'

He nodded.

'So…?'

He sighed and pulled her body closer. 'Holding Sofie's son in my arms today, he felt so fragile and innocent—so perfect, not yet damaged by the world. It made me think about my own parents and how they could have done what they did.'

Pain erupted in her chest at the thought of him ever suffering.

'How could a mother abandon her child? How could a father hurt his own son? And leave him with such scars, inside and out,' he said.

She shook her head. 'I don't know. It's unthinkable.'

'It made me angry,' he said. 'Thinking back to what they put us through.'

'I can understand that. It was a good look for you, seeing you holding the baby,' she said, nudging him in the ribs, trying to lighten his mood a little. And yet she bit her lip as she felt the need to voice her own concerns. 'Viggo, should I be with child by now?'

He lifted his head to look at her.

'Do you want to be?'

She shrugged her shoulder. 'I don't know. Seeing Sofie with her baby, seeing you hold him, it made me wonder if we would like to have a child of our own one day. We have never discussed it—a family, children. I was worried that you were angry with me, perhaps wondering why there were no signs yet of me making you a father yet.'

'How could you think that? I'm not angry with you at all, Helena.' He kissed her forehead before lifting her as he stood up, before placing her back down on her feet. 'I am certainly not waiting to hear that you are with child, that we will be parents.' He walked to the edge of the balcony, before turning around. 'But neither am I sure I'm either suited or qualified for that role.'

'What? Of course you are,' she said, stepping towards him.

He crossed his arms over his chest, leaning against the wall. 'I want you to know I would never do what my father did. I would never behave like that.'

'Is that what you're worried about?' she gasped, stepping forward. 'I know you're nothing like your father, Viggo. I know what kind of man you are, and you are the only man I would want as my husband and the father of any future child I might have,' she said, coming to stand in front of him.

She didn't know why he felt he needed to reassure her. And then she realised—he was trying to reassure himself. She placed her hand on his cheek. 'I believe it. But you need to, too. You need to trust yourself just as much as I trust you.'

He dropped his arms and held her around the waist, gathering her to him.

He pulled back to look into her eyes. 'Why are you so kind to me?' he asked.

'Because you deserve it. You never meant to hurt him, Viggo. It was an accident. The fact you feel guilt when he never did proves you're not the same as him.'

He looked at her. 'I never thought of it like that.'

'You need to start being kinder to yourself. See the good in yourself. Everything I see.'

'I'm working on it. With your help.'

'Well, it's about time I taught you a thing or two. After all, you saw the potential in me. Brought it out in me. If I have to remind you every day of all the incredible things about you, so that you finally believe it, I will. It won't be hard.'

He suddenly pulled her close to him, grinning a predatory smile. 'Do you know what is hard?' he whispered, and as he held her naked body, she felt the solid ridge of him against her hip.

'Finally!' she said and he threw his head back and laughed.

'Come with me,' he said, taking her hand, leading her back into their room.

Reaching the bed, he toppled her on to the furs, turning her over on to her stomach. He put one knee on the bed and his body came over her. She glanced back at him over her shoulder, watching him push down his breeches, and she whimpered, excited about what was to come. He had made her wait too long. He held her by the hips and, somehow knowing she needed no warm-up, he entered her from behind, all the way, in one slick thrust, his groin pressing against her bottom. And she cried out, nearly coming apart, immediately.

'Do you like it like this?' he asked.

'Yes,' she whispered.

He tugged her up on to her hands and knees, rearing over her, spreading her legs wider with his knees, and he thrust again. And when she cried out his name in pleasure, it made him do it again and again. She loved the way he took control of her, the way he made her feel protected and safe. She'd felt that way since the moment she'd met him.

He brought her back up against his chest, so he could hold her breasts, pinning her to him, as he moved his hands over her taut body, and down, to touch her between her legs while he surged inside her. She began to pant, knowing she was close.

She ground back against him, telling him she wanted more of this insane pleasure they had discovered they could give each other, because they were made for each other, and he quickened his pace, taking her harder than he had before, as if he needed her more than he'd ever needed anyone in his life.

'I feel like I'm where I belong,' he whispered.

'Home,' she said, her hands reaching up to come around his neck. And when they came together in stunning synchronicity, she felt him surrender his whole self to her, everything he had to give.

He brought her back down on to the bed with him, so she was curled up in his arms.

'That was intense. Every time I think it's the best and then it just keeps getting better.'

'Yes, it is the same for me,' she said.

'You know, at the rate we're going, a child could come sooner than we think.'

She pulled away slightly and turned around to look at him. She raised her hand to his cheek.

'Seeing your sister today…has it made you…*do you* want a child?'

He looked down at her. 'One day, yes. If it happens, I will be delighted. But I am quite content for now, aren't you?'

'Only quite?' She smiled, teasing him.

'I don't think I could be happier.'

'Me either.'

'We both grew up living for someone else, Helena. I raised my sister and you were brought up to be someone's wife. This is our time now, isn't it? Just for us.'

She nodded. 'What if I can't have children?'

'The same goes for me. But there's no reason either of us wouldn't be able to.'

'I don't know.' She shrugged. 'I just never want to disappoint you.'

'And I told you, you could never. You need to believe that, too. You are everything to me, Helena. I have everything I want right here.' He kissed her, fiercely. 'If children should come along in the future, then that will be wonderful, but if they don't, you are enough for me. I have everything I want, right here in my arms.'

And as she pulled him towards her, to hold him tight, so did she.

* * * * *

If you enjoyed this story,
then you're going to love
Sarah Rodi's other captivating romances

Her Secret Vows with the Viking
The Viking's Princess Bride
The Warrior's Forbidden Viking Bride

And why not pick up her instalment in our
A Season to Wed collection

Only an Heiress Will Do *by Virginia Heath*
The Viscount's Forbidden Flirtation *by Sarah Rodi*
Their Second Chance Season *by Ella Matthews*
The Lord's Maddening Miss *by Lucy Morris*